HOMOSASSA SHADOWS

by the same author

Brandy O'Bannon mysteries

Trace Their Shadows

Shadow over Cedar Key

HOMOSASSA SHADOWS

A Brandy O'Bannon Mystery

Ann Turner Cook

iUniverse, Inc.

New York Lincoln Shanghai

HOMOSASSA SHADOWS

A Brandy O'Bannon Mystery

iUniverse books may be ordered through booksellers or by contacting:

iUniverse
2021 Pine Lake Road, Suite 100
Lincoln, NE 68512
www.iuniverse.com
1-800-Authors (1-800-288-4677)

ISBN: 0-595-34466-6

Printed in the United States of America

For the *Hillsborough County, Florida, Sheriff's Office,*

who valued my husband, Jim, for all the right reasons:

his honesty, compassion, and unfailing respect for others.

Foreword

The settings in this novel are real and the Seminole and Safety Harbor Indian lore accurate, although the characters and situation are, of course, imaginary. Anyone familiar with Florida's "Nature Coast" along the north central Gulf of Mexico will recognize the fishing community of Homosassa and the impressive, if short, Homosassa River. If they join boaters on that river, they will pass Bird Island, the Salt River, and Tiger Tail Island. From the Salt they can cruise the Little Homosassa, past the site where a hidden Indian mound actually exists, although it has never been excavated.

The fictional United States soldier's journal is based on similar historical journals, and the events in the Second Seminole War are historically accurate, even to the capture of the wily old warrior, Tiger Tail.

When the novel moves to a Tampa location, the former Seminole museum and outdoor exhibits play a key role. A 1980 excavation in preparation for a municipal parking garage in the city's downtown uncovered the nineteenth century Fort Brooke cemetery. Among the burials here lay the skeletons of many Seminole Indians, which led to the creation of the Tampa Seminole Reservation, a memorial, and a burial site for these forgotten tribesmen. This novel is set in 2000, because the Seminole museum, gift shop, and zoo on the Tampa Reservation, featured in the final chapters, were swallowed up the next year by the Seminole Hardrock Hotel and Casino. Before that date, the Seminole Cultural Center in

Tampa, its museum, and outdoor exhibits were well worth a visit, although legendary Old Joe had already passed on to an alligator's reward.

Most Florida visitors—and even recent residents—do not know the fascinating history of this extraordinary state. It is rich in drama, and the state's natural beauty exceeds that of the artificial tourist meccas most people see. Old Florida, the Real Florida, still remains for the discerning eye.

*   *   *   *

I want to thank Sheriff Walter C. Heinrich, Retired, of the Hillsborough County, Florida, Sheriff's Office, for checking the crime scene, and to my friend and indefatigable editor, Staci Backauskas, for her invaluable suggestions.

My thanks also go to anthropologist Patricia Riles Wickman, Ph.D, former Director of Anthropology and Genealogy, Seminole Tribe of Florida, for her help in translating words from English to the Maskókî language, more popularly known as "Muskokee." I am grateful, as well, to archaeologist Frank Gilson, who very kindly described in 1998 the work of Florida state archaeologists. Unlike the Indiana Jones of our imagining, he said, they labor largely at salvage operations on Indian mounds, repairing damage caused by pot hunters and keeping just ahead of the bulldozers. Any unauthorized person who took away human remains would be in serious trouble. Generally such remains are turned over to an Indian group, who reburies the bones with private ceremonies.

A list of reference materials for the novel follows the text.

I had forgot that foul conspiracy of the beast Caliban...

The Tempest. Act IV, Scene 1

PROLOGUE

▼

Timothy Hart pushed himself out of bed. He could scarcely breathe. His legs wobbled and his head felt light. He clutched his stomach. Painful cramps again. He'd spent half the night in the bathroom. In a rising panic he glanced out the window at the alien land, at cabbage palms, palmettos, scraggly oaks hung with Spanish moss, stunted cedars, all still and quiet in the morning light. An island, worse luck. No roads, no bridges. Only a broad river on one side and a creek on the other three.

Thoughts skittered in and out of his brain. He should've hidden the briefcase. He didn't want the others to show the journal to anyone else. No time to worry about it now. Most of all, he should have gone to a doctor yesterday. Had to be one in this god-forsaken place. Instead, he kept eating those berries and green herbals he was told would settle his stomach. Now he had to get help. He had to reach the boat. It was half an hour up river to town.

He stretched a shaky hand for his clothes on the chair. His vision dimmed. He tried twice before he could force his legs into his shorts from last night, then pulled on the shirt, and without buttoning it, thrust his feet into unlaced shoes. Next he dragged himself into the kitchen. He caught the scent of bacon, but the house was empty. The landlady had left a box of dry cereal, a sweet roll on the counter, yesterday's newspaper, Wednesday's. Today was Thursday. He'd been here a week. His dream was within his grasp. But he had to find help.

The sight of the food made him gag. No hope from the phone. It had been out of order for a week. Maybe he could catch the old woman before she took off in her own boat.

He staggered through the living room, onto the narrow wooden porch, stumbled down a few steps, and felt his legs falter. He had a dim memory of a woman reporter. She was to come to see him. He needed her now. His breath came in gasps. He was aware of water glinting in the sunlight, and the fresh smell of a breeze over Tiger Tail Bay. In the distance a motor droned, far down river. Faintly, he heard his feet crunch over oyster shells. He'd dragged himself into the yard, but his landlady's boat was gone. He could make out the shape of the skiff he'd rented, pulled up on shore, but his vision was hazy. He'd have to shove it off, find the strength to pull the cord to start the engine.

A wave of nausea swept over him. His knees buckled. He reached for the boat and everything blurred. At the last second of consciousness, he felt a shock of recognition. He'd been too trusting. The roots and berries and stalks weren't safe. Poison, he thought. Poison! The herbs…

CHAPTER 1

▼

Brandy O'Bannon sat at a Tiki bar, watching the wide Homosassa River glide past, its black waters shimmering under the oudoor lights. She nursed a margarita and toyed with a crab cake, reluctant to return to the rented house alone. Tomorrow was Thursday, the official beginning of her vacation, but it promised to be a solitary one. Her husband could only visit on weekends.

When a splash sounded in the dark cove behind her, she turned to see a narrow head surface, then submerge again, only bulging nostrils still above the water—the small resident alligator. She gazed past her own pontoon boat, bobbing beside the restaurant pier, toward the shrimp boats moored where the river's curve began.

At first Brandy ignored the three men seated near her at the bar. She shut out the clatter of dishes and the muted chatter around her and imagined the river's past. She could almost see the shadows of natives gathering clams and oysters along the shore, or Seminole Indians hiding out among the cabbage palms and cedars.

An excited voice intruded on her thoughts. The oldest of the three men talked eagerly to the male bartender, his glance sweeping the other patrons at the bar. "N-name's Timothy Hart," he said, leaning forward and thumping the counter with one palm. "You folks b-be hearing about me soon. News will k-knock y-your hats off." Brandy pegged the speaker as a tourist. He was about sixty-five and balding, his forehead and nose pink from exposure to the sun, a plaid shirt stretched tight across his pudgy stomach. He couldn't have been in Homosassa long. His khaki shorts still looked crisp and fresh.

He turned toward the man seated next to him, who looked a lot like the Indians of Brandy's imaginings—dark skin, coarse black hair pulled back in a plait, Asian eyes. But instead of a loin cloth or a colorful Seminole costume, he wore faded blue jeans and a long sleeved shirt. One hand relaxed around a can of Coca Cola. Brandy listened.

"I was h-hoping you could help me," the older man said to the Indian. He picked up a scrap of paper lying on the bar. Brandy could see words scrawled across it. "These w-words are Greek to me, b-but they're important." His voice rose again. "These w-words are the k-key to everything."

The Indian glanced at the scrap and his voice came from deep in his chest. "Sorry, Mr. Hart. They're in a different language. Not all Florida Indians speak the same one."

Hart settled his chubby frame against the back of the bar stool "S'all right. My f-friend here can g-get them figured out." He nodded toward the man seated on the other side, smiled at the bartender, and shoved his empty glass toward him. "My friend's g-got connections. He'll g-get a translation. He's an arch—arche—whatever."

Brandy looked at the man Hart had pointed out. He was middle-aged and blond, with a deep tan and a University of Florida tee shirt. Curious, Brandy inserted herself into the conversation. "An archaeologist?" she asked.

Hart swayed slightly on his stool. "Bingo," he said.

The blond man gave her an appraising glance, a slight smile lingering on his lips. "My Seminole friend and I are working together on a project off the Little Homosassa River." He closed and pocketed a small spiral note pad, and his gaze met that of the Indian. Brandy shifted her gaze to the excited tourist. "His Indian b-buddy's a m-medicine man," Hart added, clearly impressed.

Maybe the April sun didn't agree with Timothy Hart. He looked ill, those bright eyes in his cherub face sunken, his mouth drawn. When he began to slur his words, Brandy was surprised. He had finished only one short whisky and water. The bartender stroked his wispy beard, hesitated, raised one eyebrow, and finally pushed another glass across the bar.

The round face lifted and Hart raised his voice again. His eyes shone."Be a b-big find soon, a discovery, you c-could say. R-right in this little ole' town of Hom—Homo—"

"Homosassa," Brandy said. "A Seminole word." She looked at the Indian. "Means 'place the wild peppers grow.'" The expression on his broad face, the color of leather, did not change.

The man in the university tee shirt set aside his half-empty mug, slipped from his stool, and took Hart by the arm. The firmness of the gesture, and the way he slapped a credit card down on the bar, convinced Brandy that he was in charge. He had a tall, compact build, like an athlete, and hands that were scarred but clean. "Come on, Tim," he said. "You're not feeling well. Let's go. The landlady should have our dinner ready." He looked again at the Indian. "I'll run you on up to your camp."

The Seminole set down his Coke and stood beside him, also tall, but sturdier. Brandy gave the trio her warmest smile. "Take my business card." She handed it to Timothy Hart. "I'm from the *Gainesville Star*. When you make your big discovery, I'd like to be the first to know." She flipped it over and jotted down her Homosassa address and phone number. "I'm on vacation now, renting a cottage from a friend. Call me here or at the paper."

The archaeologist bit down on his lower lip for an instant, then turned electric blue eyes on Brandy and smiled. "Don't get your hopes up for a story, young lady. Sometimes my buddy here gets carried away."

Ignoring his friend, Hart thrust Brandy's card into his shirt pocket. "R-remember Timothy H-hart, Miss." He tottered to his feet. "I'll c-call s-soon's we're ready to m-make the announcement." He leaned closer, lips almost brushing her cheek. "I'm not doing t-too good. If you don't h-hear from me in a day or two, c-come see me. Our phone at the c-cottage—it's not w-working now, but I've got a b-big story for the papers. My friends here, they s-say I'm on a w-wild goose chase. But I got p-proof I can s-show you." With a weak grin, he straightened up. "Just r-retired. Staying at a p-place on T-tiger Tail Island." He drew himself up. "I'm going to b-buy it. It's the only h-house on the island. C-can't miss it."

Brandy knew the house. She didn't know it was for sale. "I'll be there," she said. "I'll be glad to write your story."

The bartender picked up Hart's unfinished drink. "The island's named for a Seminole war chief," he said. "He once hid out there with his band."

"Whatever," Hart murmured. He slumped a little as the other two loomed up on either side, and taking his arms, shepherded him toward the dock. Above them a sliver of moon, white as bone, slid from beneath a cloud. Brandy watched Hart stumble onto the deck of a stripped down pontoon boat. The Indian cast off the lines, the archaeologist took the wheel, and the red and green bow lights flickered on. As the three headed down river, the white stern light receded into the growing darkness.

*   *   *   *

The following morning, Brandy put down a dish of Friskies for her friend Carole's Persian cat, who was her charge during Brandy's vacation. Then she doled out dog food on the small porch for her own golden retriever. Once Meg had finished her dog food, Brandy staked her on a long chain in the front yard, gave her a vigorous belly rub, and left her to enjoy the attentions of passing friends in the development. Then Brandy turned toward the boat slip in front of the black and white concrete block home, untied her pontoon boat from its mooring in the canal, and stepped aboard.

She loved it as much as her husband did, its sleek aluminum hull, its movable canvas top, the eighteen-foot deck, the vinyl covered benches, and the small table. After she raised the top against the mid-day sun, she took her seat behind the wheel, and backed into the canal that ran in front of the house, eager for a spin down river. She cruised past shrimp boats and fine mansions along the upper Homosassa, swung by Marker 72, and crossed the mouth of the Salt River.

Brandy relished boating on the river, watching the herons and egrets fish along the water's edge, admiring the gnarled cedars, the turkey oaks, the clusters of black mangrove, and the ragged head of an occasional cabbage palm. Wheeling in an arc around Tiger Tail Bay, she scanned Tiger Tail Island for the solitary house where Timothy Hart was staying. At breakfast she'd decided to follow up the pudgy little man's story.

John wouldn't drive up from Tampa until tomorrow evening. She might as well do the interview now, possibly uncover a fresh story, maybe even a feature. When she finally spotted the roof and pier, she drifted close to the narrow riverbank and picked up her boat hook, ready to pull the pontoon to a post where she could tie up. A quick glance made her aware of oyster shells spread across the yard and cattails growing in the shallow water. Then her heart jumped. A body sprawled in the weeds.

Pulling the throttle to low, she idled nearer, tossed the boat's fenders into the river, and with a trembling hand, threw a line around a post on the pier. The man lay on his back, arms flung wide. She glimpsed the crown of a bald head, and thought she recognized the plaid shirt. Near the house a slight wind lifted palmetto fronds, and she heard the hoarse cry of a heron, but the log house itself stood in total silence.

She reached into her canvas bag for her cell phone, then slung the bag over one shoulder. First, she had to make sure. Stomach churning, she stepped across the uneven wooden pier and knelt beside the body. She flinched at the sight of the clenched fingers, the pale, sadly familiar face, the startled eyes. She could see no sign of injury, no blood on the face or shorts or shirt, could smell nothing but the odor of vomit spreading under the head.

Willing herself to remain calm, she placed her fingers on the cool wrist. No pulse. She dialed 9-1-1. When a female voice at the Homosassa Springs Sheriff's Office answered, Brandy made an effort to control her voice. "I'm Brandy O'Bannon, *Gainesville Star.* I found a body on Tiger Tail Island, past Marker 70. It's near Alma May Flint's house." Anyone who knew Homosassa knew Alma May. Brandy had spent enough time in Homosassa to know the old lady herself. She cleared her throat. "I think I can identify the body."

After the dispatcher agreed to send help, Brandy crossed the yard to the house and called out "Anybody home?" to the blank windows and closed door. Her voice was unsteady as she knocked loudly, but the only answer was the rustle of cabbage palms and the buzz of flies among the cedars. A sense of unease settled over her. It didn't seem to come from the cottage itself, but from the very land she stood on. The feeling isn't surprising, she assured herself. I just found a dead man.

Hurrying back across the yard, she sidled past the body, stepped up onto the pier, and took her seat again behind the wheel. For a moment she paused, listening to the slap of water against the posts, then heard a motor-boat pick up speed as it zoomed out of the slower manatee zone.

From a pocket on the console she pulled her small reporter's notebook. Jotting down every detail was important, not only for the Sheriff's Office, but for the story she would eventually write. Careful notes were her hallmark. She began recording her observations. Near Hart's corpse a Carolina skiff with a marine decal had been dragged out of the water and turned over; Alma May Flint's own fishing boat was gone; above the high water mark on the pier hung a faded sign: *Rooms by Week. Meals.* Brandy scanned the yard, barren except for tufts of wiregrass, a scattering of oyster shells, and a large Grapple Realty *For Sale* sign.

Apparently, fishermen didn't provide Alma May with enough income to make ends meet. Maybe she'd grown tired of life on this isolated island, of boating into town for all her supplies, and realized at last she was too old for the routine. Maybe she had grown tired of her hobby, scavenging among the island's sugar plantation ruins. Behind a satellite dish and the Realtor's sign, the Flint family's historic log house had been painted a bilious green, in a pitiful effort, she imagined, to pretty it up for the market. Still, it offered a choice Florida location to sports fisherman: access to tarpon offshore, as well as to gulf flats and the river. But Brandy didn't think for a minute that Timothy Hart was excited last night about catching tarpon or grouper. There was something else—something he said would be a momentous "discovery."

The story she would write might not be the one Timothy Hart had expected. After all, he didn't know he would die. But when Brandy looked at the still form in the weeds, she remembered how eager he had been to make his great find and report it to the world. Last night she had found

Hart oddly endearing, stutter and all, and vulnerable. Whatever had almost been in his grasp, now was forever lost to him. She made a silent vow. She would learn if some kind of treasure did exist in this old town. If it did, she would report it as Hart had wished, not only for herself, but because she had promised him she would.

Brandy laid down her pencil and ran her fingers through her clipped, reddish hair, damp now in the April sunlight. She remembered with a shudder the black vultures that squatted in turkey oaks along the shore. She wanted to see Hart's body covered. It deserved to be treated with dignity

She shifted her gaze to the river ahead and spotted the Sheriff's Office patrol boat, slicing toward the island. A youthful deputy in a deep green uniform moored near her boat and stepped out onto the pier. A stick of a man in slacks, carrying a black bag, followed close behind.

The deputy looked at Brandy and removed a green cap with a white star. "Much obliged for your call, M'am," he said, forehead glistening with perspiration.

She walked across the dock where he stood and stared down at the body. "I've got some information about the dead man that might help," she said, "I met him and his friends last night. He said he wasn't feeling well, said his name was Timothy Hart."

While the deputy printed her current phone number and address in careful letters in his notebook, the medical examiner sat back on his heels beside the corpse, thin legs bent like coat hangers. "Autopsy should show something," he reported in a dry voice. "No obvious cause of death." He poked, listened, sighed. "Might be stroke or heart. Not my guess, though." He stood and brushed the seat of his trousers. "Before we move him, better give homicide a holler."

While the deputy made the call to the command center, Brandy watched with a puzzled frown. Hart had symptoms of an illness last night. Probably the doctor couldn't detect the disease that killed him and wanted to cover all bases.

"For one thing," the examiner added, "looks like the guy was searched. Pockets are wrong side out, and he's been turned over. A person doesn't usually collapse on the back."

Brandy had not thought about the body's position. "Last night Hart said he expected to make some important discovery here in Homosassa."

The deputy shook his head. "Tourists," he said, disdain in his voice. "I could've saved him some trouble. There's sure nothing valuable in old Homosassa."

He began stringing yellow crime scene tape far out in the yard around the body. "I walked across the yard myself," Brandy explained.

The young man made more notes, then flipped the pad shut. "You know Mrs. Flint, old lady lives here?" Brandy nodded. "She'll be fit to be tied. A dead guy on her property, probably a tenant, won't help her get more renters." He gazed for a moment at the river. "You live in a small town, you get to know folks' habits. Mrs. Flint's likely in town grocery shopping, or poking around the old plantation grounds, like she does."

Brandy remembered Alma May Flint as self-sufficient and elderly and much admired by Brandy's Homosassa friend, Carole. "Met her a couple of times at craft shows," she said. "Hart claimed he was buying her house." She glanced at the 'For Sale' sign, still posted.

The deputy lifted his cap to let a light breeze ruffle his sand-colored hair, and resettled it at a smart angle. "You're free to go now, Miss. I'll tell the sergeant where he can reach you."

On her own note pad Brandy doodled a stick figure with a round head, lying face up. "Believe I'll wait," she said. "I'd like to talk to the detective." She added, not quite truthfully, "I might be able to help Mrs. Flint."

The young deputy shrugged. "Suit yourself, Miss. The sergeant will want your statement, all right, but he won't want to talk to the press. He won't like it, you're being a reporter. He won't like it one cotton-pickin' bit."

Brandy stepped back into her boat without answering. She dropped into the captain's chair, relieved to be off her feet. She felt weak, overcome by more than the death of Timothy Hart. The history of Tiger Tail Island was riddled with violence. She'd read about the sugar plantation that burned during the Civil War, and an earlier Seminole Indian massacre. Even before that, the Spaniards led a deadly clash with the first Indians along the river.

A cloud passed over the sun and cast a shadow across the island. Brandy felt a gathering force. A chill crept over her, in spite of the morning heat. The sensation was stronger than the unease she had felt earlier. She wrapped her arms protectively around herself. Timothy Hart was not the only person who had died on this island, and most died violently. She could almost feel the impact of all that fear and tragedy. Some would say she could still feel their anguish.

CHAPTER 2

▼

Brandy heard Alma May Flint's jon boat churning down Petty Creek before she saw it. The old lady herself was perched at the tiller, strands of gray hair flying from a crude knot at the back of her head. Another woman sat on the middle seat, a scarf wrapped around her head, a large cloth bag clutched in one hand, the other gripping the bare plank. Alma May maneuvered the boat into her slip, tied up, and clambered onto the pier, a long, shapeless smock clinging to her legs. Without waiting for her companion, she stalked across the dock, a wiry figure, not more than five feet tall, a set look on her small, pinched face.

"Seen your boat at my place soon's I come around the last turn," she said to the deputy. "What's the problem, son?"

The young deputy removed his cap. "Sorry, Mrs. Flint. This lady here," he motioned toward Brandy in her pontoon boat, "she called us about an hour ago. I'm afraid she found a body near your house. I'm waiting for the detective."

"Well, I swan," Mrs. Flint said. She marched over the rough boards and peered down at the still uncovered figure near the shore. "Dad-gum! He's my boarder, all right, poor soul, and my buyer, too. I told him he needed a doctor." She turned toward the other woman, now struggling up onto the dock. "You hear that, Melba? We lost our Mr. Hart."

Brandy studied the older woman's tall, bony friend with interest. She must be Melba Grapple, the real estate agent who had sold half the properties in Homosassa. The woman pulled off her scarf, thrust it into her bag, shook out her short, bleached hair, and followed Alma May as she started across the yard.

"It's okay to go on in the house," the deputy said. "Couldn't find any tracks. Shells are too hard packed."

Mrs. Flint turned sharp blue eyes on him, an edge to her voice. "Indeed, young man, I hope to heaven I can always go into my own house."

"Someone's been here before Miss O'Bannon," he explained, his tone more subdued.

Brandy stood quickly. "Mrs. Flint!" she called to the old woman's retreating back. "Remember me? The reporter from the *Gainesville Star*? We met through my friend Carol Brewster." As Mrs. Flint paused, Brandy strode closer. "I'm waiting to talk to the detective. I feel awful about what happened to Mr. Hart. I met him last night."

Alma May squinted at Brandy for a second, a hand shielding her eyes. "Carol Brewster? I knew her mama." She beckoned with one bent finger. "C'mon in out of the heat. Have a bite to eat. Reckon it's about lunch time."

Brandy swung in behind Mrs. Flint's stooped figure. "I'd like that," she said. "I see you plan to sell your house. Maybe a story in the papers about the history of Tiger Tail Island and the house would help the sale." She was picking her way past the satellite dish toward the front steps when another boat engine growled up to the riverbank. While a deputy threw a line around a post, a tall black man in a sports shirt and slacks stepped from the second patrol boat. Brandy halted.

"Reckon we got to put up with more law men," Alma May said from the doorway. "Go on now, see him if you got to, and Melba and me will rustle up something to eat."

Brandy started back toward the pier. The detective stood beside the body, back very straight, hands on his hips. Brandy hoped the deputies would soon cover the corpse and move it to the lab. She felt an obligation to Timothy Hart. She had believed him. Instead the detective began directing both the first young deputy and then second, who now walked carefully about, snapping photographs of the yard and the body from every angle. Brandy had reached the dock before she recognized the detective. She had not expected to see him again, certainly not in Homosassa. Their last meeting had been in Cedar Key in nearby Levy County. Brandy had been persistent about a homicide case there. She had begged this detective to help her with a scheme and at last he had agreed, mainly to get rid of her.

She stood patiently without speaking while he knelt to make his own examination. He carefully scooped up a sample of the vomit, then paced around the yard and shore, noticing every blemish in the soil, every indentation in the coating of oyster shells.

"Detective Strong!" she called finally, smiling. "Are you working in Citrus County now?"

Puzzled, Sergeant Jeremiah Strong turned. His slacks and shirt were as crisp as the leaves of a cardboard fern, his expression as unbending. She had hoped for an answering grin. Instead, he clapped one large hand to his forehead and shook his head. "Lord, protect me," he said. She waited for his hallmark Bible quotation. It came, perhaps predictably, from the book of Job. "The thing I have greatly feared is come upon me. How long will ye vex my soul?"

Brandy stepped forward and held out her hand, which he took briefly, then sighed. "I never know what to call you women who don't use your husband's last name. Are you Mrs. Able or Miss O'Bannon?"

Brandy smiled. "Neither, actually. I'm the wife of John Able, whose name is Brandy O'Bannon. But come on now, friend. Working together in Cedar Key wasn't all that bad, was it? After all, you caught the bad guy red-handed. I thought you were pleased."

He dropped his head. "Almost lost my rank over that case, O'Bannon. Your little plan wasn't exactly accepted procedure. I put a civilian in danger. You."

She moved a few feet closer. "But I'm sure that's not why you're in Citrus County now."

He crossed long arms over his chest and looked down at her. "No. Better pay. A bigger county, and one that's growing. In spite of a certain reporter, I had a good reputation. It saved me. We moved to Inverness two years ago so I could take a job at the Sheriff's Office there." Brandy remembered hearing about Strong's family. He had a patient wife and two children, one a boy he coached in Little League. She'd liked that about him.

The body of Timothy Hart, covered with a sheet at last, was being lifted into the patrol boat on a litter, accompanied by the medical examiner. The deputies glanced at Strong, seeking his okay. He nodded.

"Now looks like we have another death," Brandy said. "May be natural, of course. Mr. Hart said he was sick. Still, the medical examiner was a little suspicious, and the victim did ask me to get in touch with him. He had a story he wanted to tell."

Strong put his hand back on his hips and leaned forward. "Look, Miss O'Bannon or Mrs. Able, or whatever you call yourself, let me be clear. This is law enforcement business. Sometimes you got a problem with that. The Sheriff's Office has a spokesperson, a nice lady you'll find at the Command Center in Inverness. Go talk to her tomorrow. I have the statement you gave the deputy. I'll call you if I need you."

Strong did not wait for a reply, but began stalking toward the house. Brandy followed. "Forgive me for coming along, Sergeant," she said sweetly, "but I've been invited for lunch by Mrs. Flint. She lives here."

Brandy thought she heard him groan as he knocked on the door, but she also thought her presence made Alma May more welcoming when she admitted them both. They stepped into a living room with sturdy maple sideboard and table, a fireplace with a mantle, a stiff looking sofa and two upholstered chairs. The detective asked to use a separate room. He would first speak to the realtor, Melba Grapple.

Alma May headed back toward the kitchen. "Beats all," she said. "Finally get a buyer and he passes away. Thought he was looking poorly. I've still got one other boarder, but he's leaving tomorrow." She paused and glanced at Brandy. "Hope you and Melba like home-made vegetable soup. I'll heat up some from last night. Early this morning, I brought in a mess of greens and fresh tomatoes." She gave Brandy a no-nonsense look.

"And don't come into the kitchen and try to help. I work quicker by myself."

While her hostess banged pans around, Brandy peered at black and white family photographs on the mantle—Alma May as a child with stern looking parents in front of this same house and a portrait of an elderly man with a white beard she supposed was a grandfather. A small shelf under the window held two chipped green bottles, a cream pitcher with a broken spout, and a pewter spoon. In a few minutes, the realtor came back into the living room, while Detective Strong coaxed Mrs. Flint to join him. Next Melba took a seat on the sofa and pulled a lighter and a pack of cigarettes out of her bag. She held the flame beneath the cigarette until the end glowed, then dragged an oyster shell ashtray across the maple table toward her. Her middle-aged face had an aristocratic cast—a beak-like nose, high cheekbones, large clear eyes. Her jeans were designer, her hair job professional. Brandy wondered how she had come to live in Homosassa.

"This house seems to have an interesting history," Brandy said. "A feature story might help it sell."

Melba swung her cigarette in a graceful arc. "Perhaps. The Flints were early settlers. And, of course, there was the Yulee Plantation here. Alma May and I like to explore the grounds. It's a hobby. Sometimes I find broken pottery or glass bottles. I sent for an Archaeological Site short form. It lets us poke around and record what I find. Alma May's picked up a few items, too. There's never been a proper survey, though."

"Any chance of valuable artifacts there?"

Melba ran her fingers through her ash-blonde hair and shook her head. "Anything of value would've been found over a hundred years ago." In the library Brandy had read about David Yulee's extensive sugar plantation. The crew of a Union gunboat had burned the main house, slave quarters, and chapel, but Homosassa still prided itself on the town's remaining sugar mill ruins.

Alma May and Sergeant Strong appeared in the doorway. "I'll let myself out," he said. He nodded to Brandy and Melba, opened the front door, and crunched back over the oyster sells.

The old lady began slapping bowls and small plates on the table, then carried in a wooden bowl of salad greens and sliced tomatoes. Brandy could see Alma May's vegetable garden through the dining room window. "Law's started poking and prying, all right," Alma May said and sighed. "We won't have a moment's peace."

Brandy shifted the subject. "I was asking about the history of your house, Mrs. Flint."

"Flints were here long before David Yulee," she said, her voice sharp. "They had a little old cabin here before the county was settled. Passel of durned Indians burnt it to the ground. Killed everyone with knives and hatchets but my great-grandpa. He was just a boy then. If he hadn't been out duck hunting, I wouldn't be here."

Melba took another lady-like puff on her cigarette and said in a quiet voice, "The massacre happened during the second Seminole War, of course. In the mid-eighteen-thirties."

Brandy remembered the bartender's comment last night. "What about the Seminoles who hid out on the island?"

Alma May's lip curled downward. "Durned savages. I don't allow no Indians on my place."

Melba spoke up again. "Of course, there haven't been any Indians around here in more than a century. They were all sent west, except for the few hundred who escaped into the Everglades."

Brandy glanced at Alma May. "I saw one last night—with Mr. Hart."

The old woman's eyes glinted. "Well, he ain't staying here. I hear he's camping out on the island. It's a big island. Can't stop that."

After they were seated at the table, Brandy broached the subject of Hart's search. "Last night Mr. Hart talked about making an important discovery around here. I don't know if it was something worth a lot of money, or just something of historical interest." She watched their faces.

Melba looked up quickly, maybe surprised, maybe concerned, and murmured, "Of course, the Seminoles who came through here owned nothing of value. They were impoverished people, on the run." Alma May paused in the kitchen door, holding a pan of steaming soup with a pot holder, eyebrows raised. "Thought you was interested in my house, young lady. I don't go snooping into a boarder's business, thank you very much."

Brandy's tone softened. "I am interested in your house, Mrs. Flint. But everyone's going to ask you about Mr. Hart. Did you see him before you left this morning?"

Alma May ladled a thick broth of vegetables into three bowls. "Not this morning. Most often he didn't get up early. I set some cereal and sweet rolls out for him before I left to pick up Melba. He'd been looking peaked. Only been here about a week. Said last night at supper he was going in to see a doctor. He had the trots, I think, and stomach cramps. He'd rented his own boat, so I went on down the creek."

"Who's the other boarder you mentioned, Mrs. Flint?" Brandy asked.

"The fellow who's working at the Indian mound on the Little Homosassa. Sent down here by the state. Mound's not far from here, so it makes it easy for him to go back and forth in his own boat. He leaves the house even earlier than I do."

The archaeologist, Brandy realized. Hart's attractive friend in the University of Florida tee shirt. He and Timothy Hart were fellow boarders. That was why they were together last night. That fact didn't explain the Seminole.

"Just my luck," Alma May added. "He's fixing to leave, too. Taking a couple of rooms at a motel in town. Says he needs the extra space for a few items he wants to study."

They finished their meal in silence. Brandy kept glancing out the window. How would she react if she were a settler and a warlike face appeared suddenly above the sill? When they had savored the last morsel of soup and salad, she rose and helped carry the plates and silverware back into the kitchen. "I really appreciate the delicious lunch," she said, and meant it. "It's a rare treat to get vegetables fresh out of a garden." She picked up her canvas bag and moved to the door. "I'd like to come back, if I may, talk to you more about the house and Tiger Tail Island."

"I reckon that would be all right," Alma May said slowly, her blue eyes wary.

*   *   *   *

In the late afternoon Brandy swung her boat into its slip at the concrete block house she was renting. For months she and her husband had paid Carole to leave their boat there so that it would be in the water when they wanted to fish or cruise the river. Now Brandy tied the pontoon securely fore and aft, crossed the narrow road, and knelt to hug her aging golden retriever. After she unsnapped the long lead that allowed Meg the full range of the unfenced yard, she banged through the front door. The home itself included three bedrooms, a screen porch, living room, and utility.

In the kitchen Brandy again set out dry cat food and water for her friend's haughty cat and fed Meg, then poured a small glass of Merlot and passed on into the living room. Carole gave her a deep discount for a two-week vacation here, as long as she cared for the Persian. Carole had scheduled her own vacation for this time, and those plans locked in the dates for Brandy. Weekends her husband John would make the two and a half hour drive up from Tampa, where his architectural firm had assigned him to work a temporary job.

Brandy paused at a bookcase by Carole's easy chair and noted the row of Folger Library copies of Shakespeare's plays. Carole was one of her more literary friends from university days, where they had both majored in English Lit. Only two weeks ago, Carole had driven to Gainesville to join Brandy for a University of Florida theater production of *The Tempest*. Brandy pulled out the slender volume of the play and flipped to a few favorite passages before returning the book to its alphabetical place. She had made a curious connection. Timothy Hart died under suspicious conditions on an island that also appeared to house a sorcerer—medicine man Fishhawk—wandering spirits, and a witch or monster capable of murder. Unfortunately for Hart, the monster on Tiger Tail Island ranged unchecked. In any case, his sad fate promised a dramatic human interest story.

Brandy sat for a while at the wicker table on the porch, sipping her wine and watching the boats gently rise and fall with the tide. The shadows of tall pines lengthened across the canal. Overhead, a cloud of turkey vultures swooped past on their way to roost on the town's water tower. Although the birds were valuable to the ecology, she never saw them without a sense of dread. For the moment, the approaching night seemed to gather its forces of secrecy and darkness.

Brandy tried to shake off the somber feeling by planning for tomorrow. She would call the Sheriff's Office and ask about the spokeswoman Sergeant Strong had mentioned. She would have time for a briefing. John wouldn't arrive for the weekend until the evening. She would use Carole's Chevrolet for the drive to the Citrus County capitol of Inverness and the Sheriff's Office Command Center. Because Carole had asked Brandy not to let her car sit idle for the whole two weeks, Brandy had left her own Toyota coupe in Gainesville and driven to Homosassa with John.

After a restless night, she finished a solitary breakfast of grapefruit and English muffin, then telephoned the Sheriff's Command Center and learned she could sit in on a press briefing of the Hart inquiry at 2:00 P.M. For the next hour she transcribed her hasty notes of the day before, filled in the details she could remember, and noted the facts she knew about Alma May Flint and her friend, Melba Grapple. At the top of the first page she drew a pencil sketch of the log house, the small boat pulled up on shore, and a stick figure lying beside it.

Next Brandy phoned her editor and brought him up-to-date. He agreed that she should look into the circumstances of Hart's death, as long as she was already on the spot. She was to let him know if it promised a story of interest to their readers. Brandy sighed. John already had a reason to argue with her. This case would give him another. He would not be happy to find her investigating a feature story, one that again might involve a murder, and that might occupy her time this weekend.

At 1:30 P.M. Brandy drove past pastures, lush with new spring grass, and groves dotted with oranges, and into the old town of Inverness. She passed the elegant British style Crown Hotel on North Seminole Avenue and the historic Citrus County Courthouse, in the process of restoration. Finally, people seemed to appreciate historic buildings. A similar job was keeping John busy in Tampa. She noted the quiet waters of Lake Tsala

Apopka flanking the downtown area and tried to remember its Seminole meaning: something like "fish eating place." The tribe had left its mark here, too.

After parking at the Citrus County Sheriff's operations center, she found the briefing room, signed in, and joined a reporter from the *Citrus County Chronicle* and a stringer for the regional section of the *St. Petersburg Times*. A neatly groomed brunette in a tailored navy suit faced them across her desk, backed up by an imposing row of sheriff's portraits.

She pulled down glasses that had been perched on her head, surveyed a page before her, and read aloud: "The body found on an island on the Homosassa River yesterday morning has been identified as Timothy Hart of Danville, Illinois, age 65. This morning the Sheriff's Office located his next of kin, a younger sister, Mrs. Harvey Blunt, also of Danville. A local officer there went out personally to tell her about her brother's death. Mr. Hart had been in this area a week. He rented a room on the river from long-time resident, Alma May Flint, 75."

When the woman paused to adjust her glasses, Brandy raised her hand. "Has the medical examiner completed an autopsy?"

The woman frowned. "I'm getting to that," she said a little testily. She glanced at the reporter sign-in list. "Miss O'Bannon, *Gainesville Star?* Wouldn't have thought there'd be much interest in Gainesville. We don't see the *Star* here."

"Actually, Mr. Hart may be of wide interest in Florida," Brandy said with emphasis. The others turned to look at her.

"The cause of death is being investigated," the spokeswoman continued. "We're waiting for a report from the lab." She looked up and spoke with more hesitation. "I think I can tell you that Mr. Hart was interested in surviving off the land. But suspicious facts remain."

"You're waiting for a toxicology report?" asked the reporter from the *Chronicle.*

The woman's expression became bland. "We're looking at all possibilities."

"Might be poisoning," the man from the *Chronicle* said. He grinned at Brandy. "They send the stomach contents off for testing. Pleasant to think about, isn't it? May take a while." Brandy remembered that the detective had removed vomit from the scene.

But she wasn't thinking as much about Hart's ample stomach and its contents, as about Mrs. Flint's garden. Tiger Tail Island was uninhabited except for the old lady and her tenants—and the Seminole Indian Alma May said was camping out on the island. What could Hart have been eating? Where could it come from? Would he eat a quantity of some kind of vegetation without guidance? She remembered that Alma May and Melba Grapple hiked over the island, looking for artifacts from the nineteenth century plantation. They would know what grew there. If the Indian was familiar with his people's history and culture, he would know a great deal about surviving off the land.

Brandy looked around without success for Sergeant Strong. "Is Detective Jeremiah Strong handling this case?" she asked.

The woman did not answer. "This is still an unexplained death. That's all we have for you now," she said.

Brandy made rapid notes. Pitiful Timothy Hart. Detective Strong must already know if the medical examiner suspected poisoning. Of course, it could be unintentional or self-inflicted. Strong must be talking to people who knew Hart like Alma May and Melba, and his companions the night before he died. The spokeswoman had not mentioned Hart's quest, or his belief in some great discovery. Hart had said the archaeologist would be able to explain it, so the specialist must know something about his story. Hart had complained that his companions did not take him seriously. Maybe Sergeant Strong didn't either.

Back at her friend's home in Homosassa, Brandy checked her watch, sat on a stool in the kitchen, and picked up the telephone on the counter. It would be an hour earlier in Illinois—3:00 P.M. She dialed long distance information.

Danville, it turned out, was not a large town. After speaking to a Thelma Blunt, who was her husband's cousin, Brandy located Timothy Hart's sister, Adele Blunt.

"Mrs. Blunt," she began after identifying herself, "I'm so sorry about your brother. I met him a couple of nights ago. A very nice fellow. I—"

A crisp voice cut her short. "Yes, of course. But to tell the truth, also a fool."

Shocked, Brandy paused. Then she said, "Before his death Mr. Hart spoke to me about some discovery he expected to make in Homosassa. Do you—"

"I warned him," she said. Her tone did not soften. "He never should've retired from the furniture store. Management still wanted him. He got a puny little pension, and he'd begun to waste that on this fool hunch he had." Her voice rose. "But you see, he inherited an old farmhouse and some land from our great-grandmother. Well, we were both actually entitled to the farm, but she always favored Tim. The boy in the family, you see."

Brandy waited.

"Well, he found a wretched old journal in the attic, and it got him all in a dither."

Brandy sat up straighter. "And did you see the journal yourself?"

"He showed it to me, but to tell the truth I couldn't make out the handwriting. All faded and spidery, you know. I don't think Tim really read it, either. But he got very secretive." She wound up triumphantly, "Then he rushed off to Florida like a chicken with its head cut off."

Brandy slipped a pencil out of a cabinet drawer. "Do you know how old the journal was or who wrote it?"

Adele Blunt now sounded bored with the conversation, and more hesitant. "Tim claimed it was written by an ancestor. A soldier, I think, in Florida. Served in some Indian war or other."

"Can you recall a name or date?"

The other woman's tone grew acidic. "I've told you all I know. Tomorrow I've got to find someone to sell Timothy's old rattletrap car he left there and make arrangements with a crematorium. It won't be easy. His funeral policy might not be good there. Then I've got to have his ashes flown back home."

Inconsiderate of Hart, Brandy thought, to put his sister to so much trouble. She kept the sarcasm out of her voice. "You don't plan to come to Homosassa yourself?"

Indignation spiked in Mrs. Blunt's voice. "I see no reason to. I can't do anything for Tim now except bury his ashes in the family plot."

Brandy tried another question. "Mrs. Blunt, has anyone from the Sheriff's Office talked to you about the journal?"

"Some man did call, told me they hadn't decided yet what he died of. Might be something he ate. Tim was gullible about alternative medicines, herbs and things not properly tested. A fool, like I said. The man from the Sheriff's Office didn't ask about a journal."

"Did you tell him—"

"I've given you quite enough time," Mrs. Blunt snapped. "I can't believe I've talked this long to a reporter. The family doesn't want a lot of ugly publicity. That's all I have to say." She hung up.

Brandy still had a couple of hours before John would arrive. On the screened porch she recorded highlights of the conversation in her notebook. At the end she jotted her first goal: *find the journal.*

CHAPTER 3

▼

As the porch clock neared six, Brandy pushed thoughts about Timothy Hart, his murder, and his mysterious search out of her mind. Her husband would be there soon. Early yesterday Brandy had not been thinking of death. She had cruised down the river, worried only about her on-going disagreement with John. Tonight she would try again to make him see her point of view.

The sun was low when John drove into the carport. Charcoal clouds, rimmed in scarlet, hung in the western sky. He emerged from his minivan, two heavy books under one arm, the other hand dragging a small suitcase hooked to a stuffed briefcase. She knew from the sag in his shoulders and the weariness in his brown eyes, that he was not only tired, but disappointed. Probably not with his job, even though he was bringing work with him on a holiday weekend. His frustration, she knew, was with her.

When he stepped into the screened porch, she lifted her face to him. "Looks like you need a couple of days off."

He brushed her lips with his, set down his briefcase and bag, and laid his books—a biography of Alexander Hamilton and one of his favorite sources, *Classic Cracker Architecture*, on the wicker table. Meg jumped up from her spot beside Brandy's living room chair, rushed onto the porch, and raised her creamy muzzle, tail wagging. He gave her copper-colored head a rub as his eyes sought Brandy's.

"I missed you," he said. "Hope you're having a good vacation." He dropped into a chair beside the table and fingered his mustache, a habit when he felt tense. His was a firm, square face. Its strength, the upright set of his shoulders and his lean body had always thrilled and somehow comforted her—until this obstacle had risen between them. Tonight he slumped and ran one hand through his dark hair.

She wanted to avoid the inevitable discussion. "Let's relax. It's nice out here. Sit down, and I'll get two beers." She hurried through the living room into the kitchen and lifted the cans from the refrigerator. "I had an adventure today," she called brightly. A delaying tactic. She took mugs from the cabinet. "I found a body yesterday. It was horrible. I'd met the man…"

"Bran," he said as she came back with the drinks on a tray, "you can tell me about that later. Our problem won't go away. I'd like to have an understanding, one way or the other."

Brandy had a good track record for getting what she wanted. It helped as a reporter. Wheedling demeaned her, but it was called for now. "Come on," she said. "I'm not thirty yet. There's lots of time to have a baby. I'm just getting off the ground at the paper. One more truly great story and I could be a feature writer."

He rubbed his forehead. Wistful eyes searched hers. "Won't you even look for a job in Tampa or St. Pete? It would make everything easier."

She shrugged and took a seat beside him. "There isn't a vacancy at either newspaper. Anyway, you may not stay in Tampa after the old courthouse is renovated."

He reached over and took her hand. "That's not the point. I want a family. I thought we agreed on that in the beginning. It's the point of getting married."

She was not making him understand. "I'm not like your mother, you know," she said gently. "I don't want to give up everything I've worked for. I don't know any men who would quit a job they love to bear and take care of a child. Especially when they're just getting started."

"I've waited five years."

She poured some beer into her mug, her mouth tighter. "I've got friends with children. They worry all the time about baby sitters. They've got no freedom. They're always rushing to get home. With a schedule like that, how could I cover a story like the one I just ran across in Homosassa?"

He hadn't touched his drink. "No one's asking you to totally give up your career."

"Later, honey, when I'm established. I'm not saying 'never.' I want to plan a baby when we have a good, steady income." She spoke quietly. "I want to be able to take a few years off. Have money saved up to tide us over. See our way clear to fund a college education."

He dropped his head, his beer forgotten. "There'll never be a time for you," he said. "Never quite enough money. There'll always be a story you want to do next. I've read about older couples who wait. Then they spend thousands at clinics, and still don't have a baby."

Disturbed, Meg rose from where she had flopped down and again wagged her fluffy plume of a tail. The peace-maker, Brandy thought. John rubbed her head again. "Meg would be wonderful with a child."

Brandy felt a rising sadness. There was no good resolution. When she did not respond, John swept up his briefcase, shook his head, and tramped into the dining room. A few minutes later Brandy heard him in the bedroom. He would be hanging his jeans and a suit to wear back to the office Monday. For a long time she sat in the growing darkness, staring at the boat in the canal. She had meant to make a good supper—cook roasting ears, snap beans, maybe grill a steak on the back deck overlooking the tidal creek. Now she didn't feel like it. When she finally went into the house, she saw John had set down his laptop, and spread his papers and sketches over the large dining room table, along with a few Mozart and Bach CD's. Working and listening to music was apparently how he planned to spend the weekend. Well, she had a project, too: Timothy Hart.

"Let's go out for chicken wings," she said. They climbed into John's minivan in silence, not quite hostile but devoid of intimacy. He did not reach over and give her a pat as he usually did. John wheeled into the parking lot of a small, cypress-paneled restaurant near the ruins of the nineteenth century sugar mill. When they were seated, the conversation quickly returned to their chronic problem.

"I've been asked to fill in as a coach on a boys soccer team," John began as a waitress set out plates of wings and Greek salads. "I used to play in college."

Brandy smiled. "Why don't you? You'd get some exercise during the week."

He stirred his salad with his fork. "I'm afraid it would be too painful. The other coaches are all dads." They finished in silence.

*   *   *   *

Back at the house, Meg lay unusually still on the living room carpet between their chairs, her brown eyes turning from John to Brandy, sensing something wrong.

John switched on the television to the local public station. The National Geographic was airing a program about baby animals. Brandy abandoned him to a den of wolf cubs and returned to her notebook.

That night in bed she patted his arm and gave him a quick kiss on the forehead, but he pulled away, silent, as he often did when they had quarreled. Brandy rolled over, her back to him, feeling rejected. Probably just as well. Now anytime he touched her, she assumed his desire was not for her but for a baby.

As she lay there, Brandy's eyes grew moist. Her father had encouraged her, his only child; he had been certain she could be a first rate journalist. Now he was gone, dead of a heart attack before she earned her English lit degree or added the specialty in print media, or had her first newspaper job. He had faith in her, even if John didn't seem to care.

The image of a tanned face with a lock of blond hair falling across his forehead floated into her mind—Hart's archaeologist friend. She remembered him in the soft light of the Tiki bar. They might meet again when she paid another call on Alma May Flint. Brandy finally fell asleep and dreamed John and his minivan lifted into the air above Homosassa and vanished, while below the archaeologist stood at the bar, a protective arm across the shoulders of Timothy Hart.

The next morning John and Brandy shared bacon, eggs, and toast on the screened porch. She asked a few questions about his Tampa restoration job, but he showed little interest in the death of Timothy Hart. Clearly he viewed it as one more distraction for Brandy, one that complicated their weekend.

After breakfast he strode into the dining room and began poring over computer print-outs of the historic courtroom. He had a problem with the placement of its amber-colored windows. Brandy stood for a few minutes at his elbow and gave him a weak smile. "Want to get in some fishing today?" she asked, "Or just get out in the boat? We could go down to Tiger Tail Island, and I could show you where I found the body. The old lady who lives there's a character."

He rubbed his forehead. "No, thanks. I've still got some work to finish before I go back. If I have time, I can fish just as well in the canal." He stood, walked to the music console, and pulled out a CD. "I know you want to get back to your story. I'll be okay."

She sighed. Why did her work always seem to interfere in their lives, while his did not? Still, maybe she wasn't being quite fair. If he complained about her hours on the job, it was only because he wanted to be with her.

As she loaded the dishwasher, she made her plans. She would take the boat to Mrs. Flint's, try to talk to her remaining boarder, the archaeologist, and find out more about the Indian mound dig. She would like to locate the elusive Seminole and discover why he was camping on the island. Most important, she wanted to learn what had happened to the journal Hart had found. She left John at the dining room table again, Meg at his feet, while the intricate strains of a Mozart concerto filled the room.

Brandy pulled into Alma May's rickety pier about 9:30 A.M., in time to see the archaeologist crossing the yard toward his own pontoon boat. On its deck she could see a shovel, screens fastened to frames, hand spades, small boxes, and an ice chest.

"Brandy O'Bannon," she called to him. "*Gainesville Star.* Remember, we met at the Tiki bar the other night?"

He halted, walked over to her boat, and placed a tanned hand on the railing. "Grif Hackett," he said. "Short for Grifton. Don't think I introduced myself that night. I was too worried about poor old Hart." He gave his head a mournful shake. The blond lock fell across his forehead. "With good reason, it turns out." His was a narrow face with high cheekbones, his eyes a startling blue.

Brandy hoped for an interview, but she didn't pull out her notebook. She would ease into it. "What do you think was the matter with him?"

Again Hackett shook his head. "My Seminole buddy Fishhawk Pine told him about a lot of stuff the Seminoles used to eat. Hart was into that herbal stuff. You have to be pretty careful, though. Experimenting could've made him sick. I didn't know him well, and no one here knew his medical condition."

He glanced toward his boat. Probably he's eager, Brandy thought, to get started for the mound. The hour was late for an early riser. "Did he show you an old journal he'd found?"

Grif bit his lower lip and paused. "A journal?"

"I called his sister in Illinois. She told me about it. She was not his biggest fan. Not much sympathy for him there. He says the journal was the reason he came here."

Hackett gazed across the bay where the Salt River joined the Homosassa, as if trying to remember. From its nest atop a tall channel marker Brandy watched an osprey rise on broad wings, flashing white breast feathers, and circle the bay. "Seems to me he said something about finding an early record of some kind," Hackett said. "Might be interesting to Florida historians. I usually saw Hart only at Mrs. Flint's. We didn't talk much." The osprey plunged into the water, then flapped free, a fish in its claws.

"Did Hart spend his time fishing?"

Grif waved one arm toward the hard wood hammocks in the center of the island. "Mostly he tramped around the island. He was negotiating for Mrs. Flint's house. First day he was here I took him to buy some heavy boots. Natives call them Homosassa Reeboks. You need them here. But I didn't see him fishing. Maybe he planned to after he bought the house."

The white-breasted bird settled into its nest. Brandy could see tiny heads shoot forward. Hackett had called his Indian friend "Fishhawk," another name for "osprey." She wondered if Fishhawk, the man, also was a skilled hunter. "I'd like to meet the Indian you were with at the Tiki bar."

He hesitated a few seconds. "That could be worked out, I guess. He's from the Seminole Cultural Center in Tampa. We've got an arrangement. He's a spiritual adviser for the work I'm doing at the burial mound near here. It's been disturbed. The state wants me to assess the damage and try to put things right. They have to have a Ph.D. archaeologist on site."

Something else to check out—the Indian's connection to Hackett. She had read enough Florida history to know that Seminoles were not mound builders. But then, mound builders no longer existed. Spanish diseases and guns had seen to that. "I'm going to be in the area about ten days. Could I visit the mound, too? I've never seen an excavation under way."

Hackett stepped forward and extended one hand. "No problem. Brandy, isn't it?" His handshake was firm, the hand callused but scrupulously clean. "We don't actually do much excavating anymore. Repair work is more like it, and inventorying what turns up. Come aboard and I'll run you down to Fishhawk's camp first." She found herself hooked by a pair of clear blue eyes, then his gaze dropped. She supposed he noticed her wedding ring. It was just as well. "Fishhawk's place isn't far. I need to see him anyway. Then I've got to pick up a graduate student who's been helping out at the mound." He turned his lips down in disapproval. "At least, she thinks she's been helping. Fortunately, this is her last day. She didn't find field archaeology as exciting as she expected. She didn't care for the dirt and the heat and the bugs, especially the spiders and gnats. Understandable, really. Tie your boat up here and come aboard."

In a few minutes Brandy had thrown a half hitch around a post at the end of the pier and swung up through the gate of Hackett's larger pontoon boat. He switched on the engine, reversed, and started down Petty Creek on the western side of the island. After they had cruised about a quarter of a mile, Hackett nosed into shore, jumped from the bow, and pulled the boat up onto the sloping bank. Brandy tucked her jeans into the tops of her walking shoes and followed him over the railing and onto a narrow path. It wound upward through wire grass and beside a wide marsh of silvery black needlerush and marsh grass. Near the creek a long, slender canoe lay bottom up.

"At the Cultural Center Fishhawk shows how the Seminoles made these," Hackett said. "It's almost a lost art. They were hacked out of the hollowed core of a cypress log. This one's about fifteen feet long. Back breaking work. Of course, this is a clone, not an original."

On a rise several yards before them stood a cluster of cabbage palms, turkey oaks, hickory nut trees, and cedars, a typical coastal hammock. "The guy's getting back to his roots, you might say." The archaeologist stopped to give Brandy a hand. "He says Seminoles are losing their own culture, even their own language. I suppose they are. There were never many Florida Seminoles. At the end of the Second Seminole War only about three hundred were left in the state."

A thin coil of smoke lifted above the trees. From the shadows came the low monotone of a chant. Hackett paused to shout, "Hey, there! Company here. Fishhawk!" The voice halted. A cedar rustled at the outer edge of the hammock and the Indian emerged. He wore a long-sleeved cotton shirt, jeans, and boots. If he owned the traditional brightly colored Seminole jacket, he must save it for special occasions.

Up a slight slope stood the "chickee," a replica of the open-sided housing that nineteenth century Seminoles learned to build when they were constantly on the move, sometimes only a day or two ahead of the army. Four cypress logs supported a roof of palm thatch woven together with vines and thin rope. To make a crude floor, planks had been nailed to the supports a couple of feet above the sandy soil. In the shade of hammock and chickee, Fishhawk did not wear the black, deep-crowned hat that lay on the floor.

Hackett lowered himself beside the chickee to perch on his heels. "You remember seeing this young lady when we had a drink with Hart the other night?"

Fishhawk gave her a curt nod and squatted next to his friend. He looked to be in his early forties. The broad, copper-toned face and black eyes disclosed nothing.

"She wants to ask us a few questions about poor old Hart. I told her we didn't know much." Fishhawk remained silent. "Got your chickee up with no problem, I see."

"You got it," he said. "A few days ago a friend barged in the cypress logs and palm fronds and a crew of guys to help." He spoke in a resonant baritone.

Brandy glanced around for something to sit on and finding nothing, sat uncomfortably on the ground beside the archaeologist. "Dr. Hackett tells me you're exploring your own Seminole culture," she said. "Kind of re-living it. I understand a band of Seminoles stayed on this island for a while during the Second Seminole War."

For the first time the Indian looked at her, then shifted his gaze quickly away. "Tiger Tail's band." His deep voice had a bitter ring. "Not long before they were taken at Cedar Key. The old man was the last Seminole war chief sent west. He died in New Orleans. Of a broken heart, they say."

Brandy hurried on. "I read that a thirty acre plantation was built on the island in the 1860s. I mention it because Hart said he hoped to make a valuable discovery here. Looks like you're exploring the island." From her chart Brandy calculated Tiger Tail must be about three miles long and a mile and a half wide. Big. "Can you tell me what you've learned about the island?"

Fishhawk looked around him, at the oaks with their long fingers of Spanish moss, at the creek beyond, at the saw grass stretching toward Alma May Flint's house. "We don't need to explore this island, Miss O'Bannon," Fishhawk said. "We need to purify it—and ourselves." He turned toward the shadows. "There's evil here. Your people wouldn't understand. I'm one of the few left who knows about these things. I'm trying to drive out the evil. You Christians call it casting out demons."

"You're talking about witches," Hackett said.

The Indian glanced at him, the look in his glistening eyes guarded. "I know how to protect us. Hart wouldn't listen. Mrs. Flint and a bunch of white people with money may think they own this island. But to the Master of Breath it belongs to us."

Brandy knew that many contemporary Seminoles had only a fraction of pure tribal genes, but Fishhawk's weathered, red-brown face looked a hundred percent Indian to her. He seemed as natural to the island as its cabbage palms, its hammocks, and its water birds.

Still, Brandy wondered if Fishhawk was casting out demons or searching for treasure, but she only smiled. "I read about the settler's cabin that was on the island. I believe a family was killed there by Seminole warriors in the nineteenth century." Brandy felt sure he knew about the massacre at the Flint's pioneer homestead.

"There was a lot of death on this island. A lot of the white soldiers hadn't much use for settlers themselves. A surgeon with the army about that time called the settlers' children 'little white-headed responsibilities.' But because of them, soldiers drove my people off their land."

Brandy had no answer. There were many other deaths, of course, Indian ones of more than one tribe, slaves, soldiers, too. The area had known two wars. Evil had struck the island time and again. Brandy remembered the eerie feeling she had while she waited on Tiger Tail Island for the detective.

"Fishhawk was raised by his grandfather. A respected medicine man," the archaeologist said in a quiet voice.

He pointed to an iron skillet, brimming with green leaves, over a charcoal fire. "Getting the black drink ready to purify yourself?" When the Indian nodded, Hackett added, "One treatment was enough for me. You want to go to the mound with me today?"

Fishhawk scowled. "Not unless I have to. But I got to stay around, anyway. That big Sheriff's detective told me I had to."

So Strong had interviewed him already. Brandy wondered if the detective had more success in getting him to open up.

"Annie called," the Indian said to Hackett. "Wants friends to drive her up from Tampa to join me. Wants to bring our little girl." A suggestion of a smile lit his dark face, then vanished. He took a sober look into the black brew. "I'm afraid it's not a good idea."

Hackett stood, stretched, reached one long arm to help Brandy up, and looked at the Seminole. "You'd enjoy the company. They'd keep you busy, all right." He frowned at the chickee. "But your wife's going to want more comfort than you've got here."

"Yeah," the other man said with another fleeting smile. "She do hug her air conditioner."

"Is it safe for your little girl?" Brandy asked, glancing around at the crude shelter and the woods.

Fishhawk snorted. "You ask a Seminole that? Children survived a lot worse camps than this. I can protect them. Anyway, I shouldn't be here much longer."

"I'd like to meet your wife and daughter when they get here." Brandy smiled. Fishhawk didn't seem to know how to respond. He remained silent, but Brandy was not easily discouraged when she thought she might learn something new. "Maybe I'll drop back by."

In the silence Hackett turned to Brandy. "Come on. Fishhawk's busy getting purified and ready for his family. We'll go to the mound after I pick up my student. It'll give me a chance to tell you about my own search." He smiled, led her back toward the path, and dropped his voice. "Actually, I'm the one who's made the real find, not poor old Hart. Only mine hasn't any value except to research, and no museum can keep it." He shook his head. "Fishhawk's my friend, but don't ask him about studying burial mounds. He doesn't approve. Disturbing the dead's a big negative."

"You must've found Indian bones."

Grif nodded. "I didn't create the problem. Thieves who steal from Indian graves did."

CHAPTER 4

▼

"Fishhawk isn't my friend's English name, of course," Hackett said as they pushed his boat off the shore. Brandy scrambled to find a seat among the sifting screens, trowels, and a small tool Grif identified as a probe. "Fishhawk's American name is Franklin Pine. But he likes to use the name he got at a naming ceremony as a boy. Comes from a dream his grandfather had when Fishhawk was a baby. Something about an osprey swooping down and plucking something valuable out of water. Even the name Fishhawk is Anglicized. It's really a Miccosukee word I can't pronounce. Still, his mother had him baptized. Go figure."

"Must be confusing for contemporary Seminoles, not knowing which is their real culture."

The archaeologist turned the key to the engine and it roared to life. "Fishhawk knows. His boots are firmly in the chickee. Now Annie—she's different. She's a full-blooded Seminole, but she's more into white culture."

Brandy watched Hackett skirt the oyster bar that lurked below the water where the creek joined the Homosassa River. "I'm to pick Bibi up at the dock nearest the Florida Marine Patrol trailer. She'll be waiting there. He frowned and shook his head. "She won't be eager to go back out to the mound. I warn you, the mosquitoes are fierce, and it's dirty work. Bibi will never make a field archaeologist. I guess it's just as well she finds out now.

She volunteers at the Crystal River Archaeological Site Museum. She should study native pottery and specialize in ceramics instead."

Grif turned back upriver, skirted Bird Island with its roosting flocks of cormorants and anhingas, and skimmed past a row of shrimp boats docked along a pier.

"But you prefer field work?"

Grif gave her a wry smile. "Yes, but in an area where new discoveries are being made, like Mexico."

When he passed the Marine Patrol station, he maneuvered into the closest marina. A tall, solidly built girl in jeans stood by one of the gas pumps, watching Grif. An attendant in coveralls hurried to the edge of the pier and helped pull Grif's pontoon into a slip.

"I'll fill the tanks while we're here," Grif said to Brandy. "You may want to get out, grab a Coke or something." He called across to the girl, "Brandy O'Bannon here is going to ride out with us. She's a reporter from Gainesville. Brandy, meet my student, Bibi Brier."

Brandy stepped up onto the dock. "I've never seen real archaeological field work in progress," she said to Bibi, who did not move from her place beside the pump. Instead she began encasing her long brown hair under a tight fitting scarf. She barely nodded to Brandy, then turned to Grif. "I'd about decided not to go this morning. But I've changed my mind." She focused large gray eyes on Brandy, who thought young Bibi wore a lot of carefully applied eyeliner and mascara for grubby work in mosquito-infested woods.

Grif watched the attendant finish with the first heavy plastic tank next to the engine and start filling the second. "Today I'm planning to bring several items to the rooms I've rented at the motel," he said. "I've taken an agitator there for washing pottery shards. We won't be long at the mound."

With languid grace, Bibi sauntered over to stand next to Grif. For a large-boned woman, she moved with a surprisingly liquid quality. Brandy thought she'd probably had training in dance.

"I can help you clean the fragments with a toothbrush," she said.

Grif did not reply directly. "Bibi not only volunteers at the museum," Grif said to Brandy. "Last fall she went to the Chassahowitza Wildlife Refuge a few miles south of here and helped build an observation blind and a pen for the winter's incoming whooping cranes."

Brandy turned to Bibi Brier with renewed interest. "You've been very busy."

"I grew up in Crystal River," Bibi said, eyes still on Grif. Brandy recognized the hero worship gaze.

If Grif was affected, he didn't show it. "Well, let's go. It's already late. Fortunately, I don't have to do anything except bag a few items."

The three stepped down into the pontoon. Grif took his place at the console, while Brandy and Bibi crawled over the tools and perched on a bench in the rear. "I've got a suggestion," Brandy said before Grif cranked the engine. "Drop me off at Alma May's to pick up my own boat. I'll follow you to the mound. I need to get back to my place by lunch time." John would be waiting.

He shrugged. "Suit yourself, but after we turn off the Salt River into the Little Homosassa, you'll need to watch for rocks. Stay right behind me. The river's pretty shallow this time of year."

A few minutes later he stopped at Alma May's dock, then idled off shore while Brandy settled herself behind the wheel of her own pontoon. Beside Alma May's small craft rocked a sleek Grady White boat with a 150 horsepower engine. Brandy glanced up at the house. Through the open living room window she recognized Melba Grapple, and beside her, a tall, bulky figure. Brandy remembered Alma May was a widow. As she turned the key, shifted into reverse, and cut in behind Hackett, she wondered if there was a Mr. Grapple.

After about a quarter of a mile, Grif wheeled his boat into the Salt River. For a moment Brandy had the incongruous view of the Crystal River nuclear power plant tower thrusting up above distant hammocks. Grif cruised through Shiver's Bay and into the narrower Little Homosassa, where he beached his boat across from the mouth of a shallow creek. Both Bibi and Grif jumped out and dragged the bow further ashore. Brandy pulled in beside him, tugged her own craft up beside his, and climbed once more over the bow railing. Beyond the tiny beach rose a slope, dotted with red cedars and cabbage palms. A few slender trunks curved out above the water. Brandy did not see a mound.

Bibi stretched, stared at the ground lifting up before them, then wrapped her arms around herself. Although she wore a long-sleeved shirt, she didn't seem confident it would protect her. "I'm staying with the boat," she announced. "I'll help with anything you want to take back. I don't need to go up there again."

Grif frowned. "Mosquitoes, I suppose," he said. "Well, suit yourself." He sighed. "I've got two people who're supposed to help me, and neither one's willing to work on the mound." Brandy realized Fishhawk did not want to come even this close.

Shells popped under his feet as he walked toward Brandy, holding out a can of insect repellent. "The mosquitoes will be fierce. The Seminoles used fish oil mixed with juice or ashes of indigo. This probably works better." He watched while she sprayed her arms and legs and rubbed some of the liquid on her face, then reached back into his boat and dragged out a bedraggled jacket. "Better put this on, too, for the long sleeves. You wear a wedding ring," he added quietly.

Brandy's cheeks reddened. He hadn't noticed it before. "I do. But..." She paused in confusion. She had almost confessed that she and John had problems.

After a few seconds Hackett said, "I understand about the 'but.'" He turned, started up an overgrown trail that wound among the cedars. "I was married for a time," he said. "It didn't take." He glanced over his shoulder as she toiled up behind him. "But I've got no kids, thank goodness. And you?"

She shook her head, remembering how John felt on the subject, then looked up. They now stood on top of a hill about eighty feet wide and twelve feet high, overlooking both river and bayou. Brandy realized they had been climbing the mound itself, its summit hidden by thick cedars. "We're on state land," Grif said. "Florida owns about 80,000 acres here that are protected from development. Safety Harbor Indians lived here, long before the Seminoles came. They were in the area when the Spanish first came to Florida." He looked west toward the Gulf, perhaps two miles away. "Treasure ships from Mexico sailed past here on the way to Hispaniola. A few wrecked on coral reefs off shore because of the hurricanes."

Brandy tried to picture the mound, river, and woods as they had been then—scores of Indians, men casting nets for fish and crabs, digging for clams, women pounding maize, children scampering among them.

"The state sent me here as a repairman, you might say," Hackett said. "A Florida Marine Patrol boat spotted pot hunters up here a few weeks ago, digging up native pottery. The officers scared them off, but they could never identify the thieves. They notified the state archaeology department. Enter me."

Brandy gazed around her. Across the top and sides of the mound the soil had been disturbed, but she didn't see open holes. Apparently Hackett had begun restoration work.

"In these cases, a committee that includes Seminoles meets in Tallahassee. They decided I should preserve what's not disturbed and turn the pottery fragments over to the Natural History Museum in Gainesville. I'm a regional curator on the staff."

"You can't just put things back the way they were?"

"Once a site's disturbed, it's ruined for the Indians and the archaeologists. We needed a spiritual advisor for the job, but fortunately, I knew Fishhawk. Of course, there aren't any Safety Harbor people left, but the Seminoles could be very distant cousins. Some anthropologists believe a number of the original Indians survived the plagues of small pox and other diseases and joined incoming Creeks. After all, white men wrote the histories that said all the original natives were wiped out. Some may have survived far from the Spanish, farther inland. In any case, we know southeastern tribes were influenced by the mound-building culture."

Brandy noticed that several spots were covered with fresh dirt. "Must make it hard to be an archaeologist in Florida. Don't archaeologists usually collect what they find from the past?"

"Not at American Indian sites. Most American Indians believe the earth is damaged when it's plundered. They think even burial goods like pots are animate. Certainly they don't want Indian bones displayed, like museums did for years." Hackett stooped and carefully withdrew a plastic cover. "I've followed Fishhawk's advice—to a point. He was only near here once. Indians don't like to be around the dead, or even look at a graveyard. He didn't come as close as Bibi is now. Traditional Seminoles don't even want to speak of the dead, but Fishhawk does have a job to do later."

Grif pealed back the plastic sheet, and where it had been, Brandy could see a square hole in the soil and beside it a vertical shaft several feet wide. He squatted next to it. "Spent several days working here," he added. "The pot hunters bored a six inch hole and partially uncovered this burial. Fortunately, the water table here is high. That helps preserve things. I've taken out several pots with holes knocked in them. The holes let out the spirit." He rose, and then bent down, hands on his knees. "The pot hunters got a few all right, but they weren't big time dealers. They worked with long handled shovels, not back hoes."

"There's a market?" Brandy swatted several mosquitoes on her jacket sleeve.

"Sure. Private collectors will pay. Maybe some museums, if they don't know the sale items are loot. Here, look down." She bent over the shaft. Even in the warm April sun, she felt a sudden chill. She could see bones, not an articulated skeleton, but what looked like diminutive leg bones laid side by side, a ragged piece of cord still binding them to earth-colored fiber. Near the slender bones Brandy could make out a fragile jaw bone, a few tiny teeth, parts of a small, broken skull.

"Skulls are sometimes stored separately. Sometimes set on the bones," he said. Brandy's voice dropped, as if in church.

"They seem so little."

Grif Hackett stood and stretched. "A small child. Probably a girl. Kids had a high mortality rate. They led a hard life." Brandy turned away from the opening. She wondered if the grave goods had included a doll, perhaps, or a toy necklace. She didn't ask. After all these generations, what else could be left besides bones and clay and shell?

"You'd be surprised," Hackett added. "There's even a market for Indian bones."

Brandy stood and faced away. "That's barbaric. If this is the work Fish-hawk doesn't approve of, I can understand."

Grif pulled his lower lip down in disapproval. "To scientists bones are just a mixture of calcium carbonate, calcium phosphate, and fibrous tissue. Nothing to get upset about. But I'll keep the bundle burial moist to preserve it, and Fishhawk will re-bury it with the proper ceremonies." He gave a crooked smile. "Superstitious stuff, of course. He has to consult the committee and decide where. Probably not here again. Too isolated."

"Pot hunters might come back?"

"Remember, bones have been sold." He pointed to a small one-room clapboard shack half hidden among the cedars. "That's what's left of a fisherman's old place. That and a dry cistern. I've stored some pots in the shack before I take them to the lab." He glanced once more into the damp shaft. "This burial ought to be studied. For one thing, I found blue beads with this child. Shows these Indians did contact the Spaniards. We can even tell from the bones what their diet was."

Brandy knew that until a few years ago excavations were commonplace; museums had been filled with aboriginal artifacts and bones. "And the great find you made?" she asked "The one that won't bring any money?"

"You've just seen it—a bundle burial. Much better preserved than ones found near here in the fifties. Now re-burial is the law, if burials are disturbed at all."

Brandy thought again of her study of Shakespeare. She remembered a line from the epitaph on his grave, and murmured, "Curst be he who moves my bones." The meaning was plain enough for the most illiterate gravedigger. Indians weren't the only ones who thought bones were sacred. A slight wind stirred the cedars, then the air became still. Brandy shuddered. How many skeletons were buried here? The very air seemed charged. She could understand why Fishhawk did not want to be here, maybe Bibi, too. The feeling welled up again that she experienced at Tiger Tail Island, waiting for the detective.

She tried to put the renewed sensation out of her mind. "And what exactly is a bundle burial?"

Hackett gave her a wry grin. "You won't like this. These Safety Harbor people weren't the only ones to use bundle burials. Anyway, the corpse was kept until it decayed, then the remaining flesh was boiled off, the bones arranged properly, bound by cordage in fiber mats and re-buried. It's called a secondary burial. Nice, right?"

Brandy swallowed. She tried not to picture the process or the priest who must have supervised this grisly practice. And yet was the procedure really more repugnant than the modern embalmer's art, the eviscerated, visually enhanced cadaver in its ornate casket? "I guess it actually shows respect for the dead," she said softly. She became aware of swarms of mosquitoes, no longer deterred by the repellent.

"These folks were not pure primitives. The Spanish recorded a lot about them."

Brandy glanced at the re-covered shaft. "It's good to learn about them, I suppose. We owe them that." She still felt overpowered by an aura of death. Years earlier on a vacation to England with her father, she had this feeling in Bath when she toured an underground passage where archaeologists had discovered first century Roman skeletons. She had fled back into the daylight.

Hackett did not seem to feel the same suffocating presence of death. Instead, he calmly replaced the plastic. "Fishhawk not only believes we shouldn't study burials. He believes the ghosts of the dead still linger, and they can make you sick. Most traditionals think that."

"I can see Fishhawk's point."

"Well, it's not a stupid belief. The dead do cause disease. Not these guys, though. They've been gone for about four centuries."

She watched his expression carefully. "Do you think this find could have anything to do with Timothy Hart's search?"

He gave a surprised shake of his head. "Not a chance. No real money here."

Grif took her arm as they turned toward the downward path. "I've always wanted to talk to a genuine archaeologist. I appreciate the tour," she said.

He threw back his head and laughed. "I'm not Indiana Jones, you know. In Florida we barely stay ahead of the bulldozers. Mostly we inventory what developers turn up." His expression grew more somber. "It takes years of study. For my job, I had to have a graduate degree in Archaeology with a specialization in Historical Archaeology. Takes years to repay that cost. Then two and half more years of full-time experience." His tone became sharper. "And then we don't get rich. Far from it. Sometime soon, I'd like to pack it in here. Try working in a more receptive environment." Jaw set, he swatted a cluster of mosquitoes lighting on his arm. "Mosquitoes will eat you alive here. Get back to the boat while I collect the pottery fragments I stored in the shack."

Among a buzzing swarm, Brandy descended to the riverbank. Bibi sat in Hackett's boat, picking at a torn fingernail and looking bored.

"Fascinating stuff here," Brandy said. "But a trifle eerie."

Bibi pressed her lips together and frowned. "Dr. Hackett's wasted professionally in Florida. He earned scholarships and worked like a dog at odd jobs to earn his degrees. He never had it easy. This kind of repair work wasn't what he studied for. He's got bigger ambitions."

"Oh." Brandy stood next to Grif's boat, not eager to start back through the narrow, unmarked channel on her own. "What would he rather do?"

Bibi gave Brandy a knowing look. "He should be in Mexico or Guatemala. He says exciting work's going on there in Maya research. He's only an associate professor at the University, but he should be a full professor." She studied Brandy for a few seconds, lapsed into silence, and resumed work on her broken nail.

Brandy crawled back into her own boat and waited until they heard Grif inching back down the hill, carrying a large canvas bag. Gently he handed it to Bibi, who set it on the deck. As Grif prepared to shove her boat off the beach, Brandy scrambled out to help him. "Remember, I hope to meet Fishhawk's wife," she said.

Grif hesitated. "Fishhawk said Annie's arriving tomorrow," he said finally. "If you go to the camp, it's probably best that I come along. Give me your number and I'll phone you." Brandy glanced up at the lean, brown face. Compared to John's, now so withdrawn, Grif's looked welcoming. She reached into her boat and dug into the canvas bag she'd set on deck and handed him her card, Carole's phone number scribbled on the back.

But the image of a third face lingered in her mind, an older one, more vulnerable. "I'll be in Homosassa a few more days," she added. "I'm not finished with Timothy Hart. My editor's interested. I think everyone's too eager to say he was dumb. I don't believe he was. Gullible, maybe. I think he learned something about this area that excited him. Probably from that journal his sister described. She said a soldier kept it. Maybe it's because of that journal, he's dead."

Hackett cocked his head. "That's a serious charge."

"It's what I think. I intend to find out."

He lifted the bow of her boat and they began shoving it off the riverbank. Just before the pontoon boat floated free, she climbed in. Grif's brows lifted as he gave the hull a final push. "Your looking into Hart's death could be dangerous,"

Brandy shrugged. For the first time he sounded like John. "It won't be the first time I've poked around in a murder case."

As Hackett heaved his own craft into the water and backed around to start for Homosassa, Bibi knelt beside a box on the deck and lifted out paint brushes, a screen, and picks, checking that they had what they needed. At some point he would expose to sunlight the long dead. A dark thought.

Still, as Brandy chugged back down the winding river after him, her mind shifted from Hart to the native Indians and then back again to the archaeologist. A rugged, knowledgeable fellow. She wondered how Hackett's former wife had let him get away.

As they cleared the Salt River, and Grif veered off toward Alma May's house on Tiger Tail Bay, she glanced at her watch. Already 12:45 P.M. As she eased into the no-wake manatee zone, she picked up her cell. Two pontoon boats and an inboard cruised passed in the weekend river traffic. She dialed John. No answer. Maybe he had decided to fish, but he should be ready for lunch. When she swerved into the mouth of Carole's canal, she saw him sitting on a plastic chair beside the concrete bank, a line in the water, a bucket beside him.

"Mullet fishing," he called as she reversed and pulled into the boat slip. "Got a nice one. Must be two pounds." He stood up, drew in his line, and removed the plug of fatback from the hook.

Brandy tied up and hurried down the dock to peer into the bucket. "You want it for tonight? I've got cornmeal and onions. I could make hush puppies."

He rubbed his forehead and started back to the front door beside her, carrying the bucket. "Don't I wish. No such luck. Had a call from my assistant on the job. He's got a problem with what a contractor is doing to a bearing wall. I need to check it early tomorrow morning." Inside the screened porch he set down the bucket of water with its great fish.

Brandy looked up at him. "And that means?"

"I've got to leave. I need to pick up some papers at the apartment before I go to the site." She knew he meant his Tampa apartment, not theirs in Gainesville.

In the small kitchen Brandy lifted ham and cheese slices out of the refrigerator. "You've got time for a sandwich and a glass of iced tea." She decided to tell him about Fishhawk, although he hadn't seemed interested. "I interviewed a Seminole from the Tampa Cultural Center this morning. A fascinating guy. He's called a spiritual advisor." She hesitated before mentioning Hackett—and then wondered why. She had done nothing wrong. She hurried out to the porch and set their sandwiches and iced tea on the wicker table. "A University of Florida archaeologist took me to see him." John probably pictured an archaeologist as an elderly academic with a grizzled beard. Just as well. "The Indian's camping on Tiger Tail Island."

For a minute John stopped eating. "You're talking about the island where you found the body? Bran, you sometimes get in trouble on these stories. Promise you'll be careful."

She nodded. "Not to worry. I plan to talk to Alma May Flint again, like I said. Then I'll see if I can wring some information out of homicide. Guess who's on the case? Jeremiah Strong. We met him in Cedar Key a couple of years ago." She pulled her note pad from her canvas bag and patted it. "There's something odd about the whole situation. Timothy Hart's dead from unknown causes. I don't think he wanted to buy Mrs. Flint's property for fishing. He thought he was going to find something valuable in Homosassa. Now the old lady and her friend are searching the island. The Indian just decided to camp out there, although he's as welcome as the small pox. I'm curious about them all."

John brushed fingers across his mustache. "I hope you'll leave the investigation to professionals. I remember Strong. A good guy, and savvy. He doesn't need your help. He'll give you the story when he's ready."

Her gaze settled on the note pad. "I won't be foolish. I just want a few questions answered. Don't worry."

John laid a hand over hers. "But I do." He sighed and carried his plate into the kitchen. "And I especially worry about us." She shrunk before the earnest expression in his eyes. "Please think about what I asked yesterday. Talk to mothers you respect."

"Okay," Brandy said, not convincingly.

At the door John stooped to pet Meg. As he put his arms around Brandy to say good-bye, she wondered what was happening to them. She had been deeply in love with John. In most ways she still was. She remembered their joy in exploring Florida rivers together, holding hands at orchestra concerts, their pleasure in reading the same books. She remembered their honeymoon in the funky historic inn near Mount Dora, tender nights in tiny apartments from Tavares to Gainesville. But she wanted to control the timing of a family herself. "You know, I'm the one who'd make the sacrifices," she added, submerging a twinge of guilt. "This is not the right time."

His dark eyes turned graver. "You need to find the time, Bran." He walked to the minivan and looked back from the driveway. "Go on while you're here and get your story. Do your own thing."

"Call," Brandy said, "about next weekend."

She stood, hands plunged into her pockets, watching John's minivan pull out of the carport.

CHAPTER 5

▼

When Brandy picked up the kitchen phone and dialed Mrs. Flint, the old lady answered. After identifying herself, Brandy began with a statement she thought might even be true. "I'm working on a story that may help you. But I need to talk to you again. Could I come out in about thirty minutes?"

Alma May paused. "I reckon," she said at last. "Might as well. Everyone else has."

"Sheriff's Office?"

"A whole battalion," Alma May said and hung up.

By 2:45 P.M. Brandy drew into the dock at Mrs. Flint's. She had expected to see Alma May's boat tied to a post, but a Sheriff's Office patrol craft had also pulled in on the other side. Getting crowded here, she thought, as she looped a line over a cleat near the end of the pier.

As soon as she stepped onto the porch, she could hear Alma May's shrill voice through the open door. "All this trouble on top of the problem with your old man!"

The answering voice soothed. "This will be over quite soon. And I'll handle Tugboat."

"It gets my goat."

Brandy rapped on the door. "Mrs. Flint?"

Alma May answered, "Come on in. Rest of the world has."

In the living room Melba Grapple raised her well-coifed head from the newspaper and faced Brandy with a well-bred smile. She was seated on the couch, leafing through the day's *Chronicle*, a cigarette burning between slim fingers. Although her features were jagged, almost eagle-like, they were somehow genteel. Under her veneer of understated elegance, Melba had a jaunty, raw-boned look, like steel under silk. An odd friend for Alma May. What had Alma May meant about Melba's husband? Tugboat? Melba didn't seem like the wife of a man called "Tugboat."

Alma May faced Brandy from the kitchen doorway with a resigned expression. "I suppose you've got a passel of questions, too." Brandy slipped a note pad out of her canvas bag. "Not many. Any calls about the house?"

"We aren't listing it again until the Sheriff's Office is finished here," Melba said. "We're only asking seventy-five thousand. Of course, that's because transportation is by boat only. But it's quite a nice vacation place. Plenty of room. Three bedrooms, two baths, desalination, historic. Not to mention the river access and view."

Brandy made quick notes, then watched the two faces closely. "I thought I'd focus on the history of Tiger Tail Island. Since your house is the only one on it, the story should arouse interest in the house. I can add a lot of good detail if we can find the nineteenth century journal Mr. Hart said he had. It's probably connected to the island, since he came here for some kind of search. Did he mention a journal?"

Mrs. Flint paused before she shook her head. "Don't recollect such a thing." Her eyes sought her friend's.

Melba nodded in agreement. "Of course, we weren't in his confidence, and that's a fact. I scarcely knew the man." She still gripped the newspaper but her eyes were on Brandy. She didn't notice the burned down cigarette until the ash reached her fingers, and then she quickly stubbed it out in an oyster shell ashtray already dotted with scorch marks.

Brandy was certain the two knew something, but she did not want to badger them. "If the Sheriff's Office has finished with Hart's room," Brandy asked, "I'd like to see it, too. Considering the circumstances, anyone interested in the house will want to know something about the man who just died here."

Alma May nodded toward a door off the hall. "Cops is out tramping through the brush right now. That detective, too. Don't know what he thinks they'll find. They was in the bedroom long enough. Nothing to see. I got to get the room ready to rent again. Got to clean and set out fresh towels and the like." She lifted her shoulders in a helpless gesture. "I reckon it won't hurt to let you in, just this once."

Brandy smiled and strode down the short passage leading past the kitchen to the bedrooms. Hart's room looked especially bleak—a twin bed, stripped, a dresser, the drawers pulled out about an inch, a straight chair and a small table, bare. Men's clothes still hung in the closet, a jacket, jeans, shirts, dress pants. Quickly Brandy felt the pockets, although deputies would have confiscated anything important. The bathroom was equally non-productive—shaving gear, soap, comb, aspirin.

Brandy sighed. What did she expect? A trap door to the basement or attic? Alma May followed her and peered into the room. "Got to bundle up Hart's things for charity, I reckon. The cops say his sister's not coming to get them. Pretty heartless woman, if you ask me. She arranged for some dealer here to sell his car. Nothing else's worth anything, anyway." Alma May retreated down the hall.

Brandy felt renewed pity for Timothy Hart. Through the back window she stared out at the water oaks, the bristly trunk of a small cabbage palm, and beyond it, circling the end of the island, the black waters of a canal, dug forty years ago by land speculators. Several times Brandy had explored it in her boat. The more canals, the more waterfront. But if any houses had ever been built along it, they were long gone now. Past the bank lay a broad vista of tall grasses, a tall water hickory tree, and a hard wood hammock in the distance. Somewhere to the south lay Fishhawk's camp.

Brandy focused again on the ground directly behind the house. At the spiky base of the cabbage palm she could see a slight mound. The sandy soil looked uneven. On a hunch, she called out to Alma May in the living room, "I'm leaving now. Thanks. I'll go out the kitchen door."

Then she hurried out into the side yard, glad that Alma May and Melba were in the front of the house. Where would a sick man hide something if he didn't want to leave it in the house, and didn't feel well enough to venture far? Or where would someone else who found it be likely to hide it in a hurry?

In the back yard Brandy examined a tottering storage shed, the door sagging open, and several garden tools. With a hoe she carefully pulled loose dirt away from the palmetto trunk. After probing for several minutes, she felt the blade touch something solid; her heart thudded. Deputies were still threshing through undergrowth on the other side of the canal. Gently she brushed away the gritty soil. Under it lay a leather briefcase.

For a moment Brandy hesitated. Then taking a tissue from her canvas bag, she pulled back the zipper. Inside she saw a thin, battered notebook. She considered taking it out, but her conscience intervened. Strong was out there among the cedars. Her find might be important evidence. She glanced back at the house. If she left it and went for help, it might be gone when they returned. All was quiet. Again Brandy was tempted and again resisted. Maybe she could strike a bargain with the detective. Using the tissue, she re-zippered the briefcase and picked it up by the handle. Then pushing her way past the saw palmettos and cedars, she followed the voices and footfalls of the officers. When at last she glimpsed the back of a green uniform, she called out. Startled, the man swung around.

"Get Sergeant Strong, quickly," Brandy said. "Tell him there's something here he needs to see." Better not identify herself yet, or he might leave on the next boat. When the puzzled officer raised a cell phone to his lips, Brandy started back the way she had come. Beside the clump of palmettos, she placed the briefcase behind her and sat down on the sandy ground to wait. Her mind swirled with questions. Who planted the briefcase? Three were often in the house besides Hart—Alma May, Melba, Hackett, and maybe even this man Tugboat. Did Mrs. Flint hear her call to the deputies just now? Where was Fishhawk? Was Melba Grapple still in the house?

Within fifteen minutes Sergeant Strong's head appeared above the wax myrtle and scrub oaks. He took one look at her, paused, shook his head, and muttered, apparently to himself. "If thou faint in the day of adversity, thy strength is small."

Brandy pushed herself up and brushed the back of her jeans. "Sounds like a useful proverb."

"Advice to myself," he said. "I thought you'd gone out of my life. But show me what you found. We got to go over this whole blessed island."

Brandy raised an eyebrow. "And you're looking for what?"

"As curious as ever, aren't you? Now show me what you've got or I'm leaving."

Brandy hooked her thumbs in her jeans pockets. "Maybe we can make a deal, Sergeant. I want to do the right thing, but if this briefcase holds what I think it does, I want to see the contents myself. I promise I won't write about anything until you give the okay. I proved last time my word's good."

Strong passed one large hand over his close-cropped hair. Sweat dripped from his glistening forehead. He's exasperated, all right. Brandy hid a smile. Maybe he's also intrigued. "You know the law can confiscate anything related to this investigation," he said. "But let's see what it is."

Brandy stood, lifted the case a few inches, careful not to touch any part except the protected handle, and set it down again. "Your guys didn't spot this. I did."

"You know better than to tamper with evidence."

Brandy shrugged. "I didn't leave fingerprints. I was afraid the briefcase would grow legs."

The detective stalked back toward the patrol craft and signaled to the officer on board. In a few minutes a stubby crime technician came hurrying around the house, nodded to Strong, and knelt by the briefcase. After he made a note of its original position, he took a snapshot, then pulled on a pair of gloves from his kit, and carefully picked up the case. "If it belonged to Hart, we need to get it to the lab," Strong said. "Somebody buried it for a reason. Might be fingerprints inside."

Brandy gave him a beguiling smile. "I didn't touch anything but the zipper, but I did take a peek. The case holds some kind of a book. It might be an old journal of Hart's. His sister said he had one. I could've looked through it first, but I didn't. See how good I can be?" She squinted up at him. "How long will it take the lab?"

"Depends. May take a couple of weeks at least."

Brandy dared to put a tentative hand on his arm. "You're not going to look at it until then? Why not take a peek now? You don't have to smudge any prints."

For a few seconds Strong stood silent, his dark face a study in concentration. "You have a point," he said. "I'm going to take it to the boat. There's a table there."

As they walked down the dock, Brandy glanced over her shoulder. A living room curtain rose and fell back into place. Alma May Flint's boat still lay moored to the pier. Apparently she had not yet taken Melba home. The technician laid the briefcase on the table, unzipped it, and with expert care, slipped out the long, narrow book. The detective glanced at the technician. "I need gloves." The tech handed Strong another pair, then moved to the bow, sat down, and began filling out a series of cards.

Brandy's gaze fixed on the tattered volume. The binding was loose, the gray, hard cover pock marked. "Everyone claims they don't know about this journal," she said, her heart racing. "I wonder if Hart buried it, or someone else?"

Strong's lips contracted in a grim line. "We know someone else is involved. Someone searched the body."

Brandy nodded. "I heard the M. E. say Hart's pockets were pulled inside out."

Strong positioned himself squarely at the table. "Hart's body was turned over, that's clear. When someone found the victim, why didn't they call for help?" The detective's gloved fingers touched the edge of the first page and flipped it. "There is nothing hid that shall not be manifested," he said.

A hopeful Biblical quote. Brandy hovered at his shoulder, then pulled her notebook and pencil from her bag and began to take notes. The journal had no preamble. At the top of the page in faded ink she read aloud *Lieutenant Henry Hart, United States Army, Third Infantry—In the Year of Our Lord 1840.*

The first entry was dated that December.

I've been stationed at Fort Brooke on the Gulf Coast since September. Constant drilling. Continuous forays into the field hunting stray Indians and bringing them in. Burning their crops. Last month we had several war chiefs in camp for a parley. They were supposed to agree to be deported to the west. But they drew rations and liquor for weeks, and never made up their minds. At last the rascals left and General Armistead declared hostilities resumed. More monotonous scouting. Word came yesterday that a Mikasukee Seminole war chief named Halleck Tustenuggee—that last word means he is a great war chief—and his band attacked an escort party near Micanopy, killed an officer's wife, a lieutenant, and three enlisted men. Must catch Halleck

January, 1841. *To date General Armistead has shipped out 450 Indians. He has captured 236 more and has them ready to leave. Only about 300 savages remain in the whole miserable territory, but still Congress says we must fight until every single Indian is sent west. A settler family was murdered this month with arrow and hatchets. Shows the savages are running low on ammunition.*

April 1840: I came down with the sickness that has put a lot of the men in bed with a fever. I've been getting better for the past 3 months at Fort Brooke.

I've picked up a lot of Indian lingo from the Seminoles held here. I can translate if I need to, but it's more useful to listen and not show I understand. I don't know both Indian languages. I understand the one called Maskoki.

May 1841: General Armistead relieved. Col. Worth now in command. Coacoochee—we call Wildcat—finally captured. That should help. He was a fighter. Col. Worth and his men rounded up the Seminoles hiding out near the Crystal and Homosassa Rivers.

December : War Chief Halleck killed a group of settlers near Mandarin.

January 1842: We've been holding old Thlocko Tustenuggee, the trickiest war chief of them all, here at Fort Brooke for months. Everyone calls him 'Tiger Tail.' He's been living off the fat of the land. Yesterday he escaped at night under the guards' noses.

April 29, 1842. That Indian devil Halleck came in to Fort King and was trapped. Now he'll go west at last......Wretched, unclean water, eaten up by bugs and mosquitoes, suffering now from unbearable heat, no fresh meat. We're treated worse than the savages. Rations now are parched corn ground with sugar. When we do stumble on a few chickees, the savages disappear. They make no sound. They crawl through the wild grasses and hide in trees. We struggle on through terrible swamps searching for a few pitiful renegades.

July 14, 1842:, After Halleck emigrated today, we found his band had hidden their goods in hollow trees and palmetto sheds in the swamps, burying such stuff as cotton cloth, blankets, calico, even canisters of powder. Looks like they think they will come back, but 40 warriors and 89 women left on a steamer for New Orleans. They had to be issued clothes. Many of the women were wearing flour sacks. At Fort Brooke I saw squaws collect corn dropped from the horses' mouths. They used it to make a kind of gruel they call 'softi.' We can't help but pity them.

August 1842: Third Infantry is in Cedar Key. Conferences with the last of the war chiefs going on. Much celebrating. Whiskey and corn and beef handed out to the savages. Tiger Tail is still the trickiest, though he's old. The old war chief has escaped three times but promises now to emigrate. Settlers still being murdered in the middle part of the territory. The chiefs say they cannot control the young warriors. The young men have never known anything but war. That may be so, but does not improve the mood of the settlers.

October 4, 1842: "Terrible storm hit Cedar Key. Water 27 feet high, blew the hospital from its foundation. Two steam ships and a sloop broke loose and wrecked. Indians all fled."

December 1842. Tiger Tail hiding out near Cedar Key. Sends word that the storm was a message from the Great Spirit. He says his people are not to go again to Cedar Key, so the army will not send Tiger Tail any more rations. With the help of a squaw, a surgeon and Lieutenant Spague finally found the old rascal nine miles from Cedar Key. The officers came back and said the chief was in bad shape and drinking heavily.

Dec. 20, 1842. Sprague is sending Lieutenant Jordan and myself with twenty men to bring them in. We don't expect any trouble. Sprague says the band only has six men, eight women, and several half-starved children.

Dec. 29, 1842: The last of the Seminole war chiefs has finally been sent west. Taking old Tiger Tail was an experience. The chief was scratched up, bleeding, and seemed drunk. Sprague thought he had probably been fighting with someone in his own band. Personally, I think Tiger Tail was sick. We had to make a litter to carry him to Cedar Key. On the trip back to camp I overheard a comment from one of the Indians that considerably aroused my curiosity. The Seminole warrior said 'I hid something the white men want. This is a thing the white men always want. They will kill for it. We found it digging for clams near the great water. Near our old camp on the river, I helped make a kill. Burned a house and took some food.

I did not want to bring this thing with me for the white men to steal. It is powerful medicine. A medicine man needs it for his medicine bundle. It did not help our people. Maybe it will kill the soldiers. It is very frightening.'

I listened, pretending not to understand, while the warrior's friend asked the warrior where he hid the powerful medicine. I have written the translation as well as I can, but I did not know all the words. I am writing them as they sounded to me. The warrior said he put it in a sugeha hoo chek—I think that means a tobacco pouch—and then hid it in we enkokee, near the burned house. He said it will be safe there.

He fears all his people will be thrown off the big boat as soon as they cannot see land, but if he lives and can come back from the far away place, he will recover this thing and take it south to a medicine man. Of course, these Indians will never come back. When I get out of the army I plan to see if I can find what the Indian hid. I think it must be very valuable, and in a safe place. It shouldn't be hard to locate the massacred settler's land. Several months ago we heard about an attack on a lone family near the Homosassa River.

"That's it," Brandy said. "That's what brought poor Timothy Hart to Tiger Tail Island. I wonder if he worried because his ancestor called the object frightening. It didn't bring luck to the Indians, and it sure didn't bring luck to Hart." She drew in her breath. "Tiger Tail the lieutenant wrote about—he's the Seminole war chief the island's named for." She also thought of the Flint family massacre on the island and raised her eyebrows. "The Flint family were the only people killed by Indians in Homorassa that I know about, except for a postal rider later." She looked again at the old journal, a few pages faded and almost illegible, one torn. "I wish the lieutenant hadn't skipped over so many months."

"I expect that war was like all the others. Months of boredom and misery and then a few of real terror. The man wouldn't have the time or the place to write every month."

The detective flipped a few more pages. "The journal says Henry Hart's Third Infantry lost three officers and sixty-five enlisted men during the Seminole War. The rest were shipped back to Illinois in February, 1843."

Brandy dropped onto the bench across from Strong and turned back through her note pad. "Do you think Henry Hart ever did come back? Ever came to look for whatever it is?"

"That record is almost the last in the journal, but maybe he did search later. After about thirty years he wrote one more long entry:"

> *June, 1870. Came back to Florida, now a state, and managed to catch a ride from Jacksonville to Pensacola and a steamer down the west coast to Cedar Key. From there I got a coach to the miserable little fishing village of Homosassa.*
> *I hired a farmer who knew the land where the settler's house was burned almost thirty years ago. He said the same family still owns the land, but I couldn't find the owner. The farmer took me there, but my luck ran out. No one I talked to could translate the key words to the hiding place. I told no one why I wanted to know the meaning. I found nothing of interest except the burnt ruins of Senator David Yulee's plantation, now only a tall limestone chimney among scrub oaks. When the country people and fishermen saw I wanted to search the grounds, they warned me off—one with a shotgun. They believe the slaves buried silver and valuables before they fled the area, but no one knows where. My guess would be under the chapel. It stood at the end of the major road and is where the slaves would have gone for safety. I suspect a good deal of digging has been going on there. The plantation owners were very rich.*

Strong held the journal by its edges and closed the book. "The End." He shook his head, then gazed out at the dark river. "Interesting that Henry Hart wasn't the only one who thought something valuable was hidden on Tiger Tail Island."

CHAPTER 6

▼

While the detective read from Lieutenant Hart's journal, Brandy had jotted down the pertinent facts, including the Maskoki words, spelled phonetically. "Looks like we need a Seminole translator," she said, remembering that Fishhawk had told Hart he did not know the translation. But was he telling the truth? She did not speculate. Instead she said, "Of course, poor Timothy might've been after the Yulee plantation treasure instead."

Strong slipped the journal back into the briefcase. "I'm not sure which lead the Captain will want to follow. Maybe both. We're waiting now on the lab. We've got to know what Timothy Hart died of." He fitted the case into a plastic sleeve, saying softly, "Lord deliver us from battle and murder and sudden death.'"

Brandy recognized the quotation from *The Book of Common Prayer*. "Amen," she said. Maybe Strong felt the same tragic aura as Brandy had when she waited near Hart's body.

She dropped her note pad into her bag and cast a last, lingering look at the riverbank where the dead man had lain. "How long will it take for the lab to examine the contents of Hart's stomach?"

Strong grinned for the first time, his teeth white and even in the deep brown face. "Captain got a special deal. Usually takes six weeks at best. But a new lab just opened in Tallahassee, and someone owes the Captain a favor. They're not real busy yet. We may know what killed Hart as soon as tomorrow." The detective glanced up at the house and the saw grass flats and hammocks behind it. "I'd better round up the troops."

Brandy stepped out onto the dock, suddenly aware that both Alma May Flint and her guest had not yet left the house. They could be watching.

✳   ✳   ✳   ✳

By six o'clock Brandy had fed Carole's Persian cat, given Meg another belly rub, and filled her bowl with dry dog food. Then she sat down on the screen porch to transcribe her scribbles into her larger notebook. Within a few minutes she stopped, caught up in the horror of what she was recording. Across the canal cabbage palms and live oaks were nothing but twisted shapes against the darkening sky. Above, the nightly clutch of vultures circled toward their water tower roost.

"Deliver us from battle and murder and sudden death," the detective had said. For seven years, soldiers and settlers and Seminoles had endured all three—the Indians slow starvation as well. Battles and murder and sudden death under a canopy of Spanish moss, beside rivers, deep into swamps.

She thought, too, of the terror felt by women and children, facing the pitiless arrow and knife, knowing the certainty of scalping and death; she thought of the famished Seminole women, huddling in wind and rain with their own hollow-eyed little ones. Brandy shivered. Amid all this horror, on a nearby island must lie some haunted, yet treasured thing. Something even now a man would kill for. She thought again of that other haunted island, the one created by Shakespeare. *The Tempest* had its spirits, too, its sorcerer like Fishhawk, and its own "thing of darkness," the monster Caliban. He also sought to kill.

When the phone rang, Brandy hurried into the kitchen to pick it up, relieved to have her lurid thoughts interrupted. She expected to field a call for her friend Carole. Instead she recognized a deep, now familiar voice. "O'Bannon, girl reporter?" the voice said. "Grif Hackett here. Want to meet Fishhawk's wife tomorrow?"

On her note pad Brandy doodled a round head and gave it black hair, pulled back in a plait. "Sounds good," she said. "My husband had to go back to Tampa. I have the day free."

He paused for a second. "That puts a new spin on this evening. How about a drink and a bite to eat tonight out by the river? We can set up the time to see Annie."

Brandy thought of her bare refrigerator. She hadn't taken time to shop. She also thought Hackett might have a theory about who buried the journal. By now everyone might know about her discovery; news travels fast in a small town. People might hear from those two watchers, Alma May and Melba, or from some loose-lipped Sheriff's deputy. She might as well tell Hackett. His guess about who buried the journal could confirm her own. And, she had to admit to herself, she enjoyed his company.

"Sounds good," she said. "What about including Bibi?" Brandy had not found the graduate student welcoming, but she did have an interest in Grif's mound project.

"She'll be at a meeting in Chassahowitzka with other volunteers. They're planning to observe the whooping crane migration back north. It'll begin any day now. Besides, teacher-student fraternization outside of working hours isn't very wise."

*　　　*　　　*　　　*

The Tiki bar and surrounding deck rose beside the shadowy river like a bright oasis. Grif and Brandy threaded their way between crowded tables toward two empty stools at the counter. She recognized the bartender by his neat beard and his trick of elevating only one eyebrow. The same man had waited on them the night she met Timothy Hart. Now he delicately touched his small, well-groomed Vandyke.

"Too bad about your chubby pal," he said to Grif as they settled at the bar. "Read about him in the paper. Seemed like a nice guy."

"A real tragedy," Brandy said.

Grif nodded. "He was a sweetheart, but a little goofy. Didn't know him well. We both stayed at Alma May Flint's place down river a few days." He turned to Brandy. "I'll take a Scotch and water. What about you?"

"Merlot. Chilled."

The barkeep slid a drink toward Grif, dropped a few cubes of ice into a glass, swished them around, dumped them out, and poured the ruby-colored wine. He grinned at Grif, again raising one eyebrow. "Where's your Indian buddy? Out tracking something?"

"On Tiger Tail Island, as a matter of fact," Hackett answered. As he reached for his glass, Brandy noticed his Rolex watch, the smart cut of his jacket. Grif Hackett could have stepped out of *Gentleman's Quarterly*. Obviously, he cared about fine things. John was always neat, but he would just as soon shop at K-Mart.

The bartender wiped long fingers on his apron. "Fisherman stopped in from the Gulf the other day. Says he saw a panther come right to the river-bank around marker 47. Snatched a cormorant out of the water. Couldn't believe his eyes." To another customer he added, "People have seen black bear, too. Just south of here around the wildlife sanctuary at Chassahowitzka."

Up and down the river lights began to wink on. Brandy thought how dark and filled with wild animals the area had been when Tiger Tail and his ragged band hid here. She could not imagine the skills it took to survive in those swampy woods—skills that Fishhawk now wanted the world to remember. But Fishhawk's wife planned to stay on the island also. And they had a child.

At a nearby table a boy of about three slid out of his chair. Brandy watched him reach small fingers into the bread basket. "How old is Fish-hawk's daughter?" she asked Grif.

"Younger than that little guy. Almost two, I think."

The little boy held out crumbs to a gaggle of eager mallard ducks. "No, no, Tommy," his mother scolded, taking him onto her lap.

The father leaned across the table. "The sign says, '*Don't feed the ducks*.'" When the toddler cried and struggled to get down, she gave him a hug. The father added, "The sign also says '*Don't feed the alligator*.'"

"Not a place for kids," Hackett said, frowning. "Now ducks will be littering the walkways."

Brandy turned away. "Not a relaxing meal for the poor mother."

Hackett raised his mug and peered at her over the rim. "Not a relaxing day for you, either, I hear. Mrs. Flint says you and the detective made some sort of a discovery this afternoon. Tell me about it."

Brandy hadn't meant to launch immediately into finding the journal. She had wanted to use the fact to leverage information from Grif. But she was prepared for Alma May and Melba to have been observant.

"We found the journal, all right. The Sheriff's Office has it. They'll run it by the lab." She watched him carefully. "Interesting that it wasn't in Hart's room. It was buried outside."

Hackett shook his head. "Unlikely the poor guy did that himself. Not if he was so ill."

Brandy took a sip of wine, studying the deeply tanned face beside her. "Detective Strong figured it hadn't been buried long. It rained the day before Hart died. It hadn't been washed up or damaged. I figure Alma May had the best shot at taking it. After all, the journal must've been in her house, and she wasn't too hospitable to the Sheriff's Office. The Sergeant had to get a search warrant. Alma May would've had time."

"Could be." He picked up a menu and turned through it. "And did the journal help you decide what happened to Hart?" He didn't bother to look up.

Brandy hedged. "I don't think the Sergeant wants me to discuss it yet. I suppose the contents will all come out eventually."

They ordered seafood salads. "About meeting Annie," Grif said "I told Fishhawk I'd pick her up at the marina. She's to call me on my cell. All he's got is that cypress canoe, and no kicker. I'll give you a buzz after I find out when she'll see you. Probably be afternoon. Chances are you can help by giving her rides into town for groceries. If I know Annie, she won't live on sofki and fry bread, and she won't want to paddle that canoe all the way to the marina."

"Fishhawk said a friend was driving her up from Tampa. Does Annie work at the casino?"

The corners of Hackett's mouth turned down. "No way. Seminoles themselves don't work there. Anyway, Fishhawk doesn't like the casino. They both work at the Cultural Center. It tries to preserve the history of the tribe and the old ways. I wouldn't say the casino does."

"Your Indian friend seems to think whatever Hart was looking for belongs to the Seminoles."

"You're on the money there," Hackett said. Brandy remembered that the journal said the Seminole who found the treasure wanted to give it to a medicine man. Presumably one like Fishhawk.

Hackett's blue eyes locked with hers. "You're really into finding out about Hart, aren't you?"

She began her answer slowly, "There's a story in it, I'm sure." Then she finished in a rush. "Besides, I think somebody killed him, and his family doesn't seem to care. I don't want the killer to get away with it."

He grinned. "We're two of a kind, Brandy—independent, ambitious."

She nodded, thinking of John. She wished he understood her that well. "I'm afraid my husband doesn't realize how much my job means to me. He's ready for the whole family bit."

Hackett gave her a wry grin. "Sounds familiar. My ex was the same. Sorry, that's not the life for me." Brandy thought of her own parents. If she herself hadn't arrived in their lives when she did, her mother would've gone on for a Ph.D. and taught at a university instead of a high school.

Behind them the little boy tumbled, eyes alight, from his chair beside the railing, pointing. The narrow snout, then the scaly, five-foot body surfaced in the black river, as it had the night Brandy met Hart and his friends. "Wanna see gator," the boy called, bending down. As he thrust his small head under the top bar and squirmed between the wooden supports, his father leapt up and darted forward to grab his hand. Hackett watched and shook his head.

While the father and mother carried their whimpering son up the few steps toward their car, a Grady White boat like the one Brandy had seen at Alma May's dock pulled into the pier. At the bow a sturdy black and brown Rottweiler stood at alert. Aboard, a solitary man, well over six feet and stocky, reached out and secured the boat to a post, then lumbered onto the restaurant deck and up to the bar opposite them. His shaved head loomed above the other patrons like a boulder, his heavy chin sported a wiry, black heard. Put a few ribbons in it, and he'd be the image of the South Carolina pirate Blackbeard. He wore a tattered tee shirt and jeans. When one hand slapped the counter, he exposed a string of blue anchor tattoos up one arm.

"Give me a Bud," he called to the bartender.

The barkeep scurried to the cooler and handed over the beer. "Sure thing, Tugboat," he said. Tugboat Grapple, at last. Brandy surveyed the new arrival with interest.

"Damned good fishing today in the flats," Tugboat said. "Redfish and sheepshead almost jumped in the boat." He grinned at the man with his wispy goatee behind the bar. "Why don't you grow real face hair." He rubbed the bristly thicket on his own face. "Look, kid. This is a real beard."

The bartender flushed.

Tugboat downed the first beer. "Two more, to go." He grabbed the next two bottles by the necks, threw down a few dollars, and had started back to the pier, when he stopped abruptly and looked back at a restaurant table on the deck behind the bar. Brandy swiveled her stool to watch. Alma May and Melba were turned away from the bar, talking, salad, sandwiches, and coffee before them. Melba was speaking rapidly, accenting her remarks by making jabbing motions with her fork.

Tugboat spoke with a voice that could boom over the sound of roaring gasoline engines. "Well, lookee here! My wife and her friend. How's the house sale going, now you gals don't have no buyer?"

Alma May's sharp face glanced back. "We're doing just fine, thank you very much. I might even decide not to sell for a spell."

Melba's regal figure seemed to shrink in her chair. "I'll be along home soon. We're just finishing up here."

"Been another hard day…" he paused, "picking up knickknacks from the old plantation?"

"Melba'll get home directly, Tugboat," Alma May said, her voice as decisive as ever. "We still got business to talk about."

He threw back his head and gave a harsh laugh. "I know your business. Bingo down at the Seminole Casino in Tampa. Guess you gals got money to waste."

"If we go, reckon we might see you there again," Alma May snapped.

Tugboat grinned. "My own friend's waiting on deck." He sauntered back toward the dock, swung aboard his boat, and stooped to stroke the delighted Rottweiler. After licking his hand, the dog jumped back to the bow. As his master gunned the engine, the big dog leaned again into the wind. Brandy moved closer to the bar. "That guy lives in Homosassa?" she asked the bartender.

He began rinsing glasses. "Yep. Long time resident. Pleasant customer." He lingered sarcastically on the word "pleasant." "Bet that Rottweiler's his *only* friend."

"I gather he's married to Melba Grapple." He nodded and elevated the eyebrow, as if to show he had not been intimidated.

"I met her a couple of days ago. Seems like an unlikely match." Grif nodded, as if he already knew the story.

The bartender gazed down river at the rear of the Grady White. "He used to be a fishing guide, before he started drinking too much. Had a loyal clientele then. Knows the river and the gulf better than anyone. That's how he met Miss Melba. A well-fixed lady from up north."

Brandy sipped her wine without taking her eyes off her informant. "Still, he seems crude for her."

The bartender slipped a row of glasses one at a time into an overhead rack, his words as slow and deliberate as his hands. "He knew the Gulf, like I said. Miss Melba was a tourist several years ago. She went out fishing with some friends. Their boat broke down. Storm came up quick, like they do here. Caught those folks and swamped their boat. The story goes Melba was scared silly. They would've all been lost for sure, when along comes old Tugboat on a fast track back to port. Hauled them out of the water and into his boat like drowned rats and towed their boat in. Made him a hero. He was a rugged looking guy then, too, but he had it all together. An exciting guy, I guess, to a woman who probably hadn't been courted much." Brandy thought of Melba's gaunt but elegant face, her bony frame. Again the bartender stroked his tiny beard; then he shook his head. "Now he lives off his wife, as far as anyone can tell. But he lives well."

When a waitress came from the restaurant with their salads, Brandy turned to Grif. "Sad story," she said, frowning. She had picked up her fork when she saw the two women rise. They had both noticed Grif and Brandy. Alma May's lips tightened and she turned away, but Melba had regained her self-assurance. She gave the two of them a brusque nod before they swept out.

*   *   *   *

In the morning, coffee still in hand, Brandy called the Sheriff's Office in Inverness and asked for Detective Sergeant Strong. When he came on the line, he didn't sound pleased.

"Little lady," he said, "don't expect special treatment. You want to know about the lab results, you come in like the other reporters and hear the spokeswoman's statement. Say, about eleven o'clock."

Brandy rolled her eyes upward, but she had determined to be agreeable. "Thanks for the information, Sergeant. No quotation to help start the day?"

Strong paused, then said in his give-me-patience tone, "Seek not out the things that are too hard for thee, neither seek the things that are above thy strength."

Brandy smiled. She had no intention of following this advice. "Thanks again, my friend. I hope you'll let the press know whose fingerprints are in the briefcase."

"All in good time," he said and hung up.

After putting out fresh water for Meg, she fastened the retriever again to her chain and stake in the front yard. Brandy was glad the dog enjoyed socializing with the neighbors, who kept an eye on her. Still, Meg lay down under an orange tree in a huff, disappointed that again she wouldn't share the day with Brandy. Brandy gave her a final pat before stepping into Carole's small sedan for the drive to Inverness.

At the Sheriff's Office, the brunette with the starched face and heavy glasses addressed the press in a careful monotone. "The lab report is in earlier than we dared hope," she began from behind her desk. "Timothy Hart's stomach contents have been analyzed. He died of poison. Pokeweed, a native Florida plant. His death may have been accidental, but because of the quantity and parts of the plant ingested, the Sheriff's Office is treating his death as homicide. He continued to eat only the poisonous roots and berries and leaves after he would've been quite ill. Likely someone else is involved."

The *Chronicle* reporter raised an eager hand. "Has the Sheriff's Office discovered the source of the pokeweed?"

The spokeswoman studied her nails, considering. Then she said, "Deputies found a possible source on Tiger Tail Island, where the victim was staying, but it was relatively inaccessible." Hart tramped all over the island, Brandy remembered. Grif had helped him buy his high boots. "The press can help the investigation," the spokeswoman went on, "by alerting the public to the danger of pokeweed, and asking readers to notify the Sheriff's Office of other locations in the area."

Brandy knew it would be useless to ask about the briefcase. The results would not be in, and why tip the others to its existence? The interview was clearly over. She jotted a few notes. She knew her editor wouldn't give a play to Hart's death unless she uncovered some truly bizarre aspect, or a Gainesville connection. The fact that Hackett worked with the Florida Museum of Natural History in Gainesville might provide that connection; also she could always hope that Timothy Hart had been right about the value of his prospective find. In the meantime, she'd stick to her story about writing the history of Tiger Tail Island.

At a library computer she quickly accessed the Internet and read an entry about pokeweed: "*A perennial with a green stem when young, later turning purple, and growing to a height of four to twelve feet with a diameter of an inch; producing greenish-white flowers in July and August.*" Unfortunately, it was spring, too early for blooms. They would've made it easier to spot the plants. The description continued, "*The deep purple berries, when ripe, are a source of red dye. Young, green shoots can be eaten when cooked, but berries, mature stalks, leaves and roots are poisonous."*

Brandy sat back, tense with concentration. The Seminoles, of course, would know these properties. They must've cooked pokeweed shoots during hard times, even into the twentieth century. They would know how to find the plant. Fishhawk, taught by his medicine man grandfather to cherish Seminole history and culture, would surely know. Would Alma May, descendant of pioneers and an island gardener? What about Melba Grapple? Brandy could see her hiking over the island in her own high boots, archaeology form in hand. She was shrewd, capable of intelligent research, of careful planning. Any one of them could've discovered the journal, even been shown the entries by poor gullible Timothy himself—could've decided to eliminate him and take up the search themselves, or already found the object, seen its value, and gradually poisoned him.

Alma May would believe that whatever was concealed on her land belonged to her. She'd probably be right about that. Melba might share her own amateur expertise with her friend and earn a reward, or she might choose to act alone, or even with her unkempt husband. Fishhawk certainly would believe the treasure, whatever it was, belonged to the Seminoles who hid it, not to the landowners. Indeed, Indians did not believe that land, created by the Great Breath Maker, could be bought by man any more than the sky. Brandy could see justification in that view.

As an archaeologist, Grif's curiosity, of course, would be aroused, but he said the Seminoles could not have anything of real value, and he was the only one with authority. Museums might be interested in the object, but they could not pay the vast sum Timothy Hart seemed to expect. And who would commit murder to place an additional artifact in a museum? Only Fishhawk might be tempted to do that. Too bad the thing had been hidden on private, not public land, where the State of Florida would have control.

Brandy realized Detective Jeremiah Strong must know about the pokeweed already, must be far ahead of her with his inquiries. She printed a copy of the Internet report and trotted down the steps to the car. At least she had been invited to meet Fishhawk's wife, and could ask a few discreet questions herself. First, she needed to know more about the Seminole culture and the basics of archaeological digs. Down the street she found the stately nineteenth century courthouse that housed the Citrus County Historical Society, ran up its white stone steps, and made her way through corridors under construction to the Resources Office. In its book store she bought the few sources she needed.

With the delicate scent of orange blossoms wafting through open windows, Brandy drove back to Homosassa, her mind on the upcoming interview. The phone began ringing as soon as she had parked and walked into the kitchen. It was Grif. "How about meeting me at Alma May's dock about 2:30 P.M.? I'll ferry you down Petty Creek. It's tricky. You need to watch for mud banks and oyster bars, and sometimes low water."

If Brandy wanted to meet Fishhawk's wife, it sounded like an offer she couldn't refuse. "That would be great."

"Her name's Annie," he added. "Not very Seminole, but she's a modern Indian. Baby's name is Daria."

"Thanks. I'll be there."

In the utility room Brandy pulled on heavy boots. Then she tucked a camera and a small note pad into a canvas bag, debated taking a tape recorder, then decided it might spook the Seminoles. When she headed for the boat alone, Meg gave a low, woeful growl, and Brandy stopped to refill the retriever's water bowl. She was glad to see the tide was coming in and the breeze was from the north. It wouldn't blow the water back out of the shallow creek, but keep it high enough for them to make the run to the island camp. She was anxious to learn details for her feature about the island, and more about the Seminole couple themselves.

CHAPTER 7

▼

At Alma May's dock Brandy did not spot the landlady or Melba. Their jon boat was gone. Hackett waved a cheery hello to Brandy. "Brought Fishhawk's wife and kid to the island late this morning," he called. The lock of hair fell across a forehead already damp from the early afternoon sunlight. "Annie's not too thrilled about leaving her apartment for a wilderness camp-out, even if it is Seminole style."

Brandy hitched her pontoon's bow and stern both to a post, then climbed aboard the other boat. She noticed that Hackett had swept it clean and stowed his crates neatly along the sides. "I don't see how Fishhawk and his wife can throw any light on what happened to Hart," she said, "but I might get a feature article about Fishhawk's experiment."

Hackett switched on the starter, the engine throbbed to life, and he turned to look behind him as he backed away from the pier. "Works for me." He looked around and winked. "It gives me extra time with you."

Flustered, Brandy fixed her gaze on the winding creek before them, trying to sort through her feelings. Attracted, yes. Flattered, yes. And yet, there was still John, crouched over computer or desk back in Tampa, annoyed with his wife, insensitive to her feelings, but not expecting her to be interested in another man.

Hackett continued smiling. "We're kindred souls." She did not answer.

He followed Petty Creek, winding upstream until at last he eased up to the mud bank, cut the engine, sprang over the bow, and pulled it ashore.

Single file they slogged up the narrow path, Brandy first. She supposed Fishhawk had beaten back the saw grass and spartina to make it easier for his wife and daughter, not for her and Grif. As she trudged up the last rise, a quick movement near an oak startled her. When she paused, a small, round face peeked around the trunk. It was a solemn little face, thatched with short black hair pulled tight at the temples. A tiny hand crept along the rough bark, exploring.

"Hello, there," Brandy called. "Are you Daria?" Shyly, the little girl inched around the tree toward Brandy, her perfect white teeth showing in a hesitant smile. Brandy suffered a sickening flashback. For a moment she saw the little teeth, the jaw bone of the Safety Harbor child in the vandalized mound. With rapid strides Hackett caught up and looked down. "How's my girl? We've come to visit," he said. "Can you tell your mother company's here?"

"I don't think she's old enough to talk yet," Brandy said. Walking upright seemed to take most of her concentration.

"Daria!" The woman's voice was high, frightened. In a flash of bright colors, Annie Pine rushed from the hammock, snatched up the child, scolded and kissed her. "No! You don't ever leave Mommy and Daddy." She spun around then, smiled at Brandy, and said, "I'm Annie. We've been expecting you and Grif. I took my eye off her for just a minute. I was spreading mats out in the chickee. No chairs, you know. Here it's only the real stuff for Fishhawk."

"You must be worried about rattlers and things," Brandy said. Unlike Dorothy in the *Wizard of Oz*, Brandy was thinking not of lions and tigers and bears but of panthers and gators and snakes.

"To tell the truth, I'm more worried about mosquitoes and chiggers. We make enough noise to keep the animals and the snakes away. Anyway, Fishhawk says we haven't angered them."

An odd statement, but perhaps not for an Indian, deeply into native beliefs. Brandy said nothing. As Annie set the toddler down again, Brandy held out her hand. "I've looked forward to meeting you. Maybe I can be of help. Getting groceries, that kind of thing."

"Thanks for the offer. I may take you up on it." Annie lifted her long, colorful skirt above her ankles. Brandy admired its combination of yellow, red, and blue cotton stripes, each with a delicate, jagged design, and each separated by slim bands of ribbon and rickrack. Around her shoulders Annie had thrown a yellow cape. Little Daria wore an almost identical outfit. "Company clothes," Annie said. "The traditional." She pointed to patchwork in each horizontal band. "Rattlesnake, lightning, and arrow designs. Seminole concerns, of course, to please Fishhawk. You can bet I'll change into jeans soon." While they walked with her to the chickee, Brandy studied the figure beside her—not plump, but rounded. The smooth, oval face, aglow with a bronze sheen, was clearly Indian, even to the almond shaped eyes.

"Fishhawk had to build the chickee platform off the ground. Annie wouldn't camp right on the dirt," Grif explained, "Most Seminoles had to in the past. Can't blame her."

Little Daria tried to scamper to her father and only lost her balance once. Fishhawk was bent over a steaming kettle. He straightened up, black eyebrows raised, and scooped the child into his arms. Then he turned to Brandy. "In a Seminole camp you must eat." He gestured at the pot. "You're our family's first guests. Old Mrs. Flint and her friend never come near us wicked Indians." His lips moved only a little and they turned down as he said, "They're banging around the island now. Make so much noise they scare the animals."

Brandy stared at the pot and suppressed images of possum and turtle. She'd read they were part of the traditional Seminole diet. Fishhawk grinned. "Not to worry, little lady. This is just sofki, a corn dish. We always have a pot on the fire." Brandy wondered how he guessed her thoughts. Maybe there was something to this medicine man routine. Now she recognized the strong, mellow odor of cooking corn.

"At least it's not coontie," Annie said, ladling up four bowls. "I'd be pounding and boiling for days." Brandy had read that historically cootie was made from the root of a plant common in Florida called Smilax. "Some make sofki now by boiling rice with baking soda or using quick grits," Annie went on. "I like cracked corn as a base."

Hackett helped Brandy onto the platform under the thatched roof. They sat cross-legged, as Annie had warned, on mats, Daria in her mother's lap. Brandy was grateful for learning the lotus position in a yoga class. Fishhawk had rolled canvas up to the eaves and laid a stack of mosquito netting to one side. He permitted himself some comforts that the nineteenth century Seminoles lacked.

"Do you ever prepare pokeweed?" she said, as casually as she could. Fishhawk's dark forehead creased in a frown. "I know," she hurried on, "that the Seminoles cooked many native plants."

"You been talking to the big detective," the Indian said in his deep baritone. "He's been here, too. He told me how Mr. Hart died."

Brandy flushed. "I thought you might know why he ate so much of it." Oh, dear, I'm not making things better.

"All Florida country folks know about pokeweed," Fishhawk said, his tone abrupt.

Brandy dropped the subject. "Well, the sofki's very good," she added, hoping he'd see the remark as an apology. Indeed, it was, once she became accustomed to the bland flavor.

"How's the experiment going?" Hackett asked, dipping deep into his bowl.

"So far okay. Early tomorrow a guy's barging in some willow saplings and stones, more blankets, and a tarp to build a small sweat lodge. He'll help me, and then I'm on my own." He glanced at his wife, who sighed. "Except for Annie, of course."

Brandy thought his wife wouldn't be much help, not with her attitude and little Daria to run after.

Hackett looked at Brandy. "Fishhawk needs a sweat lodge for purification rites."

Brandy nodded, then turned to the Indian couple. "I hoped to get pictures of the three of you, if you don't mind. I plan to freelance an article that will include your living here—with the old ways, I mean. I'm putting together one about Tiger Tail Island."

Annie looked thoughtful as she handed Daria a palmetto husk doll, dressed almost like herself. The little girl clutched it in chubby fingers. "Ta," she whispered.

"Daria doesn't talk yet, but it won't be long," Annie said. "She knows she should say 'Thanks.'" She let the child crawl onto the chickee floor. "I don't mind the photographs if they don't make us look stupid."

Clouds were forming to the west. It was now almost 4:00 P.M. "I won't use anything you don't approve of," Brandy added quickly. "It's just that Annie and Daria look so pretty in their special clothes. I want to get a shot before the sunlight's gone."

She snapped her pictures, then summoned the courage to ask Fishhawk for a translation of the unknown words Hart's ancestor quoted in his journal. "Before we go," she said, taking out of her notebook the Seminole words she'd copied from the journal. "I wanted to ask you if you could translate these expressions." As she watched both men's faces, she immediately regretted the question. Would Fishhawk know she had overheard him tell Hart he couldn't read the words? Why hadn't she simply called an expert? Still, she had been curious to see his reaction. She had not stopped to think that Hackett might be offended because she hadn't shared the excerpts with him. He looked wounded.

As for Fishhawk, his dark eyes became slits, his mouth firm. "People called Seminoles have two separate languages. Both can be written now, but this is Muskokee." After a few seconds he added, "My first few years when I learned to read, I was raised with the Miccosukees. My grandparents later moved to Big Cypress, but I never learned Muskokee." He pushed the paper back at Brandy.

Hackett stood gazing at the charcoal colored clouds. Under the cabbage palms and the oaks, shadows gathered. He did not ask to see her notations, but why should he? He was not a cultural anthropologist, would not know the language any more than she. Brandy had not said the words came from Henry Hart's journal, but these two were not slow-witted. With a start she realized Strong had been here earlier today, and he had not divulged the words. He would not be happy with her.

Fishhawk spoke again, like a pronouncement, his black eyes more on his friend than Brandy. "What people ought to be looking for on this island is a witch. I heard an owl last night."

His remark reminded Brandy of witches long ago in her own culture. She had read about the association of owls with death in Elizabethan times. Who would Fishhawk suspect were witches? Brandy thought of the two women now blundering about the island, and of Alma May's hatred of Seminoles. She looked at Annie's colorful skirt, shimmering in a ray of sunlight, at her swarthy husband and his air of invincibility, and thought again of *The Tempest*. She felt as if she had wondered into a dark section of Prospero's magical island. The monster Caliban's mother had been a witch. But who was the witch on Tiger Tail Island?

"You really believe in witches, friend?" Hackett asked with a sarcastic half grin. "You're a reasonably well-educated man."

Fishhawk sat down on the edge of the chickee platform and folded hands like worn leather in his lap. "You say you do not believe in witches. A witch is a person who can make others do evil, who can cause sickness and death, who has to be stopped, right? More than fifty years ago a man like that lived across the ocean. He caused ordinary men to do horrible deeds, he killed millions outright, and he brought about the deaths of millions more. At last the nations of the world stopped him. But you don't think Adolf Hitler was a witch?"

Brandy nodded, impressed by the logic. "Put that way, I guess we might agree."

"There's something else." Fishhawk lifted the forefinger of each hand. "Our people believe a person has two souls. One leaves right after the person dies, the other waits for four days. That ghost can be dangerous. We stay away from the dead." He jumped down from the chickee, signaling, Brandy decided, that the visit was over. "But you take Mr. Hart. A murdered man's ghost stays until his death is avenged." He looked from Brandy to Hackett. "I guess that's up to the big detective. Mr. Hart's own people don't seem interested."

"Others are," Brandy said quietly. But she wondered, too, about the Flint family, massacred by the Seminoles in the nineteenth century. "Do you think the ghosts of the settlers are still here as well, waiting for revenge?" She had a momentary image of the ghosts of the settlers rising up in territorial anger and confronting poor Timothy Hart's spirit—the uninitiated, the new kid on the block.

Fishhawk gave her a penetrating glance. "Soldiers captured the renegades and shipped them all West. I'd say the whites were avenged."

When he had begun to speak about ghosts, Annie stood up and turned away. Now she looked at Brandy and shook her head. John and I aren't the only ones who have a conflict, Brandy thought.

Fishhawk spoke into the sudden silence. "You ladies will have to excuse Grif and me for a minute. We need to discuss the re-burial." Brandy watched the two disappear behind a cedar thicket. Their voices floated up, low, indistinct, and urgent, then faded as they moved farther away.

Brandy smiled at Annie, trying to lighten the mood. "I'll be glad to come back tomorrow and take you into town. You decide what you'll need."

Annie scooted off the edge of the platform. "A Styrofoam cooler and ice and Cokes, for starters."

When Brandy knelt before Daria and held out her hand, at first the little girl clung to her mother's skirt, then pushed a thumb into her mouth and studied Brandy with a somber stare. In a few seconds the child's dark eyes brightened, she smiled, reached out a chubby hand, and fingered the cord on the camera. Brandy felt accepted.

When Hackett and Fishhawk returned, Brandy sensed tension in the air, but neither referred again to their private discussion.

"We've got to be on our way," Grif said. "Tide's running out fast." He stooped down to little Daria, reached into his pocket, and held out a wrapped candy. "It's okay," he said to Annie. "Sugar free." The little girl tore off the paper and popped the sweet into her mouth.

"Go, go," crooned the little girl, holding out her arms to Grif.

He straightened up. "Sorry, little one. Not today." He motioned to Fishhawk. "Better build some kind of a pen for the baby. She might wander off."

The Indian nodded. "I thought of that myself. I'll put it near the top of the path, so she can watch for visitors." Annie beamed. She had dashed after Daria ever since she set the child down from the chickee. A sweat lodge and a pen still for Fishhawk to build. He would be a busy man, but the structures would make excellent photographs for her article.

"Staying here isn't going to be easy, buddy," Grif said. "I hope you don't try living like this much longer."

Fishhawk turned a stern gaze on his friend. "I'll stay as long as I need to," he said.

As they started toward the creek, Brandy turned to wave. Annie held the toddler in her arms and helped her raise one plump little arm in farewell. Fishhawk turned to a small pan over the fire, and began dropping in what looked like the leaves of cedars.

Hackett smiled. "Fishhawk's already beginning to use magic against evil in this area. Next time you see him, he'll be ritually scratched with a steel needle, purification by bleeding. Brandy caught a whiff of burning cedar leaves. Before them a great blue heron flapped up from the path, squawking. Clouds in the western sky now blotted out the sun. Brandy couldn't shake a grim feeling. All the talk of witches, she supposed. Once again Fishhawk had made her aware of the island's centuries of violent deaths, especially of Timothy Hart's.

As Hackett backed out into the creek, Brandy looked past the wire grass and needlerush along the shoreline toward the island's thick spine of cabbage palms and cedars. A thin plume of smoke rose from Fishhawk's camp.

"There's sacred fire, too" Grif said. "Old time Seminoles believed fire was related to the sun. It represents the upper world—the world where you find good things like birds and plants."

"There's a lower world?"

"Snakes, witches. The Indians have to keep these worlds in balance. Right now, on this island, they're not. He's into purifying everything, including himself. His Panther Clan grandfather taught him the rituals."

"Fishhawk's spending a lot of time trying to bring those worlds into harmony," Brandy said. "How can he and Annie take so many days off work?"

The archaeologist skirted an outcropping of oyster shells in mid-creek. "No problem. In the first place, Indian people have always been pretty casual about time. Their concept is not linear, like ours. But they have a stipend from the casino money. It varies, but right now they're getting $1,500 each a month. For three people that's $4,500 per month—not too shabby. Add that to whatever they get from the Cultural Center. I wouldn't mind having such an influx of cash."

"But you said Fishhawk disapproves of the casino."

"He does. Says young people don't really have to work. Makes it easy to get into drugs and liquor. But he accepts the money, of course, and tries to keep it from corrupting the tribe. The windfall may not last anyway. The state may begin regulating the casino more strictly. People flock there now, especially older women. Lots from Homosassa, I hear."

"At least the income helped build the Seminole museum off Alligator Alley." Brandy said, lifting her notebook from her bag, and jotting a few lines. "I guess Fishhawk doesn't need Hart's treasure for the money it would bring."

"The Seminoles lost all they owned during the Seminole wars," he said. "Their museum had to borrow from other museums. Fishhawk would probably like to contribute a valuable artifact."

"Enough to murder?"

Grif raised his eyebrows and paused. "I know he's obsessed with Seminole history. He wouldn't want anyone to snatch something precious that belongs to the tribe. I don't know what he'd do to prevent it."

As Hackett steered his boat into the dock beside Brandy's, she noticed lights in the living room windows of the Flint house. Clouds hid the sun, and a chill wind from the gulf kicked up waves half a foot high in the river. "I'll follow you back to your canal," he said. "It may get a little dicey if the current's running fast. I've got business at the marina near there, anyway."

On the other side of the pier Alma May's little jon boat swayed, but Brandy could see Tugboat Grapple's Grady White boat wasn't there.

"Before we go," she said. "I want to talk to Mrs. Flint and Melba, too, if she's still here. I wonder what they found after a day's foraging. And I want to find out where that first house stood, the one the Indians burned." As Hackett tied up his boat, Brandy stepped out onto the dock. Melba Grapple's real estate sign had disappeared. If one or both had read the journal, they may have decided a sale was premature.

When Brandy and Grif reached the porch, they heard raised voices inside. Brandy recognized the waspish sound of Alma May. "Not on your sweet life! I won't hear of it!"

Melba answered, her tone not loud, but acidic. "I'm not giving you a choice." Hackett waited as Brandy rapped at the front door.

Alma May spoke again. "I reckon your man's gambled away everything, like he does. You might be obliged for my help." Apparently Tugboat had become a financial problem.

Melba spoke again. "I can handle Tugboat. Answer the door. Someone's here."

Alma May flung it open and stared at Brandy, surprised. "What do you want this time, young lady?" She remained in the doorway.

Hackett moved forward and interrupted. "I came by to say I'm staying at the motel in town tonight. I've almost finished at the mound. I'll check out with you tomorrow."

Alma May stepped aside. If Hackett didn't room here, Brandy knew she might not be allowed in again. The real estate agent had tossed her head scarf aside and sat on the couch, glaring with arms crossed at a brown bottle with a broken neck and a corroded pewter spoon on the coffee table. Beside them lay a stained pair of garden gloves and a smoldering cigarette in the ashtray. Melba swept her hand above the coffee table.

"You see before you the sole result of a day at the plantation site," she said. She unfolded her archaeological chart. "I've marked where I found each piece." When the sharp fronds of a scrub palmetto blew against the windowpane, Brandy glanced outside. A spade leaned against the wall, its blade soiled with fresh dirt.

"Digging?" Brandy asked as Grif disappeared down the hall.

Melba blew a jet of smoke to one side. "Not for Yulee silver, if that's what you're thinking."

Brandy smiled. "We've been to visit the little Indian family who's spending some time on the island."

She watched Alma May's face harden. "I've already seen more of that man than I want to," she snapped.

Brandy frowned. "I didn't think he'd ever been here."

"He wasn't no guest." Alma May stumped toward the kitchen and lifted a chunk of left over pot roast from the refrigerator. Brandy followed her and stood by the counter as the old lady took a sharp knife from a wall holder and began dicing the meat. "I was in my garden," Alma May said. "I could see over the canal there." Ker-chunk went the blade, and a cube of meat rolled onto the cutting board. She raised the knife again, face set. Ker-chunk! Maybe Alma May was visualizing Fishhawk under her knife. "He was slipping around behind the wax myrtles on the other side, like he was hiding. But I knew him all right. No mistaking that coal black hair and reddish skin. Gave me the shivers. Made me think of the Flint massacre. Blamed Indians!"

Brandy glanced back at Melba and the other woman rolled her eyes.

Brandy spoke softly. "What do you suppose he was doing there, Mrs. Flint?"

"Snooping, that's what. How do I know what he was looking for?" But, of course, they could all guess.

CHAPTER 8

▼

Brandy did not intend to leave Alma May's without having her main question answered. Hackett would not need much longer to gather up his clothes to move to the motel. "I meant to ask you," she said to Alma May, "where the original house stood. I need to know for my article about the history of the island."

Alma May wiped her hands on a kitchen towel and pointed a crooked forefinger toward the dining area. "There's an old picture on the wall took of the second house in the 1870's. It stands about where the first one was, the one burnt by the Indians." Brandy remembered the journal entry. The warrior had hidden whatever he found near that original cabin. The second one must've been built after the former soldier made his return trip and found an empty lot.

Alma May cocked her head, one thin hand poking a wisp of gray hair back into the knot at the nape of her neck. "That one weren't much more than a cabin, either. After the Indians was all cleared out, the survivor come back, re-built, and lived there 'til he was an old man. One of his sons tore the place down and used the wood in this one."

Brandy turned on the overhead light in the dining area and studied the faded photograph. It showed a two-room shingle house separated by a passage called a "dog trot" that John had told her promoted ventilation in early Florida houses. A long roofed porch spanned the front. In the rear stood a small log barn, a shed, a fenced garden with a lush stand of corn, and a narrow outhouse discreetly placed behind the garden. Next to the shed, a woman in a sunbonnet stood under a tall tree, holding a bucket.

Alma May moved up beside Brandy. "The Mrs. Flint of that day." She placed her hands on her angular hips. "That house set back a ways from the river, same as the first. In them days folks built on pilings and high ground. Didn't want no floods or snakes or other varmints in the house, thank you very much. Like I said, it was tore down for the lumber when this one was built closer to the water."

"So you can't figure out what the Indian Fishhawk was doing near this site?" Brandy asked.

Alma May snorted. "Maybe trying to find Mr. Hart's fool journal."

Melba drew in a quick breath. She realized, Brandy thought, what the old lady had said. The two weren't supposed to know about the journal. Certainly not that it had been hidden outside the house. It might be an admission that one or both of them concealed it after Timothy Hart's death. Brandy must tell Sergeant Strong. Fingerprints might show what Brandy suspected—at least one of them had handled the briefcase or turned the journal pages.

Alma May tried to cover up. She glowered at Brandy. "I seen you and the Sergeant looking at a book you found yesterday." Brandy doubted that Hart himself would bury his journal. He did not seem to keep its contents secret, not nearly secret enough. Again Alma May began whacking the roast into dice-sized cubes, her blows so forceful they startled Brandy. No delicate flower, this old lady.

"I've admired your garden," Brandy said in an effort to soften the old lady's attitude before asking her question. "Tomorrow there'll be a news story in the paper about Mr. Hart's death. The Sheriff's Office wants to know who grows pokeweed around here. Can you help? I don't suppose it's grown in a garden."

The question did not improve Mrs. Flint's disposition. "Just plumb full of ideas, ain't you? Do I grow that weed with my vegetables? No, I don't. But it's on the island and if you want to know, I've used young shoots in salads." Again her bent fingers settled on her hips. "But not lately, thank you very much."

Melba rose, shook out her short, ash blonde hair, snuffed out her cigarette, and picked up her head scarf. She left the bottle and spoon on the table and avoided her friend's eyes.

When Grif re-appeared in the hall, carrying a duffle bag, he looked into the kitchen. "Moving most of my stuff today," he said to Alma May. "We'd better get started before the weather gets worse."

"I thank you for all the information, Mrs. Flint," Brandy said.

Alma May grew more relaxed and her tone milder. "I'll be much obliged if your story in the papers gets folks interested in the house. I reckon I'll put it up for sale again shortly."

Melba stood and tied her scarf tightly around her hair. "I wonder if you'd drop me off at my place up river from Bird Island? You're going my way. No need for Alma May to run me home before a storm." Along the waterfront Brandy could see palms bent low, their fronds fluttering wildly.

Alma May stayed in the kitchen while the three let themselves out. As they walked through the rising wind toward the pier, Brandy caught up with Melba. "I've wanted to ask," she said, "why Alma May is called 'Mrs. Flint.' If this is the Flint homestead, isn't it her husband's family home, not her own ancestors'?"

The Realtor adjusted her scarf. "Alma May's husband died years before I moved here. She preferred to take back her own name. Flints are quite an old family here, and prominent. Sometimes they make their own rules. She always preferred to be known as a Flint." Melba edged onto Grif's rocking boat deck, gripping the rail, her head lifted high. "As I'm sure you've noticed, Alma May can be difficult, and that's a fact."

Brandy ducked her head against the wind, climbed into her own boat, and turned the key. The sky had darkened, and the smell of rain hung in the air. As the two pontoon boats started single file across Tiger Tail Bay, Brandy searched for the pair of ospreys. Ospreys mated for life. Would the strong wind drive either away from the nest on the tall channel marker? She caught sight of the male, feathers ruffled and head pressed to his breast, clutching the branch of an oak a few yards from the nest. The female's head was still thrust above the untidy pile of sticks and brush.

Brandy wondered if Fishhawk and Annie would weather the approaching storm as well.

Brandy slowed almost to idle, bow facing the waves, while Hackett pulled up to Melba's elaborate dock. On the pier stood the bald, thick-set man with the ragged beard, hands on hips and legs apart. Brandy recognized him from the night before at the Tiki bar.

"About time, woman!" he shouted. Again Brandy felt pity for the Realtor. No wonder Alma May thought Melba's husband needed handling. It was hard to imagine he was once her hero.

The archaeologist helped Melba ashore as the first drops of rain rattled down on the hulls, then clamored back aboard, and roared on after Brandy's pitching pontoon. "Let's have dinner again tonight," he called as she reached the mouth of the canal. He whipped his lurching boat around for the trip to the motel marina. "I'll pick you up in less than an hour. No excuses. I've got news."

Brandy was too far away to reply. Grif Hackett was getting to be a habit. And John would probably call tonight. She scooted on down the canal, relieved to be in calmer waters. From the Gulf blew a gust of wind-driven rain.

After stepping into the screened porch with Meg, Brandy watched the cabbage palm beside the house toss in the wind, and thought about Annie Pine. This weather wouldn't make Annie any happier about staying on Tiger Tail Island. She wondered if Fishhawk's wife knew about Timothy Hart and his search. Obviously Fishhawk himself knew more than he admitted. If the Indian hadn't read the journal, what was he doing more than a mile from his camp at the site of the first Flint homestead? And Brandy only had his word that he did not read Muskokee.

She picked up the phone in the kitchen and called her regional office, wishing she had done it earlier. "Look," she said to a fellow reporter, "I've got to ask a favor. It's probably too late to get an answer tonight, but see if you can reach anyone at the *Seminole Tribune* in Hollywood, Florida. Got a pencil? I need a translation of the following Muskokee words. They were written more than a century ago, the way they sounded in English." She waited a few seconds, then carefully spelled out the unknown syllables from Lieutenant Henry Hart's journal. "I need that translation as soon as possible. If I'm not here, leave it on this answering machine." She wandered back onto the porch, picked up her notebook, and jotted down a record of her visit to Fishhawk's camp.

In a few minutes Hackett pulled up in his van. Brandy settled on a raincoat with a hood, then stepped out on the front step. "It's a little wet for the Tiki bar tonight," he said, reaching across and opening the passenger door. "They've got good food at the tavern by the old sugar mill."

They drove down a road that curved under a canopy of branches cloaked in Spanish moss. "Melba's husband gets to me," she said as they parked among a throng of other cars before the small cypress building. Here she'd had the morose Friday night supper with John.

"He's a full time boozer these days, I hear," Hackett said. Brandy wondered how Tugboat was involved in the quarrel she'd overheard between Melba and Alma May.

"And your news?" she asked.

In spite of the rain, Grif walked around and opened her door. "It's almost time for me to leave Homosassa. I've taken a two-room suite at the motel to help get organized. I set up a field lab a few days ago, and I need a couple of days to pack up. I kept a few choice specimens of pottery for the museum. I want you to see the one with a bird handle." They lowered their heads to the moist air and a southeast wind, entered the little restaurant, and found a table near the bar. The piped music was soft. Fishermen and fishing guides with day old beards were perched at the bar. Glasses clinked, and from the pass-through kitchen window Brandy caught the tantalizing smell of seared beef.

It was Sunday night. That left some time before Hackett wanted to leave. "Sergeant Strong should be finished with us all by Wednesday, I'd think. I'll stay in touch with the cops, of course, in case they need me. Which I doubt."

"Does that means Fishhawk and his family will be leaving, too?"

"He's got to by the end of the week. He wants me to take the bundle burial to Tampa for him. He's arranged for it to be re-buried next Sunday.

The ceremony will take place near some Seminole graves in a cemetery near the reservation."

Brandy dropped her voice when she said the next words. "You mean, of course, to move the bones of the child?" The memory of the pathetic little skeleton made her uncomfortable, especially since she had met Daria. That child had been about the same size.

Hackett nodded. "He's taken care of arrangements for the grave. My job is to deliver the package and leave. Then Fishhawk as Medicine Man takes over. He has to make sure the disturbed spirit goes west like it should and doesn't hang around the Cultural Center."

"So you've got to go to Gainesville with the pots first and then to Tampa?"

He nodded. Rain whirred against the pane and beat on the roof. "I hate to think of Annie and Daria out there tonight," Brandy said. They ordered the prime rib special. "Grif, did you hear Mrs. Flint say Fishhawk was snooping around the site of the old homestead?"

The archaeologist's bit down on his lower lip and looked solemn. "Fishhawk's likely," he answered slowly, "to get himself in a heap of trouble."

After dinner Brandy darted into the house through the downpour and closed the door before Hackett could step down from the van. Without the weather, she might've had trouble keeping him out, and she didn't want to face a problem with Grif Hackett.

She might've been tempted to ask him in, to sit and talk, to get involved even more deeply, to hear him say again how much alike they were, and be forced to agree. Even drenched, Grif Hackett was a commanding figure.

Only one message flashed on the answering machine. Her friend at the paper had called back to report that she was working on the translation. A *Seminole Tribune* editor promised a reply from the tribe's anthropologist in the morning. John had not phoned. She felt relieved. She didn't want to listen to his warnings or defend herself, her job, or her postponement of a baby again.

In the living room Brandy picked up a book on Florida archaeology she'd bought at the Citrus County Historical Center. She didn't like being ignorant about Grif's work or Seminole culture. Here she was a native Floridian and she knew so little.

When she finally crawled into bed, she lay listening to rain drum on the metal roof. What would it be like to sleep under palmetto thatch in such a soaking? Tomorrow she would take Annie grocery shopping and invite Annie and Daria to stay with her. Let Fishhawk have his mumbo jumbo and his witches all to himself. She would also call Sergeant Strong.

Best of all, tomorrow she would know at last where the Seminole warrior had hidden his wretched and frightening whatever-it-was.

$$*\qquad*\qquad*\qquad*$$

Brandy was washing her breakfast dishes when the call about the translation came from the *Gainesville Star*. She grabbed a memo pad. "Let's have it," she said. "This better help."

"Doesn't make sense to me," her friend said. "But the guy at the *Seminole Tribune* was great. He got this from an expert. Anyhow, here goes. You already have the correct translation for *sugeha hoo chek* . It does mean a tobacco pouch. The one you really needed was for *we enkokee*. It means 'a hole in the ground with water in it,' okay?"

"That's it?"

"Afraid so. But it sounds like you may be onto something."

Brandy stared at the words. A hole in the ground could be almost anything. "I'll call if I get a real story," she said. "In the meantime, this is only vacation time."

Tiger Tail Island had changed over a century and a half, she thought as she hung up. Maybe there was once a spring in the woods, maybe still was. Springs were plentiful in this part of Florida; in fact the headwaters of a huge spring fed the entire Homosassa River. Settlers would logically build near a water source. Or perhaps they had a reservoir. Or it could mean an inlet, cut off from the river then by low tides. The fact that the plantation was built a few years after the Indians left might complicate finding it.

She stuffed her small note pad back into the canvas bag, checked her watch, and picked up the phone again. For the first time she reached

Detective Jeremiah Strong at his desk. "Nothing much to report, Sergeant," she began, "but I did find out that Alma May knew Hart's briefcase was hidden outside her house. She admitted it."

Strong did not alter his long-suffering tone. "Not surprising," he said. "Her fingerprints are on it. Both Mrs. Flint's and Mrs. Grapple's. That doesn't prove they murdered Mr. Hart, or even found his alleged treasure. It does show they were curious, but I think we knew that."

"You didn't find fingerprints on Hart's clothes? We know he was searched."

"Can't get fingerprints from cloth, young lady."

"Grapple and Flint have been combing the island. I don't believe it's all a bottle and spoon search. They may very well be illegal pot hunters." Brandy brightened. "I also got the translation of the Muskogee words in the lieutenant's journal..."

Strong didn't give her a chance to finish. He sighed. "Look, Miss O'Bannon, I have that, too. You think we're stupid? But my men went over that area right after we found the body. Nothing. Zip. Whatever that Indian hid, it's gone now. This Hart case isn't the only one I'm working on. We can't even be sure he was murdered. Maybe he was just dumb enough to gobble a whole bunch of the wrong pokeweed roots and berries."

"More than once? Even when he got sick? I think someone fed them to Hart." Brandy tapped her pencil. She had doodled an Indian head with heavy black hair and shiny eyes. "Remember, Sergeant. Timothy Hart asked for my help."

Strong's voice gathered strength. "I think you're more interested in promoting your career. Remember 'He that passeth by and meddleth with strife belonging not to him, is like one that taketh a dog by the ears.'"

Brandy glanced out the window at Meg, who lay under her favorite orange tree, red coat ruffled and silky ears blowing in the wind. Nothing wrong with taking my dog by the ears, she thought, but she didn't suppose she'd grab a Rottweiler by his. "Thanks again for helpful words, Sergeant," she said and hung up.

For a moment she actually considered Strong's advice. It always matched John's. Could they be right? If someone had killed Timothy Hart for his precious artifact, would that person hesitate to repeat the crime? Especially to be rid of a prying reporter? If she hadn't divulged the comments Hart made at the bar to the Sheriff's Office, they might not be investigating his death. And she hadn't quit nosing around.

Still, she stood and lifted up her canvas bag. She would be careful, but no one had threatened her. The island must be searched again. It didn't sound as if the Sheriff's Office planned a second excursion.

Outside the rain had stopped, but a gray sky arched over the trees and canal. The air was still washed with the clean smell of rain. Although the wind had shifted to the east, the water ran fairly high. Brandy crossed the road to the boat slip and studied the tide chart pinned to her pontoon's console. A steady east wind would blow the water toward the Gulf. That meant low water. Better get cracking. Her commitment to Hart wasn't her only one. She had also made a promise to Annie Pine.

*   *   *   *

When Brandy reached the end of the narrow trail to the Seminoles' camp, she watched Annie pluck little Daria out of her pen made from brush and cedar branches and dust off her overalls. Today Annie wore jeans, and she had pulled both her hair and her daughter's into tight pony tails. She slipped on a light-weight jacket hanging in the chickee and guided the little girl's arms into her tiny one. The child screwed up her mouth with the effort, then grinned.

"Ready for a ride to the store?" Brandy asked.

"We're ready. Daria likes to go places," Annie said. "She's not particular where."

"Go, go," cooed Daria.

Sheets of heavy plastic still hung around the chickee. Apparently the little family had weathered the rain. It wouldn't have been so cozy in the nineteenth century.

"Be back soon as I can," Annie called to Fishhawk.

He had piled flat rocks in a circle, lit a fire nearby to heat water in an iron pot, and was lashing together a ring of split saplings shoulder high to curve above the stones. On a nearby stump lay a fat pouch of tobacco. The makeshift sweat lodge, Brandy supposed. She thought Fishhawk's leathery face looked more strained than the day before. Lines cut deep in his forehead and around his mouth. He set aside the cord he was using to bind the stalks and gave his wife a brisk good-bye wave.

"No hurry. I've got work to do." As they started back down the trail, with Brandy in the rear, she noticed that Fishhawk did not turn again toward his sweat lodge. Instead he set off to the north. Brandy wondered if he again planned to survey the site of the old Flint homestead. Alma May wouldn't like it.

"Fishhawk couldn't keep the fire going last night," Annie said, helping Daria into the boat, "but I brought plenty of blankets from Tampa. Thank the Lord we have bug repellent. They don't spray out here for mosquitoes like they do in town."

Annie cuddled Daria on the rear bench of the boat as they inched their way down Petty Creek and then bucked through the choppy water toward the marina. Within thirty minutes they had pulled into the dock.

"I'd like you and Daria to move in with me for a few days," Brandy said, looping a line around the end cleat. "Let Fishhawk do his thing by himself. You might as well be comfortable."

At first Annie didn't answer. Ducking her head against the wind, her oval face solemn, she led the way through the marina lot, past the gas pumps, to a heavy pick-up plastered with "Save the Everglades" stickers— Fishhawk's truck bought with casino income, Brandy imagined. Too bad the white man's money couldn't go to the Seminoles who suffered a century and a half ago. Still, there was ironic justice in the source of the Indians' income now. She wished those dead tribesmen who'd been hounded into the Everglades could know.

Annie was not considering Seminole income, however, but Brandy's offer. "I'll think about it," she said finally. "Fishhawk warned me not to come to Tiger Tail Island, but I worry about him. I thought he'd be better off if we were with him. I don't want him to get too deep into his grandfather's stuff. He needs to stay in touch with this century. It's where we live. I'll tough it out another night. After that, we may take you up on your offer. Or maybe just hang a ride back to Tampa."

At the supermarket, while waiting for Annie to stock up on staples like bread and grits, Brandy recognized the tall, supple figure of Bibi Brier in the line at the cash register. As soon as the graduate student saw Brandy, her bored stare shifted into a frown. Brandy stepped over to speak. "How's it going in Chassahowitzka with the whooping cranes?"

Bibi shrugged. "The ground's too swampy to be good for them. We're repairing the substation for roosting." She moved forward to scoot a six pack and chips further down the counter. "The whoopers should begin to fly out sometime this month. I'm observing and helping out until they do." She tossed back her long brown hair, then peered back at Brandy. "You still hanging out with Dr. Hackett?"

A man like Grif, Brandy knew, must have many female admirers among his students. A jealous one was easy to spot. Maybe Bibi supposed Brandy was the associate professor's newest conquest. "He's giving me useful information for an article I'm working on," Brandy said, and was not surprised to see no change in the sullen expression.

When Annie finished shopping, she drove the pickup to the marina, and together they transferred her grocery bags to Brandy's boat. They had scarcely pulled away from the pier for the return trip when little Daria leaned out to starboard and pointed into the river, black eyes shining. "Mana," she squealed.

Brandy's gaze followed her finger. A circle of ripples danced in the water. Annie smiled. "Manatees. She's seen them at the Homosassa Springs Wildlife Park." Quickly Brandy cut the engine.

A broad back the color and texture of an elephant's but the size of a small walrus rose sedately to the surface. Next to it a small snout poked above water, then a four-foot, rounded body bobbed up beside the first. In a few seconds both sank again beneath the water, cruised under the boat, and swam away side by side. "Mother and calf," Annie said. "Such gentle creatures. I love to see them. They're rare because they're such slow breeders."

Brandy nodded. A sighting was always magical. Manatees, at last count about two thousand, were rarer even than Florida Seminoles, who numbered about 2,500, but this mother manatee was doing her bit. So were Fishhawk and Annie with Daria. Ironic, Brandy thought to herself. There were funds to preserve whooping cranes and manatees but none to preserve the endangered Seminole and his culture—unless the United States counted the money lost to them in gambling.

When the boat neared the Flint house, Brandy broached the subject of Timothy Hart. "Did you know the Sheriff's Office thinks a man was murdered last Thursday at this end of the Island? Pokeweed poisoning."

On the boat's rear bench Annie lifted Daria into her lap. "Fishhawk told me. You know how he is. He says he can ward off the evil on the island. So he's purifying everything—including himself. He carries around a deerskin bundle his grandfather got from his great-grandfather. They were all medicine men. It's a small one, not the big deal they use at the Green Corn Dance. The contents are secret."

Brandy recalled some references she'd been reading about the Seminole people. "Anthropologists who studied the Seminoles in the past published a few medicine bundle ingredients, like red ocher, crystals, and herbs, but I know bundles vary. Some are supposed to smell of red bay and cedar."

Annie's face grew solemn. "All have power. It's true. I couldn't tell you any real details, even if I knew more about them." She smiled suddenly. "Fishhawk collects ginseng roots. Old-time Seminoles used them as medicine. Now they're in all the health food stores. So much for dumb Indians." She shook her head. "But people today don't use ginseng to keep away ghosts. And have you heard the chanting?" She rolled her eyes to the sky. "One chant was supposed to paralyze your enemies, at least for a while. He's using that one." She shook her dark head. "Didn't do a lot of good during the wars."

Brandy was watching the pontoon boat's depth finder. The east wind had increased. The water was one foot to one and a half as she turned into Petty Creek. Pretty shallow. She pressed the electric tilt switch to lift the engine as far as possible out of the creek. Nearer the camp, the water would be even shallower. No need to worry Annie. She glanced back and changed the subject. "Doesn't Fishhawk wonder about who killed Timothy Hart?"

Annie rubbed her full lips and thought a moment. "I guess he figures that's the Sheriff's business. He doesn't expect to stay on the island much longer. He thinks we're safe. He says we don't have anything anybody wants." Brandy wondered if that were really true. What if he had found the thing everyone who'd read the journal wanted?

"Fishhawk says he's got a chore to do for Mr. Hackett," Annie added. The child bundle burial, Brandy thought.

"Is it hard, I mean, living with all the Seminole lore and not really accepting it yourself?" she asked.

Brandy knew immediately she'd overstepped. Annie bristled. "Franklin Pine is a good man," she said. "Seminole culture needs to be preserved. I believe in a lot of the same things. Christians teach about upper and lower worlds, like Seminoles do, and a God that creates everything. Seminoles call that being Breath Maker. All tribes say you should be respectful to all living things, that all living things should be in harmony. That doesn't sound too kooky to me. We have our powerful symbols and you have yours, like the Cross or the Rosary."

Chastised, Brandy recanted "I see your point."

When they beached the boat where the path began, Brandy again accessed the water depth. Farther south, parts of the stony bottom lay exposed, and over the creek hung the sour smell of wet mud. Once more she checked the tide chart. The tide was low now, which increased the effect of the easterly. Next she studied the chart of the river and its tributaries. The only other exits led through even shallower water around the southern tip of the island, or even farther south, where a waterway wound past Mason Creek to the Chassahowitzka River and its Wildlife Preserve. The wind might shift, of course, which would help. At high tide in another three hours her boat should be able to creep out. But Brandy knew she could never make it back until the water rose.

CHAPTER 9

▼

Fishhawk emerged from the hammock to carry the grocery bags up the incline. From the distasteful twist of his lips, Brandy supposed he would rather eat gopher turtles and possum with a dash of coontie root instead of Annie's choices, but he helped stack the cans and packages on the chickee platform. Then he turned a rigid back to Brandy. Obviously he didn't want her here. Still, the low water wouldn't yet allow her to leave and besides, she reminded herself, a journalist had to be aggressive with interviews.

From a pot over a low fire, Annie ladled three bowls of the rich-scented sofki, then spread Daria a peanut butter sandwich and handed her half a banana. When the toddler had finished—about as much peanut butter outside her brown cheeks as inside—Annie gave her a hug and laid her on a chickee pad for her nap. Daria would not have it. She squirmed and rolled, whined, and held up tiny arms to Brandy, eyes pleading for rescue. "Go, go," she said.

After setting aside her empty bowl, Brandy couldn't resist pulling the little girl into her lap and stroking the thick black hair. "Any idea if there's a spring on this island, maybe near the north end?" she asked Fishhawk.

He studied her, scowling, then shook his head. "Never seen one," he said.

"But there is a path through the hammock, isn't there? One that connects the two ends of the island?" She could see a dim trail curving among the turkey oaks, cabbage palms, and red cedars.

Fishhawk's frown deepened. "The big detective gives good advice," he said. "You ought to stop asking questions and leave things to the Sheriff."

Brandy had heard the same opinion from John, too. But she couldn't stop wondering about footpaths through the thicket of trees. "Let me take Daria for a short walk. It'll tire her out for her nap, and I need to stretch my legs. I can't get out with the boat until the tide comes in."

Annie sighed and said, "Sure. Take her for a walk. Just stay on the trail. Maybe I can get a few things done while you're gone."

Brandy slid from the chickee, lifted Daria down beside her, and picked up a handy four-foot long stick lying on the ground. "To scare off snakes," she said. Annie helped tuck the little girl's overalls into a pair of sturdy little boots. She seemed to understand she was going on an adventure and wiggled with excitement.

"Don't go far," Fishhawk said. He crossed over to the half-finished sweat lodge, gathered up the cord and again began weaving it between saplings, his eyes on Brandy.

At first Daria was content to patter along beside her new friend, one hand in Brandy's, with the other pointing out the "birdies," on a barren limb, black vultures that made Brandy shudder. Suddenly, with a jerk of her arm, the little girl twisted her fingers loose and trotted unsteadily on ahead, eyes on some slight movement in a clump of ferns—maybe a gopher turtle or a squirrel—then squealed with delight at the ghostly white spurge nettles that grew in clusters beside the path.

"Don't touch," Brandy said, catching up with her. "Bristles bite." With a yelp Daria drew back her hand, already stung, and scooted on ahead. While Daria toddled underneath a huge spider web between cedars, Brandy batted her way through it, an eye on the yellow and black golden silk spider in the center, its fat body more than an inch long. The thunk-thunk of a woodpecker high in the shadowy leaves of a cabbage palm startled her. Dim bands of sunlight filtered to the hammock floor. Several yards ahead a brownish snake slithered across the path. Brandy inhaled sharply as she recognized the water moccasin's triangular head. She hurried to take the child's hand, but the snake vanished among a pile of dank leaves, rank with the odor of decay. Again Daria wrenched her sweaty little fingers free and her chubby legs waddled on ahead.

They wouldn't walk far, of course. Brandy rushed again after the child. But she might yet see the lay of the land and how she could search for the original cabin site from the south, away from Alma May's fiercely protective gaze. Above Brandy, a strangler fig coiled around the trunk of a slender oak. Eventually the thick vine would kill its host.

And then the woods quieted. Birds grew silent. The squirrels vanished into tree tops. An uneasy stillness fell over the entire hammock. For a moment Brandy halted, mouth tense, eyes searching the brush, puzzled and wary.

In the next instant she heard a rustle in the grasses behind her. She spun around to see Fishhawk beside a large red cedar, standing with legs and body stiff, a rifle butt raised against his shoulder, his finger on the trigger, and the barrel pointed at her. Sudden fear exploded in her mind. Did he mean to end her meddling and her own search? With Daria safely out of the way, did he plan to scoop up Brandy's dead body and drag it into the creek for alligators?

She heard a click. Then Fishhawk spoke, his voice urgent and low. "Get Daria. Quick!"

Brandy swiveled around, sprinted a few paces down the path, and snatched up the child. The little girl gave a startled gasp.

Fishhawk spoke again, his voice still anxious. "Back up. Slowly. Don't run."

Brandy's knees went liquid. She clasped Daria to her breast and felt the small heart throb, the warm breath on her cheek. Brandy wobbled backwards, paused, inched a few more steps.

Then she glanced again behind her at the clump of cedars. Was she still a target? Her eyes followed the rifle barrel to a fallen palm trunk among scrub palmettos. In a shaft of light crouched a length of creamy fur. She could see the slight twitch of the long tail curled up at the end, and then the panther's head, ears back, held low in line with its back. Then the head lifted, the jaws opened, the white canines gleamed. The panther's face seemed to grow larger. Fur bristled around its gaping mouth, the ears flattened, and she heard a snarl, then a loud hiss. While she cowered on the path, arms wrapped around Daria, the huge cat hesitated, then in one fluid motion slid down from the log on the other side; the tawny back rippled beneath palm leaves and disappeared among the palmettos. In its wake, Brandy heard the nervous chittering of birds.

She dropped to her knees and sank down where she stood. "My God!" She stared at Fishhawk.

He moved soundlessly to Daria, bent down, and lifted her into his own arms. She clung to him, not sure what had happened but forehead creased with worry. "Go, go," she whimpered.

"It was stalking Daria," Fishhawk said. To his daughter he added softly, "Coo-wah-chokee, panther."

"I never knew you were there."

"Takes practice." Brandy remembered a passage in Lieutenant Hart's journal. Seminoles could stalk the troops, unseen, for miles, or vanish right under the their noses.

"Panthers attack from the rear," Fishhawk said. "You'd never have seen it. You were too big a victim. Daria wasn't."

"But how could it be here?" With slow steps, Brandy began following him toward the camp.

"Low water made a dry land bridge. Probably the cat came from further south, from the Wildlife Preserve. Followed a raccoon or something over here. It will leave now. This isn't its territory. Too many people. Usually panthers are very hard to find."

"You didn't shoot."

"We don't kill unless we need to. I distracted it. Big cats are cautious. It won't come near our fire." He gave a curious twist to his lips. "You wouldn't want to anger the animals, now would you? Or the evil on the island?"

Meaning the witch, Brandy thought. In a sense, he was right. Someone evil did prowl the island, but how could she know that it wasn't Fishhawk himself? Perhaps, he had planned to dispose of her until the panther appeared, and then he was forced to protect Daria instead. His little daughter's life would mean more to him than Brandy's disappearance.

For the second time she began to think Strong could be right. She would be safer not to "take the dog by the ears," to drop out, to sit on the sidelines, to wait for the Sergeant to find the answers.

✳   ✳   ✳   ✳

At 8:00 A.M. the morning after the panther scare, Brandy walked to the nearby convenience store and bought a *Chronicle* to check the wind and tide. The wind had switched to the southwest. The tide would be high at Tiger Tail in about two hours. Sunlight made bright, inviting paths in the water. She must honor her promise to bring Annie and Daria, if they would come, to her place in Homosassa. Then she could back away from the Hart case, take Strong's advice, leave the solution to the professionals.

By the time she cranked up the engine and moved down the canal, a fine mist blew in her face. The sky now was overcast. At about ten she passed the Flint house. All was quiet. The shades were drawn and Alma May's jon boat lay in its slip. After the quarrel the landlady had with Melba the day before, Brandy wondered if the Realtor had relinquished her exploration of the island, although Melba seemed exceedingly determined.

On the other side of the canal behind the Flint house, something stirred the wax myrtles. It could be a person; it could be a raccoon or an armadillo, anything. Was there another entry to the old Flint homestead site? Petty Creek was the obvious one, but a more narrow creek looped around the other shoreline, and the opposite end of the canal offered still another. Would Melba continue her search of the plantation ruins alone? Was she looking for artifacts of the Civil War era mansion, or that earlier treasure? Her husband had a fine boat, if she ever had the chance to use it.

As Brandy steered into Petty Creek, she was startled by Fishhawk's canoe spurting past her out into the bay. He bent to his task with fury, looking neither to left nor right, his long strokes shooting the slim craft forward, his dark hair flying. Brandy called out, but he did not hear.

Alarmed, she shoved the throttle as far forward as she dared and weaved past an oyster bar, eyeing the depth finder and then scanning ahead for fallen limbs or rocks. As soon as she reached the trail up the creek bank, she heard a heart squeezing sound—great, shuddering sobs. She had read that a female panther in heat sounded like a woman screaming, but these were not screams. Hands trembling, she tugged the boat's pontoons onto the riverbank and dashed toward the camp.

Annie met her, eyes wild, leaves in her uncombed hair, jeans and shirt torn and stained. "It's Daria," she cried, throwing her hands up. "Daria's gone!"

At first Brandy stared at Annie, paralyzed, then rushed forward and threw her arms around her. "I saw Fishhawk," Brandy said, "going for help."

Annie sagged in her arms. "I put Daria in her pen early, about seven. It's hard for any of us to sleep here—and started breakfast. God, it takes so long! When I went to get her, she was gone."

"Where was Fishhawk?"

Annie's face contorted into a crazed look Brandy could not interpret. "In his damned sweat lodge. We've searched everywhere."

Brandy spun around. "What am I thinking of? My cell's in the boat. You can probably reach the Sheriff's Office quicker than Fishhawk can get there. They'll send men to search."

Taking Annie's hand, she led her back down the trail. "The battery's charged. It'll be okay. But at the rate Fishhawk was moving, he may already be there."

"He's got to call once he gets to the marina," Annie said grimly. "This is faster."

At the boat, Brandy dialed the Sheriff's Office in Homosassa Springs and handed the phone to Annie. Voice choking, she gasped, "My baby's gone. Disappeared. Here on Tiger Tail Island. This morning, early."

Her voice broke and Brandy grabbed the phone. "Brandy O'Bannon here. Send as many deputies as you can. We've got to search the island. The child's not near the camp."

Annie would not sit down. Together they struggled back up the slope. "God, I don't know where else to look," Annie said, and shouted again, "Daria! Daria!"

The only reply was the whisper of wind in the cedars and cabbage palms. Across the creek a heron screeched. Brandy could not put the snarling face of the panther out of her mind. Yet Fishhawk had been so sure it would not come near fire or adults, and Annie had been nearby, stirring the sofki and toasting fry bread. Steam would have risen from the sweat lodge.

"I know that you're thinking animals. But Fishhawk says there'd be signs." Annie's voice shattered again. In a few seconds she added, "Pieces of cloth, things like that. Daria would have cried out. I know she would."

Brandy tried to feel reassured, but black bears were near and wild hogs, too. How had those earlier Indians lived in wilderness like this? All she could think of was the round little face close to hers, the breath on her cheek, the small arms tight around her neck. She felt like a rock had settled in her stomach. She could see no obvious damage to the brush and sapling pen.

She gently placed her hand on Annie's arm. "Deputies are on their way. We mustn't try to examine the pen anymore ourselves. We might destroy some clue, something that might help. But we have to be systematic. Search by grids, one block at a time. We'll start again, near the pen."

Brandy slogged along the creek bank through needlerush and spartina grasses and peered into a stand of saw grass, trying not to think about the alligators that might lurk in the mud or cruise the creek. Although alligators did not relish brackish waters, she had seen them among the islands, especially far from houses. What if little Daria had wiggled out of the pen and toddled down to the creek? What if...? But Brandy found no long, slithering track, no footprints except their own, hers near her boat, Fishhawk's where his canoe had lain. At every turn she prayed she would see the chubby little face with the sparkling eyes. Far away in the hammock she could hear Annie's frantic call, again and again. "Daria! Daria! It's Mommy."

Brandy had almost reached the southern end of the island where Petty Creek forked and wound back along the opposite shore when she heard the roar of a boat engine. A Sheriff's patrol craft came surging up the creek, a tall figure standing at the prow, another boat bringing up the rear. Relief welled within her. Jeremiah Strong and his men.

She struggled back over the wire grass and followed the men up the path toward Fishhawk's camp. Annie had already greeted them, hair in tangles, clothing coated with burs and leaves. Brandy heard her sob, "She just vanished! Disappeared." She lifted one quivering hand toward the pen. "We don't know how she got out. We can't find a sign of her. Fishhawk went for help."

Even Annie seemed reassured by the detective's firm, confident stance, his calm voice. "We'll find her," he said. "You take a rest. We passed your husband on the way back. He'll be here soon. He called the Homosassa Springs station shortly after you did." The detective turned, saw Brandy emerging from the riverbank, winced as usual, and then beckoned to her. "Miss O'Bannon, since you're here, help your friend. Get her a glass of water and make her sit down. She may be in shock."

Mutely Annie allowed herself to be led to the chickee, slumped on a mat, and with trembling fingers grasped the paper cup Brandy poured from a water bottle in the ice chest. Strong studied a clipboard with a map of the island marked in grids. Rapidly he dispatched deputies in four directions with specific assignments. Brandy could see two divers preparing to search the creek. Tears welled in her eyes; she turned away from Annie. God, she prayed, don't let them find her there.

Strong had begun a methodical questioning of Annie, jotting down times and information, when they heard Fishhawk's hoarse voice, speaking to the divers. Then he strode up the path, the lines in his forehead deepened, his eyes glistening.

"We've found nothing," Annie cried. "No one has found a trace—of anything."

Fishhawk sat down, breathing heavily. How many miles had he paddled there and back? Brandy thought about ten.

In a few minutes Strong returned. "We haven't made a complete search yet," he said. "But there's no sign of an intruder—that is, no bobcat tracks, no bear, no wild hogs. I thought you'd want to know. No sign of a scuffle."

Annie looked at him with anguish. "She'd have cried out. I wasn't far."

"But could you see the pen?"

Dumbly, Annie shook her head, "It's why we built it. To keep her from wandering off when we weren't watching."

"And your husband, where was he?"

Fishhawk clenched his fist. "In the sweat lodge."

"How long?"

"Maybe an hour."

"Did you hear any noises outside?"

The Indian shook his head.

"Did your wife see you go in and come out?"

Fishhawk scowled. "I don't know what you mean."

"I saw him go in," Annie said in a thin voice.

Strong folded the cover over his notebook. "It's good that we've found no signs. Unless the deputies turn up something, I think someone took her. Would she go willingly?"

With mounting fear, Brandy remembered Daria's childish plea, "Go, go."

Annie clasped her hands in her lap. "She would unless she was frightened. She was trusting, too trusting."

Fishhawk dropped, then raised his head. "Why would anyone kidnap her? What could anyone hope to get from us?"

Strong crossed long arms over his chest and spoke deliberately. "The motive may be different," he said. "I want you two to stay here and let the deputies search now. I'm going to make a call." They watched his tall figure march toward the patrol boat.

"I ought to give you two some time to yourselves," Brandy said, slipping down from the chickee. She set off at a brisk clip after the detective and paused behind a bushy cedar as she neared the patrol craft.

"That's right," Strong was saying into the cell phone. "Send a car to the Seminole Cultural Center in Tampa, check things out. See if a little girl has turned up there with anyone. About eighteen months old. Yes, a little Indian girl. Name's Daria. Daria Pine, Father's Franklin Pine, goes by the name of Fishhawk. He works there."

Brandy pressed her back hard against the prickly leaves, nausea in the pit of her stomach. Strong may suspect Fishhawk himself, she thought. But why? Her thoughts raced back over the last few days. Fishhawk had feared for Annie and Daria to come here, had judged the island unsafe, although he thought he could protect them. He had left early that morning in the canoe. Annie did not see him come out of the sweat lodge. Questions flooded her mind. Could he have handed Daria off to someone? What if Fishhawk had found the valuable artifact—or knew where to find it? Would he kidnap his own daughter to get Annie off the island and keep his find a secret? If the Sheriff's Office found Daria was not here, Annie would surely look elsewhere or go home.

But if Fishhawk were guilty, would Annie ever forgive him? There was, of course, an even uglier possibility. What if Fishhawk had tried to teach Daria some Indian trick she was too young to master, had taken her into the brush to learn to hide like Seminole children did in the last century, and what if she had been bitten by a coral snake or a water moccasin or rattler? For such a small child, death would be quick. He was plainly distressed. But if an accident had happened, would he dare tell his wife?

Brandy hurried back up the path ahead of the detective. She could hear the receding sound of men thrashing through the underbrush. "Look," she said to Annie. "You don't need me here anymore. I'll leave now, but would you still consider coming to stay with me?"

Fishhawk turned his head and stared at Brandy, hostility clear in his eyes. Perhaps Annie had not told him about her invitation. Annie shook her head. "I couldn't, not now. Not until..." she paused and caught her breath. "Not until they've found Daria or..." Her voice trailed off.

"I'm going to stop at the Flint house," Brandy said. "I'm sure the deputies will ask there, but I'd like to talk to Mrs. Flint, too. And that real estate woman, she'll probably be there if they made up the spat they had yesterday. Deputies ought to search that area."

"Daria could never have gone that far," Annie said in a faint voice.

Not alone, Brandy thought. Out loud she said, "Take my cell. It's good for several days. Call me at Mrs. Flint's or at my house if they find anything, please. If no one finds Daria soon, I'm going to search near the Flint house myself. The officers already failed to find something there that I later found myself. I have to try."

To the Sergeant, still standing near the chickee, she said, "I'd like to notify the newspapers. Someone in the area might've seen or heard something."

He nodded, but his eyes were on Fishhawk. "You're a spiritual advisor, I hear," he said. "I understand you believe a witch may be on the island."

Fishhawk's eyes narrowed, a muscle stood out in his cheek. "Our beliefs are not the same as yours, Sergeant. I can't explain them to you. You wouldn't understand."

Frowning, Strong ran a big hand over his forehead and said sadly, "Can a man take fire into his bosom and his clothes not be burned?"

If Fishhawk understood the Biblical warning, he gave no sign. He still sat beside Annie, his big hand covering hers, his broad, flat face without expression.

Brandy walked toward her boat, for the moment Jeremiah Strong beside her. "Fishhawk believes he's purifying the island, casting away evil," Brandy said. "He compared his belief to the casting out of devils in the Bible."

Strong paused, as if studying the proposition. "As a medicine man, Fishhawk also believes he can heal the sick," he said slowly. "It's a shrewd comparison. According to Mark, Jesus gives His disciples two powers—to heal the sick and to cast out devils. Matthew added they had the power to cast out unclean spirits. But the devils and the unclean spirits were in people."

"And so they are on Tiger Tail Island," Brandy said.

CHAPTER 10

▼

Brandy said a mournful good-bye to Annie, but before she left the island, she walked over to the detective, who stood apart now, studying his chart. "What do you think, Sergeant?"

"I don't like coincidences," Strong said. "Hart claims he'll find something valuable on the island; Hart dies on the island, probably poisoned; a few days later a child whose father knew Hart disappears on the island. There's probably a connection."

Brandy raised her eyebrows. "Did your men find anything at all?"

He shifted the clipboard to his other arm and ran one large hand through his hair. "The print of a boot beside the pen," he said. "It fits the father."

"Of course, he looked in the pen before he went for help."

"I know. The area's pretty muddied up with the mother's footprints—" he frowned at Brandy— "and with yours. If someone left prints earlier, they've been tramped all over now." He lowered his eyes, closed them for a moment, and shook his head. "I hate it when something happens to a child. If we don't locate her very soon, we'll call for volunteers."

"Count me in," Brandy said. She remembered that Strong had children of his own. She didn't doubt the strength of his concern.

As she trudged back to her own boat, she knew the detective was irritated with her again, but he would also understand her need to help. Half way to the Flint house she saw Hackett's boat approaching from the main river and throttled back at her side of the winding channel to let him by. As he passed he called out, "I heard the terrible news. I'm going to see Fishhawk. Maybe I can help."

"Good," Brandy said. "The Sheriff's Office sent deputies." He waved and swept on by.

Alma May's jon boat lay next to the dock, the house itself quiet. The only sound was the rustle of cabbage palms and the sharp cry of a seagull. Before Brandy knocked at the front door, she skirted the house and peered into the garden. She could see across the canal that curved around this end of the island before joining the river. Nothing moved among the shrub oaks, palmettos, and wax myrtle. Apparently, deputies had not gotten to Alma May's property yet. Fishhawk's camp was a long walk away.

As soon as Brandy knocked, Alma May opened the door, and Brandy pushed over the threshold. She could see Melba Grapple's scarf on the coffee table beside the pewter spoon and broken glass jar. Neither had been put away. Maybe the two had reconciled their differences. "Has anyone told you about the little Seminole girl?" Brandy asked immediately. "The child staying on the island with her parents is missing."

Alma May pursed her lips. "We're way ahead of you," she said. "A sheriff already called. Well, ain't no child here." She made a visible effort to soften her tone, but the words still came out triumphant. "Never should've been on the island."

Brandy flushed. She had the momentary image of the small, round face, the bright eyes, the black hair pulled back in a neat pony-tail. But antagonizing Alma May Flint for her heartlessness would not help Daria. She looked about for Melba Grapple. "Your friend at the plantation site again?"

Alma May shook her head. "Melba and me, we got business to talk about—privately."

A door opened into the kitchen from outside, and Melba called into the living room, "I think everything's going well." Her lanky figure appeared in the doorway, white blonde hair in tangles and sweat on her face, carrying a Tupperware box.

"We got company," Alma May said in a loud voice, looking at Brandy. "I think she's fixing to leave." Melba spun around, glanced anxiously into the living room, then hurried into the hall and disappeared inside Timothy Hart's old bedroom. Brandy heard a muffled sound through the door—a reedy whimper, a half cough. She tried to edge her way farther in, but Alma May stepped before her, arms crossed.

"You'll call the Sheriff if you see anything of the little girl, won't you?" Brandy asked. "Someone should search around here. The missing child's only a toddler, not quite two."

Alma May's answer was tart, "Then the kid couldn't of come all this way." She stepped toward Brandy, moving her toward the door. "They need to look somewheres else."

Brandy didn't argue. "Is Mrs. Grapple in some kind of trouble? I heard something like a sob from the bedroom."

"Mrs. Grapple's fine, thank you. You heard the cat. Been sickly." Alma May opened the front door. "Cat's got the heaves." Brandy found herself on the doorstep.

Brandy couldn't remember a cat. She strained to hear the cry again, but Alma May was saying goodbye. The last thing Brandy heard was Alma May's final remark to Melba in the hall. "I declare, we're not shut of that woman or the deputies yet. They'll be back, too." From outside Brandy saw window shades rattle down around the living and dining rooms.

After starting her boat's engine, she cruised slowly down the canal that rimmed the rear of the house and garden. A shovel leaned against the shed. In the opposite field she was surprised to see a series of potholes around the wax myrtles. Some one had been methodically digging test holes around the old site. She thought of the tour Hackett had given her of the Safety Harbor mound and had a sudden inspiration. These two women could be illegal pot hunters of long experience. Tugboat could have a hand in this. He'd have contacts. They all needed money, and Hackett said there was a market. She'd seen Melba carry a Tupperware container from the yard into the kitchen. The three could be in business. She wondered if they'd added Hart's treasure to their inventory.

All was silent from behind their drawn shades. But how could pot hunting or even vandalism of the mound be connected to Daria's disappearance? Brandy pictured the two intractable women—especially Alma May—and remembered Fishhawk's talk of witches. Would these two hold a friendly little girl to force Fishhawk to stop his search and leave the island?

After Brandy entered the river again and returned to her own boat slip, she studied the auxiliary electric motor in the pontoon's bow. They seldom used it, but John had wired it to the battery for the gasoline engine. Tomorrow the electric motor might serve a purpose. It was silent and drew less water than the usual prop. With it, she could move stealthily around Alma May's house and tie up in the shallow canal, unheard. She liked the idea. Forgotten was her decision to take Strong's advice. Finding Daria was more important. If she located the phantom hole of water, so much the better. If the Sheriff's Office called for volunteer searchers, Strong would know she'd answer. All of Homosassa was the target, and Brandy couldn't trust the two women to comb through Alma May's property for Daria.

Back in her temporary house, Brandy hurried into the kitchen and called the *Gainesville Star* to report Daria's disappearance. She also alerted the Citrus County *Chronicle* and advised both papers to check with the Sheriff's Office. A story in the morning papers might produce a lead. Her final call was a message to Strong: check out the Flint house. In the front yard Meg woofed to come in while the Persian cat leapt down from the living room couch and wound herself around Brandy's ankles. She fed them on the screened porch, then slumped in a chair at the table, unable to concentrate on anything but little Daria. Overhead she heard the thump of helicopter blades. A pilot had joined the search.

Brandy pulled her notebook out of a cabinet and flipped through meticulous pages of notes. It didn't help. Nothing made sense. She winced at the child's face she had doodled in one margin, the large eyes, round face, tightly drawn back hair. Perhaps she could take comfort in the fact that Daria had not been found. If Strong was right, if someone had taken her, she might still be all right. She wrote *Tuesday* at the top of a new page, carefully recorded the day's events, and ended by noting that if no one located Daria by morning, she would search the north end of Tiger Tail herself.

At last she remembered the answering machine. The red light had been blinking when she called the newspapers. Annie could've phoned. But the message did not come from Annie, but from John. "I expected you to call," he said, an edge to his voice. "I can never reach you at Carole's place, or on your cell, either."

Of course not, Brandy thought helplessly. I gave the cell to Annie. She might not turn it on except to call out.

John's voice went on. "I won't plan to drive up this weekend. You'll still be busy with this new story you're working on. Go on, do your own thing. If you see you've got some time for us, call me, but I've got to go out this evening." There was a pause. Then he added, "I hope you're thinking about what I said." The recording clicked off.

It was a few seconds before Brandy pressed the erase button. She had complained that John wouldn't share his feelings, but when he did, it hurt. She hadn't called today because she'd been trying to find a little girl. Maybe he was looking for an excuse not to join her. As it was, they'd been apart much of the year. As she punched in his number, she wondered what his engagement was for the evening.

"Got your message," she said. It was hard, trying to sound perky over a machine. "Things have been complicated here. A toddler is missing. I lent my cell to the mother. She's panicked." Brandy didn't know when to suggest John call her. "I'll try to reach you later."

With a glum face, she opened the refrigerator and was contemplating the unsavory choice of left-over fried shrimp or a frozen half-pound of hamburger when she heard a car pull into the driveway. For a moment she thought John might've found time to drive to Homosassa, after all. But the visitor was Grif Hackett.

As soon as she opened the door, he stepped in and stood looking down at her, sympathy in those iridescent eyes. "They haven't found Daria yet," he said

When Brandy dropped into a porch chair, he pulled one out for himself. "I appreciate your coming to tell me," she said. "I've notified the papers. Strong okayed it."

"Can't hurt. The divers had to call off their search. It's getting too dark. They'll be at it again in the morning. According to the local news, they've called for volunteers."

"Annie?"

"Bearing up. Fishhawk is acting strange. He doesn't want the Sheriff involved."

Brandy's lips tightened. "I suppose he thinks his spells can bring her back."

Hackett frowned and shook his head. "Look, I didn't come just to bring no news. You can't sit here all night, worrying. Let's go out and eat. Then I want to show you something." With a slight smile, he held up his hand, palm outward. "Don't worry, not etchings. Pottery. Some remarkable specimens. Remember, I told you I'd like you to see the one with the bird handle. I'm restoring a few pots in my make-shift field lab. Then I'll take them to the research center."

Brandy thought of the tedious evening before her, sitting alone, waiting for news. John would not call back, would not be back. She could, of course, spend her time vacuuming and dusting for Carole. She looked down at her sweatshirt and jeans. Okay for Homosassa, she thought. She lifted a jacket from the back of a chair and closed her notebook. "Why not?" she said and forced a smile. "Beats the prospects here."

"There's a restaurant and lounge by my motel. I had to take a suite. I need the extra room for lab work and packing my gear." After they stepped outside, Hackett paused beside his van. "Do you know when your husband's joining you?"

Brandy looked away. "He's not coming up this weekend."

"And your plans?"

"Help look for Daria, mainly. I'm still checking on the Timothy Hart case. The two may be related." She opened the door to Carole's car in the double carport. "Look, I'll take my friend's car and meet you, so you needn't drive me home." Safer that way, she thought. Keep him at bay.

"Like I said," he said, smiling. "We're a lot alike. Independent."

The lounge where they stopped first was timbered in dark wood and jutted out on pilings above the river. At the copper bar on the second floor sat a fisherman with gray whiskers and few teeth. He was flanked by a scattering of tourists. At one end of the counter hunched the heavy-set man Brandy knew as Tugboat Grapple, propped unsteadily on his elbows. He had covered his bald head with a billed cap at a rakish angle, and his belly sagged over his belt. He peered with watery eyes at the young female bartender. "Let's have a little service here, girly."

"Come on, Mr. Grapple," the girl said. "You've had enough. Don't you think you'd better go on home now?" She glanced behind her for back-up.

"God-a-mighty no, I don't wanna go home now!" The big man's voice soared in an imitative treble. "Ever seen my stick of a wife?" He laughed and looked around for support. A hush fell over the lounge while the bartender stepped to a phone.

"Another close-up of Melba's husband," Brandy whispered to Hackett.

Grif picked up his a scotch and water, took a firm grip on her arm while she gathered up her wine glass, and guided her to a table for two by the picture window. "To name that man 'Tugboat' is to insult a useful water craft," he said. "I had a run-in with him recently in Chassahowitzka."

"I heard Alma May say he gambles. I wonder why Melba doesn't leave him?"

"Getting rid of Tugboat might not be easy." He rolled his eyes at the ceiling. "But she's got leverage. He can't make her too angry. She seems to support him now."

A small man in slacks and a sports coat came in from the restaurant downstairs, stopped beside Tugboat, who was banging his mug on the counter, and spoke to him quietly. Tugboat swung around, teetered on his stool, then apparently made a decision. He slammed down a bill and glared at the man in the suit. "I'm clearing out now, you little buzzard," he said. "Next time I come back, I'll be rich enough to buy this stinkin' joint." The remark was not lost on Brandy.

Tugboat was lurching toward the door when he reached Brandy and Grif's table. He paused, bent down, and thrust his weathered face toward her. She caught a strong whiff of whiskey. Grif's fingers clenched over the edge of the table. She had never seen him angry before.

"I seen you around," the boatman said to her, his voice like gravel. "Heard about you from old Melba. Sticking your nose in folk's business." As he leaned closer, Grif began to rise. Tugboat ignored him. "Folks in this town like their privacy. That goes especially for reporters."

Grif pushed in front of the table, grabbed a surprised Tugboat by one beefy arm, and shoved him toward the door. The boatman, off balance, tried to shake himself loose, thought better of it, and staggered with Grif behind him toward the outside. In silence the customers watched the former river guide reel alone into the parking lot. The fisherman at the bar gave Grif a toothless grin. In a few minutes Tugboat wobbled onto the floating dock. He fumbled with lines looped around the pier cleats and spoke to the Rottweiler. It leaped up from the deck and stood quivering at the bow. Then the engine roared beneath the restaurant window and Tugboat's Grady White shot out into the river.

Grif and Brandy watched him go. Brandy was shaken. She ordered a second glass of Merlot.

"Don't worry," Hackett said. "He's drunk. Probably won't remember in the morning that he threatened you."

Brandy felt tightness in her throat. She didn't like having Tugboat Grapple set against her. It helped that Hackett felt protective. Still, Tugboat had given her the glimmer of an idea. He implied he was coming into money, lots of it. How much were aboriginal artifacts worth now, especially since they could no longer be removed legally? Someone had looted the mound. And she also wondered how much Timothy Hart's missing artifact was worth. Everyone seemed to know about it now.

Grif and Brandy ordered crab stuffed shrimp. The large window beside them overlooked a tiny island, encircled by water that shimmered under the dining room lights.

"Did Alma May feel bad about losing you as a boarder?" Brandy asked.

He shrugged. "She and Melba have other fish to fry. I think they were glad to see me go."

"I tried to talk to Alma May and Melba about Daria." Brandy plunked down her fork, annoyed just remembering. "Alma May sounded almost glad the child was gone. She said now the Indians will all leave. We know Fishhawk was messing around the old site, but Melba was, too—not to mention Alma May herself."

"Mrs. Flint can sound more uncaring than she actually is," Hackett said. "She just has a thing about Indians."

"I don't think either of them plan to look for Daria at all. If I don't hear she's found tonight, I'm going to search near their house myself. I half suspect them."

Hackett grinned. "Better be careful."

"I'm a volunteer. I won't get very close to the house itself. I'll start at the old cabin site. I asked Alma May to tell me where it is."

When they had finished dinner, Hackett led Brandy downstairs and across the parking area toward the lobby of the motel. "The pots I found will help take your mind off Daria. The pieces are ready to wrap and pack for the drive to Gainesville. I've seen photographs of one design, but I've never looked at an authentic specimen before. I want to take some good pictures. The pots make you appreciate what those guys did with almost no tools."

In the lobby Hackett stopped at the desk for messages. The clerk, a middle-aged woman with a tower of blonde-gold hair, leaned across the counter toward Grif.

"I took a phone message for you, Mr. Hackett," she said, her voice soft and inviting. "Also a woman stopped by to see you a few minutes ago. She waited a while in the lobby and left." After the clerk handed him a slip of paper, he looked at the phone number and stuffed the paper in his pocket. He was more interested in an envelope with a foreign stamp that had been forwarded.

"From a museum contact in Mexico City," he said. "They're showing a new Maya exhibit. I'm interested in Central America, that's where the real digs are going on. Prehistoric cave stuff is really new."

While Grif studied the letter, Brandy turned toward the plate glass window fronting the parking lot, feeling slightly groggy. She regretted the second glass of wine with dinner. A face stared back from a low slung sports car parked before the motel. Bibi Brier. She made no move to leave her seat behind the wheel. Brandy wondered if it was her note the archaeologist had poked into his pocket. Bibi did not look happy. "Look, Grif," Brandy said. "Your grad student must be the woman who came to see you."

"Forget it. She's bad news."

As Brandy walked on, she noticed the sports car stayed in its parking space.

When they stopped at Grif's door in the hall, he added, "I keep in touch with what's going on in my field around the world. We can't collect artifacts in Florida like we used to, but other countries can, and American archaeologists lead the pack."

He opened the door into a sitting room. Although its windows overlooked the river and pool, Hackett had drawn the drapes. "Don't want anyone snooping," he said. "When the word gets out you're an archaeologist, old ladies and little kids come out of the woodwork with sappy questions. Besides, I don't want this stuff swiped."

On one table along the wall he had stacked several plastic boxes with tight-fitting lids and packets of bubble-wrap. "My little field lab," he said. On a table Brandy saw pottery fragments sunk on edge in a box of sand and next to it a tube of Elmer's glue. Beside the tube sat one clay pot fitted together like a jigsaw puzzle, the missing pieces filled in with mortar of a similar color. On another table he displayed two more specimens.

"Look at the bird one. My prize." Brandy stared at a pitcher the size of a large coffee mug. On opposite sides of the short bowl protruded the finely sculpted, matching heads of two birds with big eyes and thick bills. The base was marked by incisions suggesting flowers in a heart-shaped design and decorated with dots.

"A Weeden Island punctuated pot," Hackett said. "Those Indians were here before the Safety Harbor people, but their pottery was an influence."

Brandy examined several tall pots as well. He identified them as "Safety Harbor Incised." They had squat bases and narrower necks, the whole cut with lightning-like lines and small circles. Brandy was impressed. "What would pot hunters get for these?"

"I don't know the market right now, but they could certainly sell to private collectors."

Suddenly she felt him draw near. He laid one hand on her shoulder, turned her to face him, and with the other lifted her chin. "I admire you, you know," he said quietly. The blonde lock fell over his forehead. "You're everything a woman should be. Lovely looking, bright, caring, independent."

Brandy began to shake her head.

"I love how protective you are. Look how you feel about Annie and Daria. I see how interested you are in everything around you, how talented you are." His hand moved to her waist. "Don't run off just yet. Come to Gainesville with me this week." She didn't feel clear-headed. Instead she felt the warmth of the wine. Without speaking, she looked into those spectacular blue eyes. He pulled her against him, and she felt the heat of his body, the urgency of his hands. In the back of her mind a bell rang, low. But John had said, "Do your own thing."

For the moment she swayed against him. She could smell his cologne, a brand she'd wanted to buy for John. It was too expensive. Grif pressed moist lips, open against hers, and she felt his fingers lift her shirt, explore beneath. Her knees went weak. She saw the open door into the bedroom, felt him gently ease her into the doorway. As she took a step forward, her glance swept over a large Tupperware box that sat on a table inside the room, the lid pushed to one side. Brandy could see cocoa-colored, slender shapes. The bundle burial, she thought, the aged little bones, the remains of a child like Daria, probably stuffed into the container with her tiny shell necklace and her blue Spanish beads. The sight stopped her. She stared into the box, shook her head as if to clear it, then pushed him away, her eyes still on the tiny skeleton. When John said, "Do your own thing," he didn't mean this.

"No, Grif. I'm not that independent," she said, her voice shaky. "I should leave."

Hackett stiffened, the muscles in his face taut, his fingers still tight around her arms. He had hustled a man the size of Tugboat through a door. His gaze followed hers to the box. For a moment she was frightened, he was so quiet. But he released her and stepped back. "Suit yourself." he said, "There'll be another time. You'll see."

She picked up her canvas bag and turned toward the hall door, while he remained in the center of the room, his stance confident. He did not move to stop her. "Don't stay in Homosassa this week," he said. "Come with me." She could hear the throb in his voice. "I leave day after tomorrow. Don't answer now. I'll see you before I go."

Brandy nodded without speaking. She still felt confused, but she knew she had come to her senses, and the four-hundred-year old child's bones had somehow helped.

She stumbled out into the hall. In the lobby she felt the blonde clerk's eyes bore into her back as she hurried outside and drew in a deep breath of fresh night air, glad she had driven herself tonight. Before she could step into her car, a tall woman strode toward her, moving with now familiar grace. For the second time tonight Brandy recognized the same flinty face. Bibi Brier thrust herself close enough for Brandy to see fierceness in her eyes.

"I checked up on you, you know," Bibi said, her tone measured. "I've got friends who know Carole Brewster. You've got a husband working for a Gainesville architectural firm. He's in Tampa now. He'll be interested in knowing how you spend your evenings."

Words froze in Brandy's mouth. She had never considered John's reaction to her friendship with Hackett. She wanted to say, "But nothing happened!" But Bibi Brier had spun on her heels, stepped into her sports car, and slammed the door.

CHAPTER 11

▼

No messages waited on Brandy's answering machine. She mixed a cup of hot chocolate, and sat down in the living room to watch the late news, emotions in turmoil. What did Hackett mean to her? He was attractive and he did seem to understand her, to care about her, and to demand nothing from her that she was not willing to give—unlike John. But other women could flit easily from one relationship to another. She doubted she could.

A newscaster mentioned the disappearance of an eighteen-months old Seminole girl on Tiger Tail Island in Homosassa and asked for anyone with information to call the Sheriff's Office. The station showed a shot of searchers shuffling through a tangled field and a photograph of Daria that appeared a few weeks earlier in the *Seminole Tribune*. The paper featured a section where proud parents could display their children's pictures. Tears came to Brandy's eyes. No one mentioned the death of Timothy Hart on Tiger Tail Island. A few days ago the poor man had been big news.

When Brandy finally fell asleep she did not dream of Grif Hackett, as she feared she might. She dreamed instead that she stood in a room with the drapes open, while outside the window a huge osprey flew past, its claws grasping a limp body.

*   *   *   *

In the morning Brandy awakened from a restless night. John had not responded and no call had come from Annie. Time to join the search for Daria along the Homosassa River. After coffee and toast, she pulled on high boots and a long-sleeved shirt with a pair of jeans. After picking up her note pad, she fastened Meg to her stake and gave the retriever fresh water. She was patting her canvas bag, feeling naked without her cell, when the kitchen phone rang. Hackett spoke softly.

"Thought about what I asked? We could have a great time in Gainesville before you go back to work. Pick up where we left off last night." She heard the smile in his voice. "Anyway, you'd like the people at the museum."

Brandy felt a rush of electricity, remembering his body against hers, his voice urgent in her ear. The feeling scared her. "I probably would like to see the museum," she said carefully, "but I've got unfinished business here, Grif. I don't want to go away with Daria still missing. Then there's the Hart case. I've got some theories about that."

"I'm afraid you've made enemies here, asking so many questions. You'd be wise to make yourself scarce."

"All the more reason to stay. Someone's hiding something."

Another pause. "I'll look for you before I go," he said and hung up.

Before she left the house, she tried to reach Strong. He wasn't there. "I called last night," she said to the officer who answered. "Yesterday I heard some suspicious sounds coming from a bedroom at Alma May Flint's house. Ask him to have a deputy check it out." She hung up, dissatisfied.

In the boat Brandy lowered the shaft of the electric trolling motor into the water, and holding her breath, switched it on with a remote. It clicked a few seconds, then she felt the slight vibration as it purred on, its prop inching the boat backward. Good. Its silence would be handy. After she turned it off, she hit the tilt, dropped the gasoline engine's prop into the water, cruised down the canal to the river, and turned about a mile west to the gas pump at the closest marina. When she handed her charge card to a lanky young attendant with his baseball cap on backwards and his pants at half-mast, he asked, grinning, "Out looking for another body?"

She thought of Alma May, of Melba and Tugboat, even of Fishhawk. "I just hope it isn't mine," she said.

The Grapple home was quiet as she passed, but Tugboat's boat was gone. Against a slight head wind she churned into Tiger Tail Bay and watched an osprey fly toward the nest, and settling there, drop a fish beside its mate. Soon fledglings would appear. Only two boats passed her on the way to the Gulf. A Wednesday saw little river traffic. Along one isolated shore she could see volunteers beating through the underbrush. If Daria had been hidden, for whatever reason, she could be concealed right under their noses. From Tiger Tail Island the lone houses scattered along the riverbanks would be quick for a kidnapper to reach.

Instead of first cruising on toward Alma May's property, Brandy detoured north into the Salt River and idled toward an abandoned concrete block cottage at its mouth. She switched off the engine, raised the tilt, and inserted the prop of the electric motor into the water at the bow. Behind her a crab fisherman's boat slipped past, moving toward traps that bobbed like globes in the bay ahead. The river was shallow, but a splintered pier jutted a few feet from the bank.

As the pontoon drifted toward the remains of the wooden dock, she cut off the motor and secured the boat to a post. She saw no sign of human habitation, even though campers sometimes set up tents on these islands. A charcoal fire had recently been lit further down the waterfront. Grateful for her knee-high boots, she stepped through the boat's gate, tested the rickety dock, and jumped over onto a riverbank strewn with oyster shells. A red front door on the cottage, its paint peeling, did not look tight. She pushed it and it creaked open. If anyone were here, she reasoned, it would've been locked. She called out. The scuffling she heard in response sounded like rats. She peeked inside. The room was vacant. No one had been there in years. Dust coated the concrete floor, unmarked except for the tracks of lizards and mice.

Still, she told herself, as she boarded her boat again and cast off, the investigation proved the electric trolling motor would work when needed.

She remembered seeing yet another empty dwelling—not a house exactly. Grif had pointed out a shack near the Indian Mound where he had temporarily stored some pottery fragments. He wasn't the only one who would know about the shack. Fishhawk and Bibi, had been to the mound with Grif. So might Tugboat or Melba and Alma May; any combination of the three could be the pot hunters the Florida Marine Patrol chased off weeks ago. But it was a place almost no one else would know about. The cabin wasn't visible from the Little Homosassa River.

Taking the starboard side of the Salt and skirting oyster beds, Brandy wound her way into Shivers Bay, past widely spaced houses, many deserted, perched along the shore. She avoided a thick stretch of sawgrass and the occasional crab trap, as well as shoals along the port side. At the mouth of the Little Homosassa, she slowed and studied the water even more carefully, then steered cautiously into the smaller river. The channel markers did not extend into the Little Homosassa, but in a few minutes she recognized the dead tree trunk curving above the water that marked the mound location. Here, four days ago, she and Hackett had pulled their boats ashore on the narrow beach.

She cut off the engine and switched on the electric motor again. No reason to signal her arrival. The crab fisherman she'd spotted earlier chugged on ahead toward Sam's Bayou, stopping now and then to check his traps. Before beaching her boat, Brandy waited until he disappeared behind the cabbage palms and twisted turkey oaks at the next bend. Then remembering the swarms of mosquitoes, she checked in her bag for insect repellent, gave herself a liberal spraying, and dropped the boat keys into her jeans pocket.

In a few minutes she struggled once again up the dim path, fighting not only mosquitoes but also giant deer flies. The wind had picked up and murmured among huge red cedars on either side. Behind her lay miles of interconnecting rivers, savanna, black mangroves, and distant hammocks. At the summit she paused, seized again by the feeling Fishhawk must fear—an awareness of the silent bones that lay beneath the soil. How many had been removed, even before Hackett came? As she caught her breath after the climb, she examined the ground. She could not tell where the bundle burial shaft had been dug. Hackett had concealed it well.

On one side of the mound, the clapboard hut leaned between two cedars, its windows boarded up, its door closed. A perfect hiding place, she thought, pulse quickening. Someone, still not identified, might want to force Fishhawk off Tiger Tail Island, might put on pressure by threatening his little daughter. If that were the case, Daria could be all right, but the kidnapper would need to bring in water and food. Perhaps drug her, lock the doors. No one would hear a child here. She stared back at the river. Nothing stirred.

Brandy picked her way with care, conscious that she might be stepping on four-hundred-year old graves, until she reached the shack. New planks with metal plates for a padlock had been nailed to the door, but the only lock in use was a simple outside hook, probably to keep the door from swinging open. No eighteen-month old toddler would be able to jar it loose. Quietly, she lifted the hook. The only sound was the wind in the trees, the only smells the stale odor of stagnant water from a small cove nearby and the faint scent of cedar leaves. She slung her canvas bag over a shoulder, listened, and then pushed against the door. It swung open and she slipped inside.

This time the interior was reasonably clean, but it reeked of mildew. The rough concrete floor felt damp to the touch. A streak of light sliced through a crack in the window frame. She waited until she could see in the gloom. Along one wall stretched the counter where Grif had set his pots fragments. She could still see imprints in the residue of dust, but no sign of a child. In the rear another door stood ajar. She pushed it open and found herself in a tiny lean-to storage room with a dirt floor. It was empty except for a tarp thrown over objects on a shelf along one wall.

She lifted it, trying not to disturb anything beneath. Under it lay pottery fragments, some large, some decorated like the ones Grif had shown her. Surely, he had not left these artifacts here. Vandals must again be at work. In one corner someone had stuffed a bag of white powder—cocaine? Brandy sagged with disappointment. No sign of Daria. At least she could report what she had found, only scattered pottery and probably drugs.

Smuggling had always been a problem on this jagged coast. She dropped the tarp back in place. Still, the shack had been worth checking. Deputies searching for Daria wouldn't think of it.

Brandy had turned to leave when a sound outside paralyzed her—the crunch of shells under heavy boots. She froze. Someone was tramping over the hill, then down toward the hut. She held her breath, peered through a crack in the flimsy wall, saw nothing but cedars and sky. The outer door creaked. She shoved the door before her shut and pressed against the store-room's pitted back wall, eyes wide, heart thumping. Had Grif come back for more pots? To herself she cried "Please, let it be Grif!"

The outer door banged open, footsteps echoed across the wooden floor. Then the inner door flung wide and a figure loomed before her—not Grif's. Even before the man laughed, his fleshy frame was unmistakable. A shaved head ducked under the lintel.

"Didn't pay me no never mind, did you, bitch?" Tugboat said. "No never mind a-t'all. Still sticking your nose where it ain't wanted." One meaty hand grabbed her by the shirt and yanked her into the larger room. His moist lips and beard stank of whiskey, but he hadn't drunk enough to be harmless. He dropped his grasp and stood, legs apart, hands on his hips. She felt faint with terror, knowing what he might try next.

But for now he wanted to talk. "Let's see. Found yourself a good place to poke around, I reckon. A good place. Hardly nobody comes up here. And your boyfriend's done finished his work. Now ain't that a shame." He spat a wad of tobacco into the corner of the room. A spider, its body the size of a fifty-cent piece, scurried into a corner.

Brandy said nothing. She hadn't seen his Rottweiler. Was the dog trained to attack? Tugboat reached forward and snatched the canvas bag from her shoulder. No great loss, she thought. Bug repellent, note pad, a few bills, some coins, a lipstick and comb. He rummaged through it, grinned, and threw it back.

"Reckon I'll just lock you up a spell, so's you can think about the trouble you in." He pulled a padlock from a jeans pocket. "I'd best do a little planning, before your boyfriend comes looking for you."

Brandy's throat felt like ashes; her body stiffened. Grif was busy, wouldn't try to reach her until tomorrow. John wasn't coming at all. Carole wasn't due back for another week. Brandy had asked a neighbor to feed the animals if she was out late. No one knew her schedule. She had written in her notebook on the porch that she would search the north end of Tiger Tail Island, not here, and Annie had her cell. Brandy waited, trembling.

Tugboat squinted into the room. "Got to do things right. Lots of digging been going on, what with your boyfriend fooling around up here. Oh, I know what he's up to. But he's gone now. No one's gonna pay no attention to a tad more digging. Reckon them old Indian bones won't mind a little company." He grinned at his joke. "Don't worry. I'll be back." He gave another gravelly chuckle, stepped outside, and the door slammed shut. Brandy heard the hasps snap together on the padlock. She had a few minutes, no more.

Had he gone for a gun? A man like that always had one, a rifle probably for hunting. And a shovel? Rope, maybe? She spun wildly around, raced back into the storage room, and knelt in one corner. She had seen something. It seemed unimportant then—a crack under the foundation board that supported the back wall. She thrust a finger through the opening. The dirt was almost pure sand, not shells as she feared. In the rear of the shed, rain had washed much of the loose soil down the slope.

The clay fragments on the shelf must be sturdy. She lifted the tarp and picked up a piece about six inches square with a sharp, serrated edge. It felt firm and grainy in her fingers. How much time? Maybe Tugboat would stop for another swig. Her heart drummed, hands shook. She began to dig. Once Jeremiah Strong had told her, if you can push your head through an opening, your whole body will fit. Useful knowledge for jailers, and he had served once, he said, in the county jail. Her nails broke, dirt rained down on her jeans and shirt, her face became a sandy mask. She dared not stop, even to glance at her watch. What lay outside? She would have to try to reach her boat. She couldn't find help on this lonely island.

At last she threw herself down, face up, and tried to slither under. Her forehead struck the splintered bottom board and bled. She dug some more, tried again. This time she scraped the board, squirmed further.

Pushing hard with her feet in the sand, she shoved her way into the open air, reached back into the opening for the canvas bag, and took a few seconds to swipe some of the sand back into the hole. Don't leave a clear trail, she thought, and dropped the pottery fragment into her bag. Then she squatted, quivering, her frenzied gaze searching for a route to the river. Behind the hut lay a stretch of silvery needlerush, knee high, beyond it more clusters of red cedars, a spiky century plant. A light wind felt cool on her sweaty forehead.

How had the Seminoles escaped the soldiers and seemed to vanish? They crawled.

Brandy dropped to her knees, worked her way into the tall rushes, lay on her stomach, and pulled herself along, hoping that the movement of the wind would hide her own motion. She could hear nothing. No boat engine. No footsteps. She did not dare rise and look back. Instead, she tried to remember where the base of the mound lay. She had to circle it, make her way to the water, through the reed and marsh grasses, avoiding the spines on the sharp side of the sawgrass. She had pulled the boat ashore near a stand of tall cedar. For that she said a grateful prayer.

Brandy lost all sense of time. Reaching forward with aching fingers, she pulled her body after them, writhing like a snake through high grasses that scratched and scraped. Sand spurs embedded in her hands, clung to her shirt and pants. Mosquitoes and yellow flies buzzed and stung. Her nostrils filled with the acrid odor of damp soil and soggy weeds.

Finally, she allowed herself to creep forward on her knees, keeping her head well down. Her hands began to sink into marsh. She must be nearer the river. When she reached the shelter of the cedars, she crouched forward, picked up a fallen branch, still laced with a few berries, as a shield and slithered from tree to tree. She was out of sight of the shack now, but keeping a circular distance from the mound summit. Tugboat might've left the island, gone elsewhere for his gun and his tools. Her spirits rose.

Above an osprey soared up with a fish in its claws. That meant the river. She spotted a heron poised on the low branch of a turkey oak. It must be fishing along the shore. She dropped her leafy camouflage and knelt behind a wide cedar. She could see her boat, but not Tugboat's, although it could be in the cove. Hers was about ten yards away. Again she crawled over sharp oyster shells, hands bleeding. Not daring to look up, she shoved the pontoons into the water and pulled herself through the aluminum gate. With a paddle she pushed the pontoons far enough to cover the electric prop. Tugboat had not searched her pockets, had not found her keys. Maybe he thought she had left them in the boat. She would drift out into the current, then switch on the electric motor. As soon as she could get far enough down river, she'd shift to the gasoline engine. Her pulse pounded.

And then Brandy heard the shout. "Thought you'd get away, bitch?" Tugboat stood in a clear space between two cedars, maybe twenty yards away, his Rottweiler beside him, a rifle in his hand. The dog might've tracked her. Through the silent air she heard the metallic shell snapping into place. She had been so close, so ready to sneak away. Tugboat could've been watching her, could've relished her struggle through the weeds before he finished it with one powerful bullet. A boy teasing a doomed fly. In that second, one half of her brain felt paralyzed, the other half thought: I've been here before. But Fishhawk had not meant to kill her with his rifle. Tugboat clearly did. To lose to Tugboat now—it was too much to bear.

Brandy dropped to the deck. Her fevered mind grasped one hope— where was the crab fisherman? By now he should be on his way back. On her port side she could hear the faint drone of an engine. As Tugboat lifted the rifle to his shoulder and lowered his head to sight down the barrel, the thrumming sound increased. Around the closest bend glided the flat-bottomed boat, the gray-bearded fisherman at the tiller. His engine roared, then abruptly stopped. Brandy leaped up, shouted, "Help!" waved her bag.

He steered nearer. "Something the matter? Can't get 'er going? Need a tow?" He tipped back his cap and waited. A teen-aged boy stood amidships holding a trap. At some level of consciousness, Brandy was aware of a large blue crab wiggling down the wire toward a bucket. Their engine idled.

She found her voice, did not look back at Tugboat. "Think I can get her started okay now," she shouted. "Can I follow you in?"

The man nodded and called back, "Keep to the middle of the channel."

Before she switched on her gasoline engine, she glanced at the shore. She had heard Tugboat's loud laugh, but he had now vanished. She could not tell if the fisherman had seen him. Her pontoon boat surged ahead as she shifted gear with trembling fingers, came around, and plowed along behind the crabber. Each time he stopped to check a trap, she stopped. As they made their slow way back to the commercial fishing docks, she did not hear a boat behind them.

There she waved her thanks to the man and his son, noted the name "Margaret Ann" on its hull, and cruised on to the marina. She could not bring herself to go back alone to the house. She wondered if she would ever feel safe alone again. She wanted to be around people, but her matted hair and filthy shirt and pants made her look as if she'd dragged herself out of a coal mine. The one person she wanted to see was Detective Jeremiah Strong. Fat chance. At the marina pier near the motel, she tied up and stumbled up onto the patio deck beside a small outdoor Tiki bar, sat down at a picnic table, and dropped her head on her arms. Had Tugboat laughed because he only meant to frighten her with this threats, or because he was for the moment outwitted?

A tourist from the motel, an older man, came down a gravel path toward her, concerned. "You all right, Miss?"

Brandy lifted her head. "I need a phone."

He nodded toward the restaurant wall and pay phone. She remembered her canvas bag. Tugboat had not taken her change. To the man's obvious surprise, she thumped it and shook off a shower of sand before hobbling over to dial the Sheriff's Office in Inverness.

She had never been as glad to hear a voice. "Jeremiah Strong here," it said. "What can I do for you?"

Brandy went limp with relief. "Come to Homosassa," she whimpered, "and lend me a shoulder to cry on. I'm scared."

CHAPTER 12

▼

An hour after Brandy called Detective Strong, she emerged from a hot shower, kicked her sand spur-laden jeans aside, pulled on a fresh pair and shirt, and stepped into the living room smelling of talcum powder and fresh soap. She felt human again. The Sergeant had driven immediately to the Homosassa marina, persuaded her to leave her boat there, helped her into his car and, picked up two Cuban sandwiches at a local restaurant for a late lunch. He then deposited her at her front door and was waiting on the screened porch for a briefing. She paused in the kitchen to pour iced tea and warm the sandwiches in the toaster oven before joining him. Strong sat with his note pad flipped open, his face a mask of patient resignation.

"You've learned a lesson, I hope," he said. "Almost got yourself killed. 'Be not curious about unnecessary matters,' I believe I told you."

Brandy bristled. "I'm grateful to the bone for your help, Sergeant. But what I was doing was necessary. No one else planned to look for Daria Pine in that shack, and I found what I'm sure is a stash of cocaine. I didn't interfere with your investigation. I was a volunteer in the search."

"The volunteer search, young lady, was coordinated by the Sheriff's Office. We weren't asking for lone rangers."

A subdued Brandy set down the iced tea and Cubans, while Strong glanced at his note pad where he had already jotted a few precise lines. "Tugboat Grapple has a reputation in these parts, all right. Petty stuff, as far as I can tell, but the locals figure he might be bringing dope in from ships out in the Gulf."

Suddenly Brandy was shaking with hunger and nipped into the crusty, flattened bread and layers of ham, cheese, roast pork, and salami, trying not to look greedy. An eternity had passed since breakfast, but it was only two-thirty in the afternoon. Between savory mouthfuls, she said, "I think Tugboat—and maybe his wife and Alma May Flint—are behind the vandalism at the Indian mound. Stealing artifacts and peddling them in the black market. They're at it again. It may be his side line. I overheard Alma May say Melba needed money, mostly because of Tugboat's gambling. And Alma May herself wants to sell her house, so she may be short of funds, too. They seem to have their own private agenda."

Strong folded a napkin neatly over his lap. Brandy had never seen him rumpled or his trousers without a crease. She didn't know whether to credit the detective himself or his devoted wife back in Inverness.

"I've got a detective looking for Tugboat Grapple now," he said. "Smugglers love this coast, all these little inlets and rivers. You probably stumbled into one operation, all right. We'll find out."

Brandy tried to eat as tidily as Strong, but she felt mayonnaise oozing from the corner of her lips. While she dabbed her chin, she shuddered at a sudden memory. "He was going to shoot me and bury my body with the mound builders." Her voice rose. "He could've gutted my boat and sunk it in some dead-end creek where it wouldn't be found for months." Worse, she knew no one would've found her, either.

Lines furrowed the brown forehead. "It isn't safe for you here, young lady, not until we pick him up." He looked down approvingly at Meg, sprawled beside Brandy's chair. "I'm glad you've got a dog." Meg looked up, as though she understood, and the silky tail thumped. "Will she bark? Not all golden retrievers do. Sometimes they're too friendly."

Proudly Brandy nodded. "She'll bark for sure if anyone tries to get in. But Tugboat knows I got away, that I'd talk to the law. Why would he be after me now?"

"He's probably busy getting rid of his stash, but remember, he's not a reasonable guy. If you hear anything suspicious, call. Your neighbors in the development are close. That'll help. Make arrangements to get out of Homosassa."

Brandy finished her sandwich and wiped moist fingers on a paper napkin, but she did not dismiss his advice. Perhaps she could try to get some answers from the detective while his guard was down. "Do you think Grapple could be connected to Timothy Hart's murder, or Daria's disappearance?"

Strong sighed, laid down the remaining crusts of his sandwich, leaned back, and folded his arms across his chest. "Young lady, we can't even prove Hart was murdered. We can think it, but we think a lot of things we can't prove. Maybe he had a hankering to eat weeds. I don't know why his body was turned over and searched, but that doesn't prove murder. Maybe someone found him and was curious. We can't be sure the little girl's disappearance is connected with Hart, either. Both things happened within a few days on the same isolated island, but it could be coincidence."

If the detective had news of Daria, she thought he would tell her. "Did a deputy check out Alma May's house?"

"I got the message, but we haven't yet. Not enough for a warrant, but we'll try." Strong dropped his arms and clasped his hands between his knees. "We'd have found the child if she was outside on the island or in the waters, dead or alive. I think she was taken somewhere else. People called in leads, but none of them panned out."

Brandy thought of the vanished children who are never found, many from Florida. How easy it would be to destroy Daria's tiny body! Her eyes felt moist.

Strong brought her back to the present. "What do you plan to do before we pick up Grapple?" he asked. "There's no police department in Homosassa. Folks here rely on the Sheriff's Office in Homosassa Springs, and they're spread pretty thin."

Brandy hesitated. "I'm supposed to stay through next week," she said finally, "but Grif Hackett offered to give me a ride back to my apartment in Gainesville tomorrow. He's taking some stuff to the Florida Natural History Museum for study."

Strong lifted his eyebrows and studied his hands. "Your husband's in Tampa, isn't he? Why not go there?"

Brandy gathered up the sandwich papers and folded them into a tight bundle. For a few seconds she did not answer. Once she was in Tampa, far from Homosassa and her office in Gainesville, she would lose any chance to tell the Timothy Hart story, or to be involved in either search. "I don't have a car here myself," she said. "John dropped me off about a week ago. In Homosassa I use my friend Carole's, but I couldn't take it to Tampa or Gainesville. My car's in Gainesville. I can pick it up there."

"Husband won't come after you?"

"I don't like to ask him to miss work," she added, lamely.

She knew John would drop everything and come if she asked him, but what a scolding she would get! And she was only trying to do her job as a reporter. She was not ready to see John, to feel his disapproval and disappointment in her. Their old disagreement would surface.

"Even though you were almost shot? Your husband needs to know." The detective fastened her with a direct stare. "You two now live apart? You want this man Hackett to take you home instead? I see."

He stood, replaced the note pad in his pocket, and passed his hand over his forehead, ready to erupt in a Biblical quotation. "Can you go upon hot coals and your feet not be burned?" he murmured. He'd given Fishhawk much the same advice.

Brandy did not respond. With such firm Biblical roots, of course he wouldn't approve of her seeing Grif. And detectives were intuitive.

At the door Strong said, "I'll call when we pick up Grapple. In the meantime, lock up, keep a light on and the dog with you, and don't sleep where you usually do. Call 9-1-1 if you need help. I'll ask patrol to swing by a time or two tonight. I don't think this Grapple guy will try anything now, but he might not want you to testify about the cocaine, if that's what you saw."

Brandy stood with him at the door, her thoughts again on the search for Daria and what she felt sure was Hart's murder. "Sergeant," she said, "this puzzle will never fit together without the key piece."

He paused, one big hand still on the door handle. "And I suppose you know what that is?"

"Of course. Timothy Hart's artifact."

He nodded. "Could be."

"If it's already been found, someone could be trying to smuggle it out of the area."

"We've watched, and we've looked for it," he said. "No luck so far. We can't keep the Seminole Indian from taking his canoe into Homosassa for supplies. Or Mrs. Flint or the real estate woman from going in, either. But no one's been spotted mailing anything or passing off a package to anyone. We've already searched Mrs. Flint's house and grounds once." He shrugged massive shoulders. "Probably whatever it is deteriorated years ago." But to Brandy that tantalizing thing was the motive for at least one crime, possibly two.

Strong opened the screen door. "After this attack on you, I might be able to get a search warrant for the Grapple home. I'll see if the crab fisherman or his son can confirm your story, and I'll send someone out to that shack."

As soon as the detective's Ford sedan eased out of the driveway, Brandy ducked back into the living room, her fist clenched at her side. She didn't feel safe even yet, but she wouldn't call John for help. He'd just remind her of his warnings, and how her snooping screwed up everything. Anyway, in his last message he didn't sound eager to drive back to Homosassa, and if he did, that would be the end of her investigation. In Gainesville she would still be close and in touch with events here, and she'd have her own car.

Brandy surveyed the living room. She'd been promising herself she would clean up for Carole. She should if she planned to leave town. Pants and shirts and underwear from Brandy's most recent wash draped the arm of a chair, the morning papers for the last three days littered the end tables and couch, cup rings smeared the glass-topped table, and she knew cat and dog hairs clung to the carpet. In the kitchen she had washed her few dishes, but left them to drain on the counter, and she'd spilled something sticky on the kitchen floor. Then there was the cat box. The Persian never went outdoors. She sighed.

In the utility room she gathered up a pail, mop, and broom and from the dining room closet, the vacuum cleaner. Women like Carole found satisfaction in house cleaning, in converting untidiness to order. Not Brandy. A few days later it had to be done all over again. She always grumbled that if house keeping were done well, no one knew it was being done at all. That was the problem with a neatnik husband.

By the time she finished her chores, the afternoon was fading. No call from the Sergeant, none from Annie, and of course, none from John. By 8:00 P.M. Brandy had thawed the ancient hamburger and fixed a patty, embellished with a slice of over-ripe tomato and, after removing its green edges, a week-old slice of cheese. To her Spartan meal she added a few stale potato sticks. She was sitting at the coffee table, staring at her open notebook, when the phone finally rang.

"Sorry I couldn't call earlier," Hackett said easily. "I had a request to check out a site in Chasshowitzka. I went out there, but I can't do anything now. The precious whooping cranes are still deciding when to migrate north, and everything's locked down. You going with me tomorrow?"

Briefly Brandy told Grif, without details, that Tugboat had threatened her again. She could fill him in later. She didn't want to rehash the whole experience, and she didn't relish listening to more "I told you so's."

"I'm thinking about it," she answered. "But I've got loose ends to tie up. I never got back to see Annie. For one thing, I have to collect my cell. I needed it this morning. And I still want to check out the area around Alma May's for signs of Daria that might've been overlooked. You leaving early?"

He sounded thoughtful. "I could wait. Call me tomorrow afternoon. Is Tugboat still out and about?"

"Sergeant Strong expects they'll pick him up. They haven't yet."

She hung up, then stalked about closing windows, although she hated to shut out the chorus of creek frogs, the fresh scent of the spring night, and at dawn, the mockingbird's song. Taking comfort in the neighbors' lights shining into the darkness, she called Meg in from outside. The retriever settled in her fleece-lined doggy bed in the small back bedroom, where a daybed had been the Persian's domain. Meg was bewildered at the change. The cat definitely disapproved. To establish her rights, she kneaded her claws in the bedspread, then leapt down and pranced from the room, tail high, to find a less crowded refuge. Brandy crawled onto the couch, ruffled Meg's red coat, and lay, wide-eyed, listening for the hum of the deputies' cruisers.

Lines about Shakespeare's island monster, Caliban, again drifted into her consciousness. She had always been drawn to the magic of *The Tempest*. But who was the local monster? "This thing of darkness," she whispered, "as disproportioned in his manners as in his shape…A devil, a born devil, on whose nature nurture can never stick…" Unless it was Tugboat, Tiger Tail's monster was clearly in disguise.

Outside a car rumbled down the short street, turned where the street ended at the river, and drove slowly back. A deputy's nightly rounds. Somewhere a boat's engine sputtered to life. She did not look out. Once, Meg grumbled deep in her throat, padded into the living room, and then returned to lie down with a thump. Brandy closed her eyes and tried to sleep. Finally she rose and fixed a bowl of cereal. That usually helped.

Of course, their Caliban could be a woman. She took a crunchy mouthful. A witch, like Caliban's mother. Maybe a sociopath, focused only on his—or her—own selfish needs. She thought about the missing treasure, too, a thing hidden by a Seminole warrior on the island, something the white man would value, something frightening, a seed of evil. It had certainly caused pain.

At last she returned to bed and rolled toward the wall. "This thing of darkness," she repeated, not sure whether she had in mind the perpetrator or the artifact itself—probably both.

CHAPTER 13

▼

For her morning coffee and bagel, Brandy sat at the table on the screen porch, feeling calmer. The world around her seemed routine, normal. A pileated woodpecker was already at work, pecking berries from the tall cabbage palm in the front yard. Twice he shook his scarlet crest and called out to his mate in the woods beside the creek. The early fishermen had already chugged out of their slips for a day on the Gulf.

Brandy was congratulating herself on her good luck—a night free of danger, when the phone rang. "Sheriff's Office," said an unfamiliar voice. "Detective Strong said to tell you they finally picked up Mr. Grapple."

Brandy grinned with relief. "Thanks," she said. "You made my day. Now I need to talk to Sergeant Strong." The line went silent. At last someone fumbled with the phone and she recognized the detective's exasperated tone.

"Good Lord, woman," he said. "I've got other work to do."

Brandy ignored the comment. "About Alma May Flint's house. Can you send someone now? With Tugboat out of the way, I could meet him there. I don't think she will let me in by myself."

He breathed heavily into the mouthpiece. "Might be worth checking out. You sure don't need to be there, but okay, I'll send someone."

Brandy checked her watch. She wanted time to see how Annie was doing. "About one o'clock?

"One it is, close as he can make it."

"I'm a volunteer searcher, you know. Are others still on the island?"

"Finishing up today," he said and hung up.

Brandy would visit Annie, retrieve her cell—she wouldn't go any place again without it—and take a last look around the northern section of the island, not only for signs of Daria but also for any clue about Timothy Hart's treasure. It would be her last chance. She had already dressed in jeans and a well-worn, long-sleeved shirt, appropriate for the search.

This was Thursday. Last week she'd been expecting John on Friday. No chance this weekend; he made that clear. But she'd call him when she got back to Gainesville later today. Right now she needed to focus on the tasks she'd set out for the morning. Daria disappeared early Tuesday. The two days seemed like an eternity.

Before Brandy had taken care of Meg and the Persian, she had a call from her friend in the *Gainesville Star's* bureau office. "Anything stirring on the dead man or the missing child?" she asked.

"Nada," Brandy said. "Nothing to report, not yet. I'm still working on it. I may come on home early." She didn't tell her friend why.

On impulse she dialed her own cell number. It wasn't in service. Either Annie had turned it off or the battery had run down. As Brandy replaced the phone, she glanced with satisfaction around the clean rooms. If she left that afternoon with Hackett, they would not need another dusting and scrubbing, a point in favor of returning to Gainesville today. With Tugboat in custody, she felt safe. Still, he could be slippery. It made sense to leave. After a search of the kitchen cupboard, she found a jar of peanut butter, spread it on two slices of bread, lifted an apple from the refrigerator, its skin only slightly brown in spots, tucked both in small plastic bags, and dropped them into a larger one for lunch, adding a small thermos of iced tea.

Brandy paused in the yard to administer Meg's morning belly rub, then heard her complaining growl as she drove away in Carole's car without her. She hoped Grif would be willing to transport Meg, as well. She certainly wouldn't leave without her.

At the marina Brandy parked near the motel where she had moored her pontoon boat yesterday, and paid a fee for the overnight slip. When she topped off the pontoon's gas tanks, the bony young man with the wide smile and the backwards cap was clearly curious. "Left in a hurry yesterday," he said, studying her. "Looked like you got into trouble out on the water. You okay?"

He'd probably seen her less than dignified re-appearance. "You could say I had a spot of trouble," she said. "I'm okay now." She jumped into her boat and backed out into the river traffic. No need to discuss her Tugboat Grapple problem with anyone but Strong. Still, she was relieved when a marine patrol boat passed, watching for speeders or children without life jackets. The presence of the law gave her confidence.

Moving with scarcely a ripple at the stern, she curved around Bird Island and enjoyed, as always, its clusters of anhingas and cormorants, preening and stretching their wings to dry their feathers. She would miss the water birds. Tugboat's Grady White boat rocked next to his pier. She hoped it would be tied up for a long time. She wondered if Melba had told her husband about Hart's precious treasure. Tugboat's drug trafficking and pot selling gave him contacts that could help him dispose of any valuable find.

The sun glinting on the water, the slight breeze, and the friendly waves of passengers in other boats all comforted her. Yesterday's nightmare receded. In the osprey nest Brandy could now see three heads. The fledglings would soon be almost as large as their parents. They all added to the aura of normalcy. She roared forward as soon as she cleared the last of the manatee no-wake signs, then pulled back on the throttle in Tiger Tail Bay.

She'd take that quick run up the creek to Fishhawk and Annie's chickee now, since. the tide was running high. After she found out if they had any news at all, she'd approach the old Flint home site through the end of the canal farthest from Alma May's house. By that route, the old lady would be less likely to interfere, and Brandy would have a chance to look for signs of Daria there. She would time her search for the rendezvous with the deputy. As she passed into Petty Creek, the house on the point looked as vacant as Melba's. If Daria was there, the women kept her quiet.

When Brandy reached the Seminole camp, the Sheriff's patrol craft and divers were gone. Maybe that was good news. Brandy nosed into shore, pulled the pontoons aground, and started up the path, but something was different; something missing. She had reached the head of the path and was staring at the chickee before she realized what. The long cypress log canoe was gone.

Nothing stirred around the chickee, the sweat lodge, or Daria's pathetically empty brush pen. Brandy had not passed the canoe on the way into town, but perhaps Fishhawk and Annie had made the trip earlier. Even if their daughter was missing, they would need to go into town for supplies, and unless Annie left the island occasionally, she'd go mad. Mosquito netting still hung from the top beams and the storage boxes had not been moved. Their absence, she guessed, must be temporary.

For a minute Brandy stood on the coarse wire grass that blanketed the island, smelling the blended scent of cedar and wet soil, and watching a light wind rustle the saw palmettos. Then she dug into her canvas bag, pulled out her note pad and pen, and scribbled, "Sorry to miss you. Need to pick up my cell. I'm going to take another look around the Flint home site, then I'll be back at the house. You have the number. Please call. I plan to leave town later today. My prayers are with you both and Daria." She signed the message, weighed it down with a small rock, and left it on the chickee platform.

After a solitary trip back down Petty Creek, Brandy rounded the point into the Homosassa River, churned past twisted branches of scrub oak along the shoreline, and steered into the east end of the canal. A turtle slipped into the water with a muted splash as she slowed to idle and checked her watch. It was almost noon. She had started too late, spent more time at the Seminoles' camp than she meant to, and now she had only about an hour before her 1:00 P.M. meeting with the deputy.

She checked the depth finder, noted three feet in the channel, tilted up the gasoline engine's prop, and edged in next to the embankment. In many places it was too high to clamber over. Beyond the narrow canal stretched a field, studded with arrow weeds and spike-rush, but few trees. Next to it, farther west along the canal, lay an area of thick underbrush and oaks. An egret watched her with suspicion from a low limb.

Brandy tossed the bow anchor overboard and watched it sink into the tobacco-colored water. It refused to snag the silt-rich bottom. She lifted it and crept on, scaring the egret from its fishing perch. Here she caught a line around the low hanging branch and pulled the boat in closer. After tying to the tree, she threw both fore and aft anchors in for good measure, broke out her lunch and thermos, and sat at the deck table, flipping through her note pad.

According to her notes, the site of the oldest house should be several hundred yards west, down the canal and a few yards to the south. She should have time to canvas that area, not only for signs of Daria, but for the mysterious water hole mentioned in Lieutenant Hart's journal. She could take advantage of a screen of shrubs, and hope the birds didn't screech at her approach. They could give her away to Mrs. Flint. Alma May said she'd seen Fishhawk at the site once before Hart died, so she must be able to see the area from the garden. The old lady wouldn't welcome trespassers, even those on a worthwhile mission, especially if she knew where the little girl was hidden.

Brandy listened for sounds of other volunteers threshing through the underbrush. All she heard were bird calls and mullet jumping in the canal. If only she had her cell, she would call Hackett and tell him she wouldn't be back until late afternoon. He might've finished gluing pottery fragments and cataloging his finds and be anxious to take his pots to the museum lab. By Saturday he would have to drive to Tampa so that Fishhawk could inter the Safety Harbor child's bones Sunday. Brandy could understand why Fishhawk did not want that chore, particularly now, with his own little girl missing. She might be lying somewhere, too, unburied.

Thrusting her keys and note pad into her canvas bag, Brandy scrambled through the boat gate, and clawed her way up the steep bank on hands and knees, her bag trailing by the strap over one shoulder. Leave the canal behind, she thought, creep a short way inland. She remembered the old photograph she had seen days ago at Alma May's. The canal itself had been dug by developers, more than a century after that first Flint cabin was burned by Indians. The photograph showed a nineteenth century Mrs. Flint, holding a bucket beside a tall tree that appeared to be a hickory. It rose above her garden. On this island, it was likely a water hickory. Its tough wood might have withstood the years, might even still be here. A guide told Brandy that some of the land had been planted in orange groves during the 1950s, but all signs of cultivation had long since disappeared.

She decided the grove owners had not leveled the area opposite the new Flint house, because after toiling perhaps half a block, she could see the tops of a clump of tall trees. A scraggly line of dark green wax myrtles and high grass blocked her from the canal. She could only guess where Alma May's house was, but she kept her bearings by craning her neck to see the hickory tree. Overhead, clouds were closing in from the west. Behind them the sun disappeared, and shadows fell across the island. Something shuffled in the grass. Brandy gasped and drew back, her mind filled with rattlers and water moccasins, until a gopher turtle lumbered, heedless, across her path. Before the sky grew even darker, she squatted, parted the weeds, and examined the soil, the oak scrub, and its thick, blackish branches. She could see no trace of footsteps, no broken limbs on the shrubbery, no evidence that a child had been dragged through the grass and weeds, or over the underground runners of the oak scrubs. The only smell was the tart odor of the slick myrtle leaves she herself had bruised.

Wasting my time. Deputies must've searched the area and a helicopter flown over, but I'll feel better if I look myself. Also, she had a dual mission. The journal spoke of the Seminole warrior's prize in a hole of water. She didn't believe the Sheriff's Office gave real credence to Lieutenant Henry Hart's journal entry. Even Strong assumed if the Indian's trophy existed, it had already been found, or had disintegrated in the humid Florida climate.

And then Brandy heard voices. Conversational. She paused and knelt in the sand, listening. They came from across the canal. Two women.

"I plant collards in the fall. Reckon I'll be gone by then, but I got squash and Roma beans coming up now. Tomatoes, too." Alma May, Brandy decided, talking about her own garden, probably standing beside it. "Had to tote in 'most all the top soil and a peck of fertilizer. Had me a fight with sand and oyster shells." A pause followed. A splattering sound. Maybe Alma May was watering her plants.

The other voice murmured, then grew louder. "I hated to help him, and that's a fact." Must be Melba, Brandy thought. She did not dare peer over the bushes.

"Reckon he can do us right smart harm," Alma May said.

"As much harm locked up as released. Maybe more."

"I sure figured they'd keep him longer." Brandy's heart lurched. Tugboat released? Alma went on, plaintively, "Never should've got him involved." A bitter note now in her voice. Brandy could second that sentiment.

A whining tone came from Melba. "We had to when he found out. I told you before, I want out. I don't care about the money anymore."

Alma May added, firm as ever, "We got to get more information. Then we'll go ahead with our plan. I'll stay in town. It's home, but you'll be able to skedaddle back to New Jersey." The voices receded. They were leaving the garden. A door closed. They'd gone back into the kitchen.

Brandy stood paralyzed. Tugboat released? But he couldn't be on the island. His boat was at his dock, not at Alma May's, and the deputy should be here soon. No need to panic. Tugboat had probably muscled in on their operation, illegally selling Safety Harbor pots. No surprise there. She wondered if they knew about the white powder he'd hidden at the mound. She also wondered about the scheme Alma May mentioned. Apparently, it allowed Melba to escape back to her original home.

Better get on with her search. Stooping down, she moved as stealthily as she could, pushing aside the tangle of thin branches, pulling her bag free of sticky leaves. In the top branches of the tall hickory she could already see the season's lacy, green resurrection fern. It would wither and die in winter, then by a sudden miracle, spring to life again each spring.

When she looked ahead, she halted, frustrated. A thick layer of weeds and brambles blocked her way, as if someone had cut up several shrubs, heaped them across the ground, and then abandoned the site. Alma May might mean to thin the encroaching jungle. Boards jutted out from under another heavy pile. Both sides of her path were choked off by thickets of wax myrtle and the sharp spikes of scrub palmettos and Spanish bayonet.

Bending low Brandy shuffled forward, shoving the debris roughly aside with her boots. She had moved both feet well into the brush pile, when with heart-stopping terror she felt the ground give way. She screamed, a spasm rose in her throat, and she felt herself pitch downward into nothingness. For a frantic moment her fingers scrabbled at furry stone walls, clawed through spider webs. Then she thudded into a shallow pool of stagnant water. Pain shot up her ankle. She lay panting, her whole body throbbing. Her feet and legs had taken the brunt of the fall. At last, still stunned, she pushed herself into a sitting position and glanced up.

She'd fallen into a pit, maybe fifteen feet deep. She touched her head—still attached. Her arms and hands—all right, but her foot and ankle ached. Under the fetid water, pebbles littered the hard bottom. Across one wall scrambled a fat spider, its spindly legs waving. Brandy shuddered, pulled off the boot on her injured ankle and, reaching up with a shaky hand, used the thick sole to pound the spider. She was rimmed by rock-studded limestone, shrouded in moss. More spiders had to be clinging to those walls, ones she couldn't reach. She could only hope they weren't brown recluses or black widows. Most Florida spiders were harmless, but still, they all repulsed her.

She crouched, trembling, and forced herself to take stock. The sky, now a smoky hue, shone high above her through a circle, maybe four feet across. She had fallen into a round hole, man made. What was it? The Flint woman in Alma May's photograph had gripped a bucket. Of course, Brandy thought: a cistern. Hackett had said he found one near the site of the settler's house on the mound. How else would pioneers save fresh rain water?

The Muskokee translation again shot through her mind: the treasure was hidden in a hole filled with water. Not a natural spring, or inlet, as she had supposed, but the pioneers' almost indestructible cistern. If the Indian hid his prize here, he would know concealing it in the cistern would keep it from burning when he set the wooden cabin on fire.

Brandy tried to think rationally. Although it had rained three days ago, this cistern held little water, and it was stagnant. That fact puzzled her.

She tried to rise and her leg buckled. Wait a few minutes, catch your breath, make a plan. First, surely the deputies had already found the cistern, or Fishhawk had. Alma May would know its location well. They all knew. Their knowledge could be her salvation.

She remembered the miniature flashlight in her canvas bag, one intended to shine on keyholes at night. With quivering fingers, she lifted the bag from the water, pulled out the flashlight, and directed the narrow beam up the walls. What were her chances of climbing out? The green scum was slick to the touch. Irregular rocks protruded a fraction of an inch from the concrete, but they did not make ledges large enough to stand on. In a few spots they had been dislodged and fallen to the bottom. She could not claw her way up. Surely she would fall, probably break a bone this time. She could not signal for help. She had no rope and she had no phone. The life of her tiny light was limited.

Brandy tried to calm herself. She would examine this cistern carefully. Had the deputies searched it when they investigated Hart's death and then looked for Daria? At regular intervals she would call out. The deputy should be in Alma May's yard soon. She hoped she was close enough to the house for him to hear her. Surely, he would find her boat and look for her. In the meantime, with the small flashlight she began peering at the floor and walls by grids, as far up as she could reach.

Fifteen minutes later the slender beam fell on something caught in one of the deep niches above her head—something brown and thin, the end barely visible over a tiny lip. She stretched an arm up, with another shudder brushed aside a web, and touched something leathery, rough, damp. Did she dare? Her finger and thumb closed around the fragile edge, gently dislodged it from the small pool of water in the rock, cradled it in the palm of the other hand, and brought it down to eye level where she could shine the light directly on it.

It looked like a pocket, a folded piece of deerskin, eight or ten inches long, a tuft of animal fur and the fragment of a leather strap still attached. Her heart jumped. Lieutenant Hart had written that the warrior put the treasure in a pouch before he had hidden it in a "hole of water." She'd read in a text from the Inverness museum that warriors always wore shoulder pouches to conferences for their tobacco or shot. The pouch made a perfect container for a smallish artifact, but clearly this one was empty. Maybe the object had fallen out. With eager fingers she searched under the scummy water. Nothing but tiny pebbles. Why would anyone who found the treasure leave the pouch? Maybe the thief hadn't found it. If the leather became snagged behind the rough ledge, it would be concealed in the tiny pool. The heavier treasure could drop through the open top of the pouch and fall to the bottom of the cistern.

She was certain now that there had been a thief. It would be easy for one with climbing equipment to rappel into the shaft, find the artifact, and leave behind only ripples in the stale water. But the search would be hurried. No one else would leave an abandoned cistern open for animals and people to fall into. They would cap it. That's why water had only seeped into the bottom.

Brandy fumbled in her bag for the cotton scarf she often tied over her hair on windy boat rides, dipped it in the water, wrapped the pouch to keep it damp, and laid it carefully into her bag. She remembered that unless old leather was kept wet, it would crumble to dust in the air. An expert should see the pouch, but after Sergeant Strong did. Now to call for help.

She leaned back against the wall and shouted as loudly as she could, "In the cistern! Help!" The words echoed and re-echoed around the limestone walls and floor. She waited, called again. Where were the volunteers? She might have to wait until her boat was discovered.

Above, the dusky sky deepened. Had the deputy been late? Not looked for her? It was after 2:00 P.M. Brandy rested against the wall and craned her neck upward so long it began to hurt. Her ankle was swollen. A chill from her sodden jeans crept up her legs. She worked her foot back into her boot while it still would fit.

In the past the Flint family had died, by hatchet and arrow, near here—women and children and father, except for the one son. Small wonder Alma May could not forgive. But the perpetrators, as Strong would call them, were desperate to drive the settlers out. Their own women and children were starving in the bush. Soldiers had burned their crops. Clearly the whites meant to kill them all, or send them west, which was the same thing. Word came back to them that hundreds of Seminoles died on the trip. Brandy could understand both pioneer and Indian. Now there had been a more recent death, Timothy Hart's. Brandy had felt an overpowering aura of fear near Hart's body. As she cowered in the cistern, time seemed to flow backward, then forward, murder to murder. Fishhawk believed the spirits of the dead still lingered here—even Hart's. Was it their collective fear she had sensed?

And then she heard a noise, a rustling in the underbrush, someone thrashing the way through. A thrill raced through her. Volunteer searchers, at last, or the deputy, come back. She waited. No further sound. Then the footsteps began retreating. The person hadn't seen the cistern, hadn't heard her call for help. She shouted "Down here! Look!" Fists clenched, she thought, I've got to make rescuing me worthwhile. "I found something!"

The footsteps halted. Brandy was crying now, "Something for the Sheriff!"

A heavy object was being dragged. Maybe a contraption to lower to her. No one answered her call. That made her nervous. A long, scraping sound followed.

"Hey, up there! Get me out! Please." No answer. The crunching again. Part of the sky was blotted out. At first she did not grasp what was happening. Then, like a knife blade had descended, the cistern went black. Brandy remembered the heavy boards under another pile of branches and twigs. The lid. The cistern had been re-covered. It made an excellent trap.

In a panic Brandy heard footfalls stirring through the brush, moving away toward the canal. She sat stupefied, engulfed in suffocating darkness, gripped by the memory of spiders and murder. Then behind her to the east she recognized the roar of a gasoline engine. It started slowly, then accelerated, throbbed to life, droned down the canal toward the river, and faded away. Someone was stealing her boat! If the deputy looked for her, he would never know she had been here. The volunteers wouldn't stay on the island after the sun went down. Her numb fingers felt for the square, leathery shape now in her bag and touched the empty pouch.

From the hammock above came a low moaning hooooo, the cry of an owl, Seminole symbol of death—and Shakespeare's. *The Tempest* wasn't the only play she loved. After the king's murder, Lady MacBeth said, "The owl shrieked, the fatal bellman," the harbinger of an execution, now her own. In the stifling blackness, she remembered Fishhawk's talk of an island witch and thought of the dread she had sensed on the island. She shared it now.

"Thing of darkness," she sobbed.

CHAPTER 14

▼

Night had fallen, Brandy knew, outside her prison, but inside it had been midnight since the cistern lid slammed shut. She closed her eyes tightly against the blackness, tried to relax, soaked as she was, tried to think who might come to find her. No one. No one would search in time. Without seeing her boat, how would they know where to look? The air in the tall concrete cylinder was finite. She could suffocate. Her stomach knotted. Perspiration dripped, unheeded, down her cheeks, along with her tears.

She made an effort to tamp down the panic, to wrench her thoughts away, to think of the puzzles that worried her. Who killed Hart? What happened to Daria and why? But her thoughts flooded back to the only thing that mattered now—rescue. She cringed against the cold wall, ankle throbbing, trying to block out the thought of spiders above. Twice she called out. Her voice echoed and re-echoed against the wooden barricade. It would make a muffled noise in the world above, not one that anyone in the Flint house would be apt to hear. And if Alma or Melba did, would they care?

Brandy's fingernails dug into her clammy palms. How did people prepare for death? Edgar Allan Poe wrote about being buried alive, a fate almost like being entombed in a cistern. No comfort there. Once or twice she felt something brush across her leg. Maybe a spider. Maybe there were roaches, too. She drew her legs up against her body and flipped on the little flashlight. Whatever had crawled over her had vanished. She threw the faint beam upward, then turned it off. The battery would not last. Her head swam. She felt faint, suspended in time.

Perhaps that's the trick, she thought grimly: to lose awareness, to look for that tunnel with the bright light at the end. She'd read about near death experiences. Maybe she'd see her father waiting. This time he'd say, in his quiet school teacher voice, that she'd fouled up big time. She hoped death would slip up on her, that she would simply lose consciousness at the last. Her thoughts skittered from one fear to another. She might blend with all those other spirits that haunted this place. Not a comforting idea, either. She closed her eyes and waited.

Brandy could not tell how many hours had passed before she heard a pattering across the boards above. The sound aroused her and again she felt panic rising in her throat. Some small animal. Maybe a rat. She shivered. The lid must fit tight. No mammal had come to stay inside the cistern or died there—yet.

She made herself remember favorite lines of poetry. From "Invictus": *In the fell clutch of circumstance, my head is bloody but unbowed...*That described her, all right, except her head was bowed, after all. She remembered Tennyson's "Crossing the Bar," a favorite of her father's. She read it herself with a breaking voice at his funeral.

"Twilight and evening bell/and after that, the dark..." But the poet had been an old man who saved that poem for his own epitaph. God, Brandy cried to herself, I'm not ready to cross the bar into the boundless deep. Darkness pressed down like a heavy weight. More tears ran down cheeks, already damp with sweat. Jeremiah Strong had warned her. This case, or cases, was not her business. Why hadn't she listened? Because, she answered, a helpless little girl must be found.

Brandy actually prayed herself into a light sleep. A scratching startled her, next a small panting noise, like an animal breathing out and in. Something padded across the boards again, then more scratching. Another chill shot through her. Could it be the panther? She doubted they panted. Then she heard heavier footfalls. It would be too dark outside now for volunteers.

Whoever dropped the lid shut might've returned to finish the job. But anything was better than slow suffocation. She strained with every muscle to listen, heard only snuffling around the edges of the lid. Was it only an animal? She flicked on the tiny flash and sent the beam upward. More rustling sounds, like brush being pushed aside. Then a dog barked, a blessed *woof* of discovery. Her heartbeat soared. Grif must've come looking for her and brought Meg. After all, she didn't return as promised for the drive to Gainesville.

The lid rasped partially aside. Again her pulse raced. "Grif! It's Brandy! I fell in."

A light golden muzzle sniffed through the crack. Meg and her educated nose. As the lid slid aside, Brandy exploded in sobs, too weak to stand. A wave of night air washed over her. The beam of a larger flashlight swept the cistern, but the face that peered down a second later came as a shock. It was John's. "Are you all right?" Anxious. Then a stiffer tone. "I'm not your friend Grif. Only your husband."

Her answer came brokenly. "You said—you weren't coming—this weekend."

The answer sounded even sharper. "I had an interesting phone call from Homosassa. I tried to call you, but I still couldn't reach you."

With a sinking in her stomach, Brandy knew that call probably came from Bibi Brier. Bibi had made good on her threat, but Brandy couldn't deal with that problem now. She looked down into the stale water. "I'm afraid my ankle's hurt." She tried to control the quiver in her voice. "Not really bad. I'll need a rope."

"Got a line on the boat. I'll be right back." He retreated, called, "Meg, stay," and tramped away through the underbrush. Meg lowered her muzzle next to the cistern lip and whined. Brandy felt the cool air on her upturned face, drank in its freshness, murmured her thanks to the glittering canopy of stars.

In a few minutes John knelt again at the opening and threw down a heavy line. "I've tied the other end to a big hickory tree up here. Someone else tied a rope there in the past." He tried to flick the rope near her hands. "Can you grab on and walk yourself up the wall?"

Brandy's trembling fingers grasped the end of the line. "I can try," she said. She sloshed upright in the fetid water. "Can't put much weight on my right foot."

"Try," John said. "Otherwise I've got to call fire rescue. They'd bring a ladder, but it would take time to get equipment here, especially this time of night."

Gritting her teeth against the pain, Brandy began creeping up the slimy limestone, brushing through cobwebs, canvas bag swinging against her shoulder, fingers burning where she gripped the rope. As soon as she neared the top, John reached down, put his hands under her arms and lifted her to the surface. She collapsed against him and threw her arms around his neck, gasping, "Thank God you got here."

John removed her arms. Still, she leaned against him, alarmed, her joy hedged with hurt. No matter what Bibi said, John should trust her, should be excited to see her. Yet he had not touched her except to drag her out of the cistern. He was sensitive, she knew, and withdrew when his feelings were injured, but this was different. He was angry.

"We have to get to the boat," he said, rising, his voice brittle.

Brandy sank back. "What's the matter?"

"You've had a shock. But so have I. We'll talk about it later." He pointed the flashlight at her. "Can you walk? I've got a boat at the mouth of the canal. As soon as we get to the house, I'll wrap that ankle."

"I'll try," she said again, then looked at the heavy boards he had shoved aside. "We ought to put the lid back. It was left off. On purpose."

He bent down, replaced the cover, then pulled her to her feet and guided her body against his, still without warmth, the gesture of a medic. She saw the earlier rope John had mentioned, wound around the base of the hickory tree, and chopped off just below the knot. Had someone used it to descend into the cistern and out again?

"How did you know I was missing?" she whispered as they shuffled through the underbrush, Meg trotting beside them, tail high, in a better mood than her owners.

"After the call from Homosassa, I called Carole's neighbors. They said they hadn't seen you since early this morning and the boat was gone. I drove up to look for you and eventually found your notebook on the porch. You wrote down where you planned to search for the little girl."

A spasm shot through Brandy's leg and she paused for a second. "Someone left the lid off and then closed me up in there, deliberately. I've been down there for hours, since early afternoon." She glanced at her watch. Midnight.

Across the canal, lights burned in the Flint house. "I'll ask those people to call the Sheriff's Office," he said.

She glanced up. "Don't," she said, "please. I don't want them to know about me. I can't trust anyone. Everyone knew one way or the other where I planned to search. We'll call the Sheriff's Office ourselves. A deputy was supposed to meet me."

In the dim light she could see John's mouth tighten. "If you say. You do get into messes, Bran." He helped her down the steep bank and into an aging marina jon boat moored to a tree at the water's edge. Meg leapt aboard and huddled at her feet.

"Had a devil of a time finding anyone who'd let me have a boat so late," John said. "Finally found a young fellow who works at the marina and talked him into renting it. He thinks he knows you." The skinny fellow who pumped gas for her. The talker with the inquisitive nature. He'd be quick to pass on the tidbit that she was in trouble.

She had more bad news for John. "I heard someone drive our boat away." By the boat's running light, she fumbled her way toward the bow and stumbled onto the seat. "I'd left our boat behind in the canal. I'm sorry. I don't know what they did with it."

He settled her under the bow light, and sat down next to the outboard kicker. "I'd hate to lose that boat," he said.

Brandy dropped her head. She might as well know the worst. "You said you had a shock."

John grasped the pull chord. "After I read your notes, I spoke to the neighbor who was feeding the animals. She gave me a few insights about your visitors." He knew about Sergeant Strong. She thought miserably, that left only Grif Hackett. John gave the cord a vicious yank. The boat rocked, but the engine only sputtered.

John gripped the cord a second time. "First, I looked at the marina, and I got more interesting information there. The employees suggested I check at the motel." He gave the cord a mighty pull and the engine caught at last. "The clerk at the desk confirmed what my anonymous female caller told me. Seems you didn't confine your private visit to the lobby. She also mentioned that I might learn something at the adjoining restaurant, too." Even in the dark Brandy could see the anger in his rigid face. "The reports were an eye-opener."

A weight settled in her chest. She recalled the inviting voice of the clerk with the towering hairdo. She'd had her eye on Grif; she'd been angling for him herself. Brandy had eaten at the restaurant, of course, with Grif, and then gone to his rooms. How long had she stayed? She was too flustered to remember.

John spoke in a fierce, clipped tone. "I went all through Carole's place," he went on, steering the boat into the creek, "I was looking for a clue to where you'd gone." He raised his voice above the clatter of the old engine, and she braced herself against sudden jarring as they rounded the bend into the river. "Your notebook was on the porch table. You planned to check out this end of the island today." He glanced down at Meg, and his voice softened. "Meg's a good tracker. Once we landed here she ran around, then zeroed in on the cistern." He pointed to an old shirt of Brandy's tucked around his belt. "I brought this along to keep her on target." He shook his head. "This is the most trouble you've gotten into yet."

She would have to swallow his criticism. It was better than the black hole he had pulled her out of.

"It's a shock to learn you have a boyfriend."

Brandy felt nauseated, flustered, unable to cope. "It's not like that," she said faintly. "Not at all." It could be, she thought, but it isn't.

"We'll talk about it later. I don't want to talk now."

She sank against the back of the hard bench. Before she collapsed, there was something she had to take care of besides John's feelings. What was it? It had once seemed so vital. "I found an important thing in the cistern," she said suddenly. "I found something for the Sheriff's Office." With a start, she realized she had used almost those same words earlier, much earlier, shouted them to someone before the cistern lid slammed down. That frightened statement might've sealed her fate. Whoever stole the treasure knew about the pouch from the journal, but hadn't found it. That person would not want it turned over to the Sheriff.

Her job now was to preserve the evidence. "Is there a box or a plastic container on the boat? I need to keep it wet."

With one hand he rummaged in a storage bin next to the console, pulled out a flat plastic box, and thrust it at her. "I brought my old first aid kit. It's pretty clean. You can take the stuff out." He frowned into the darkness ahead. "I thought I might need it."

Brandy eased her canvas bag up from the floor, unzipped it, and carefully extracted the folded scarf. "This pouch is more than one hundred fifty years old," she explained. "I've got to give it to Sergeant Strong. It could be a clue in a murder case." She leaned over the side of the boat, dipped water into the blue box, laid her treasure into it, and snapped the lid shut.

As John steered across the black waters and through the reflection of a silver half-moon, he did not seem impressed. The wind scoured the sweat from Brandy's face. She stared at the receding tip of the island and its thick growth of cedars, while the curve of the river vanished into a midnight of distance. Above them, a wan slice of moon glided in and out of clouds. She shivered, thinking of all those who had suffered over the centuries on that small plot of land. The fear that clutched her, she knew, was not rational, yet these forgotten souls, in some way, were here. Could the Medicine Man Fishhawk and his sacred bundle really send these agonized spirits to their final resting place in the West? He had vowed he could. She hoped he was right. When trapped in the cistern, she had felt these presences. She never wanted to feel them again.

East of the Salt River mouth, jungle gave way to darkened, elaborate stucco and frame homes, then to the black clump that was Bird Island, and next the commercial fishing docks. The only lights shone from the Tiki bar where a waiter and a barkeep were sweeping up. John nodded toward it. "The bartender told me you'd been there a lot with your archaeologist friend." He kept his voice level.

Brandy flushed. "Grif Hackett is as interested in this case as I am. I went to the motel to see some wonderful old Indian pottery."

"I see," John said dryly. He swung the boat into the short canal and nosed it into their boat slip. After tying up, he helped her stand. "I'll take the rental boat back tomorrow before I leave. Marine Patrol should be able to locate ours."

She took his hand and limped off the boat onto the dock, Meg at her heels. "John, my relationship with Grif Hackett isn't what you think. We're both trying to help with this case. And a child's missing." Her voice trailed away.

"The hotel room, remember."

"I told you, old pottery. He wanted to show me Indian pots."

"Sure he did. Most people go to museums." He took her arm and helped her through the porch door.

"Nothing happened." She hobbled into the living room.

He did not look at her. Instead he led her to the bathroom. "We've got to clean you up. Then you need to go to bed."

"I've got to call Sergeant Strong at the Sheriff's Office," she said. "His number's in my address book in my bag."

He picked up the canvas bag. "I'll call," he said.

Brandy sat down on a stool beside the shower, still feeling weak. She could scarcely tug off her muddy boots. "Leave a message," she said. "Tell whoever answers that the cistern ought to be roped off in case they can find out who shut me up there." She waved a weary hand. "Footprints, fingerprints, something. Say I need to talk to Strong tomorrow."

He left her and went to the kitchen phone. She could hear him talking quietly, an exclamation, and then he returned with a clean wash cloth and towel. "You had a message. Detective Strong called about noon. Somebody named 'Grapple,' I think, was released on bail this morning."

Not really news. That afternoon she had overheard the fact from Melba and Alma May.

"Can you stand in the shower?"

Suddenly she felt so tired she couldn't lift her arms. "Don't think so," she muttered. He filled the sink with warm water, soaped the wash cloth, and peeled off the shirt and jeans. "You won't sleep unless you're cleaned up." Gently he washed her breasts and stomach, brushed the green slime from her legs and feet, and slipped a fresh nightgown over her head.

"Lucky you're my husband," she murmured, even now she felt a warm stirring in her exhausted body.

John only looked grim. "Husband for the time being." He found an ace bandage in the cupboard, and began methodically wrapping the swollen ankle. Then he carried her into the bedroom and plunked her on down-turned sheets. "I'll bunk for the rest of the night in the back room. Too bushed to drive back tonight. I'll be gone in the morning."

She called after him, "But, John…".

"I'm old-fashioned," he said in the doorway. "One man and one woman at a time. Guess you're a little too independent for me." He switched off the light and closed the door.

*   *   *   *

When Brandy awoke in the morning, she was startled to find sunlight sliding in through the blinds. She swung her legs out of bed, felt a twinge when she put weight on her ankle, and called out for John. No answer. The weight returned to her chest. The house seemed unnaturally quiet. She peeked out the window and saw Meg lying in the shade of her favorite orange tree, fresh water beside her, and staked on the lawn. Leaning against the wall for support, Brandy wobbled into the kitchen. John's cereal bowl and coffee cups were rinsed and upturned on the dish drainer, the coffee pot full and set to stay hot. She limped on down the hall into the back bedroom. The only occupant of the neatly made bed stretched, yawned, groomed his gray fur, and gave Brandy a lordly and dismissive glance.

"Forget it, cat," she said. "I've been rejected by the master."

In the bedroom she fell back on the bed, depressed. John had made his feelings clear. Finally she fished in the closet for a pair of jeans and a clean shirt and struggled to pull the pant leg over her swollen and wrapped ankle. John had placed the first aid box on the dresser. She pulled up the bed covers and slipped it under her pillow. As safe a place as any for the tobacco pouch. She felt muddled. She couldn't concentrate, couldn't make sense of all that had happened. She did know one thing. This time she did have to get out of Dodge.

In the kitchen she poured a cup of coffee and shuffled into the living room. When she switched on the last of the television news program, Daria's perky little face glowed back at her, smiling. The first birthday photo again from the *Seminole Tribune*. The announcer said that the search still went on. Brandy's eyes filled. She had been no help in the search. She turned off the set and trudged on to the screen porch. The rental boat was no longer in the slip, John's minivan no longer in the double carport. Brandy sighed and slumped into a chair. No good-bye. No effort to show affection. He simply didn't believe her. Now her sadness was laced with indignation. She certainly had told him the truth about her own actions, if not Grif's.

Brandy set down her coffee cup, turned the pages of her notebook, and pulled a pen from the binding. While she waited for Strong to phone, she made a few notes about yesterday's ordeal. In a few lines she summarized her discovery, doodled an elongated tobacco pouch in the margin, laid aside the pen, and sighed. She wouldn't tell anyone else about the pouch until she gave it to Strong. She might be getting somewhere with the mystery of the artifact. The pouch seemed to prove an artifact had been concealed in the cistern. But what about Hart's death? And poor little Daria? And certainly her marriage was in deep trouble.

Brandy was lingering over coffee when Grif's van rolled into the carport. She realized she had not put on makeup, had scarcely brushed her hair. Grif stepped out, carrying what looked like sticks under one arm.

"Greetings," he called. "When I called this morning, I heard you had more tough luck last night. I brought you something. May I come in?"

Why not? John didn't want to be with her. She nodded. "Word gets around fast," she said.

Grif pulled a plastic chair up to the table. "Guy at the marina. He told me about your ankle this morning." John must've explained why he needed the rental boat when he returned it. Grif leaned toward her, his bright blue eyes concerned. "Someone left a second-hand crutch at the motel. I thought you might need it."

She ran a hand through her disheveled hair. "You called? I didn't hear the phone."

"Not surprising. Your husband picked it up on the first ring. He said he didn't want to wake you. He's gone?"

Her usual luck. Naturally, Grif would call, get John on the phone, and reinforce John's suspicions. "He's driven back to Tampa," she said. "He thinks something's going on between us."

Grif flashed his ultra white smile. "Isn't there?" He brushed her hand with his. "I wouldn't have gone off and left you after the night you had."

Brandy wondered how much Grif knew about last night, how much John had told him. "I'm not good company this morning," she said, "Nothing's gone right. I'm waiting for a call from Sergeant Strong. I need to find out if anyone's found my pontoon. It's missing." She settled lower in her chair. "John's bound to blame me because the boat's been stolen."

Grif patted her hand. "You were doing what you thought was right. I want to give you that ride to Gainesville, get you out of danger. You could see the work we do at the museum."

A ride home was more than John had offered. Brandy looked at Grif's clean, work-toughened hands. "I thought you were taking the Safety Harbor pots there yesterday."

He drummed his fingers on the table beside her notebook. "I tried to reach you, but I couldn't get you at the house or on your cell. When I didn't hear from you, I waited. Anyhow, I needed to make some recommendations about the site in Chassahowitzka. We can't get in there yet, but I have reports to log."

"Look," Brandy said, "I'll go freshen up. Maybe by then I'll hear from Strong or from Annie. I want to see her before I leave. I want to ask how the search is going, and I'll pick up my cell. She won't need it in Tampa." Brandy didn't want to go anywhere again without it. "Tugboat's been released."

"Yeah, I heard he'd been arrested. Too bad they've let him go," Grif settled back in his chair. "I'll take you to Annie's before we go. We'll stop and ask the marine patrol about your boat."

In the bathroom Brandy washed her face, gave her hair a few flips with the curling iron, and applied foundation cream and lipstick. Grif's offer, she told herself, was the only way to get to the Seminole camp now that she didn't have her own boat. Besides, she wouldn't go anywhere in Homosassa again alone.

When she lurched back toward the porch, Grif sprang out of his chair, came into the living room, and grasped her arm. "Here, let me help. You need the crutches."

"My ankle's just sprained," Brandy said.

He knelt to inspect the bandage, then ran his hand slowly up her leg, pushed closer, gently forced her against the wall. "You wanted me to do that. I can tell." For the second time she felt his body against her, strong, urgent. He leaned forward and his lips touched hers, pressed harder. The electric current made her gasp. Her hands went to his shoulders to push him away. He did not remove her arms as John had.

"You've been neglected," he said into her hair. "Let me put things right." Brandy was shaking her head when the phone rang.

"Let it go," Grif said, again pulling her toward him. "Let's get more comfortable." She felt giddy. He was not like John. John had turned away.

The phone shrilled again. "I told you before, I can't," she murmured. "That call could be the Sheriff's Office, or Annie. It's important."

His hands tightened on her arms. "So is this." He tried to turn her toward the bedroom door. His strength surprised her.

For the moment she felt awkward. Her voice rose. "I said, I *can't*." She tried to raise her hands, to back away. He held her for a few seconds more, in control. Then he stepped aside while she stumbled into the kitchen and picked up the phone. She would have bruises on her arms. She wondered, from passion or temper? Maybe she led him on. She might be the one responsible.

"Brandy?" The low voice on the phone was Annie's. "Are you all right? We heard you fell into the old Flint cistern." The marina attendant was still running his mouth. It was understandable. Until now, not much excitement in Homosassa.

"I'm okay now. Any news?"

Daria had been missing a full three days. Annie paused and her voice shook. "No news. I called because I'm leaving the island. I'm going home to Tampa." She halted again. "Fishhawk has to go tomorrow, too, but he wants to stay tonight. Wherever Daria is, it isn't here." Apparently, the Sheriff's Office had found no clue at the Flint house, at least nothing shared with the parents.

Brandy ached for the sorrow in Annie's voice. "I'm coming out there in about half an hour," she said.

The Seminole mother seemed to rally. "I need to return your cell. Fish-hawk charged it in town this morning. We got your message yesterday. Sorry we missed you."

Brandy realized she had written down where she was going when she left their camp. She wondered why Fishhawk was intent on staying as long as he could if Daria was not on the island. Was he still searching for something besides his little daughter, or protecting what he had already found? But he had to be in Tampa for the re-burial ceremony. Grif couldn't continue indefinitely to hold the Safety Harbor girl's bones.

When she hung up the phone, Grif still lounged in the kitchen doorway. "You're slippery." He grinned. "But the time will come."

She came toward him, braced herself against the door frame, and limped past. "No misunderstandings, my friend. I've got to stay focused." He followed while she moved on to the screen porch, picked up the crutches, and leaned on them as she stepped into the carport. "Besides, I owe John," she added. "He did come looking for me. He did pull me out of the cistern. I need to talk to him." She stooped and gave Meg a loving pat, then made her slow way to Grif's van.

When they drove to the marina, the attendant at the pump grinned, waved, and flashed a thumbs up. Brandy gave him a taut smile, climbed aboard Grif's pontoon boat, and found a seat among the boxes, screens, and trowels. Grif gunned the engine and the boat spurted into the river. She'd given the attendant more fodder for gossip.

As they neared Tiger Tail Island they could see Alma May tying her boat to the dock, while Melba, unnaturally stooped, reached for the railing. Grif idled in next to them. Beyond the canal Brandy could see a Sheriff's Office boat drawn up to the bank. Further away an officer stood near the cistern, encircled by yellow crime scene tape.

Alma straightened up and tossed her head in the direction of the officer. "Durn fools, banging on my door at the crack of dawn. Like we knew what was going on over there last night."

Grif called to her. "Hear a commotion?"

Alma May shrugged. "Boat or two went by. Not unusual. Night fishermen, I reckon." She looked Brandy up and down, her smile forced. "We cain't seem to get shut of them Indians. Reckon we cain't get shut of reporters, either."

Brandy said nothing. As Melba stepped out onto the dock, her appearance shocked her. Gone was the imperial set of the shoulders, the regal assurance on the hawk face. Brandy thought she detected a dark bruise on one high cheekbone. She looked drawn, her eyes hollow. She was taking nervous drags on a slender cigarette. For a few seconds she stared at Brandy and Grif. Then she swiveled around, stepped to one side and peered into the back yard before walking, head down, toward the front door after her friend. It was unlike her to be so silent. Brandy wondered where Melba had been the night before. Something or someone had frightened her. Surely she was accustomed to Tugboat.

It was only 9:00 A.M., so the two had been out early. Before she re-joined Melba, Alma May swung around to face them. "Just remember," she said firmly, "Anything found on my property belongs to me."

As Grif pushed the throttle forward to start down the creek, Brandy glanced back at the house. Through the thick stands of palmettos and shrub oaks she saw motion, watched as a tall, heavy man's figure, crouching down, moved toward the back door.

Brandy leaned toward Grif. "I'm glad the law is around. I think Tugboat's here."

CHAPTER 15

▼

The young deputy standing beside the yellow crime tape looked familiar to Brandy. As she wobbled on her crutches to the bow of Grif's boat, he raised his cap and settled it again on his sandy hair. He was the officer who came when she discovered Hart's body.

"The reporter lady," he said in a matter-of-fact voice, as if he had antic-ipated her rising from the creek. "Hear you had a rough night here."

Brandy flashed back to that black hole, the spiders, her helplessness, and felt a sudden constriction in her throat. "Yes, I did, Deputy."

"The guys who searched for the little girl say the lid was in place when they were here. Might be prints on the lid. It's a long shot on wood. Not slick enough." The deputy suddenly grinned. "Got news for you, though," he said. "The Marine Patrol located your pontoon boat earlier this morn-ing. Stashed in a dead end creek off the Salt River."

Grif gave a knowing shake to his head. "It figures. That wouldn't be far from the Little Homosassa and Tugboat's shack near the mound."

"Damaged?" Brandy asked.

"Not that they said. Been drained of gas. The officers towed it up river to the first marina. They've got to take it out of the water. Detectives need to check it over for prints or anything else. Maybe they can identify the perp who shut you in the cistern. You can collect it in a few days."

No reason, she decided, to explain she wouldn't be in Homosassa then. She'd tell Sergeant Strong when he called back. Brandy thought of the nineteenth century Seminole pouch, stored none-too-safely under her pillow. "If you talk to Sergeant Strong, please say I need to see him." She waved to the deputy and threaded her way between boxes and screens to the rear bench. As Grif backed around and started up Petty Creek, she said, "Good news, at last, finding my boat. Now, if someone would just find Daria."

And yet Brandy felt a vague unease. Why wasn't her boat sunk? Whoever shut her into the cistern to die surely wouldn't want her deserted boat found already. Everyone in Homosassa knew air boat rides routinely cruised that area. Still, high saw grass blocked a view of the backwater from the Salt River, and a pontoon was hard to scuttle. The perpetrator had been in a great hurry. Plainly, Grif pegged the villain as Tugboat, the monster on the island. Two days ago Tugboat was afraid she'd tell the Sheriff about his cocaine operation, but she had already done that. Why go after her last night? If he did, he must think Brandy could testify against him, or knew something—or had something that she didn't. The pouch wasn't the main prize, but its former contents might be worth killing for.

By the time they pulled the boat ashore at the south end of Tiger Tail Island, a cloud bank was rolling in from the Gulf. The Seminole camp seemed dark and silent without little Daria's piping treble. They slogged up the trail almost to the chickee before Annie spotted them and came listlessly forward. Brandy leaned her crutches against a palmetto, held out her hands, and clasped Annie's moist palms in hers.

"Still no news," Annie said. Tears glistened on her brown cheeks. Then she glanced at Brandy's crutches. "Sure you're okay?"

Brandy nodded, wondering how much Fishhawk and Annie knew about last night. No one should know about the pouch, unless John had talked and word has spread. He didn't understand its full significance.

Annie reached for the crutches and handed them to her. "I'm so sorry. I'm sure you were looking for Daria, but the Sheriff's men already combed the island." She glanced for a painful moment at the empty brush pen. "We're packing up. Fishhawk's taking me into Homosassa. Some friends will drive me home this afternoon. I can't stay here another night. The Sheriff's Office said they'd be in constant touch. The divers and the helicopter didn't find a trace. Officers and volunteers tramped all over the island and up and down the river. Not a sign of her."

Annie wore a soiled white shirt and her jeans were grass stained. Brandy knew they had no way on the island to keep themselves or their things clean.

Annie stared back at the hammock. "She just vanished. Maybe Fishhawk's right. Maybe there is a witch."

The shadows of clouds crept over the camp site. Brandy glanced at the deserted sweat lodge across from Daria's little corral and at the trail leading through the cabbage palms and cedars. She did not see the other Seminole. "When is Fishhawk leaving?"

Then, he was there—emerged, she supposed, from behind the chickee. He stood tall, knees braced, hands quiet at his sides, expression hard to read—grief mixed with some other emotion, Brandy couldn't decide what. From a small cloth bag tied around his neck came the spicy scent of herbs. Ever the medicine man, Brandy thought. He did not look at her, but faced Grif who lingered in the trail behind her.

Brandy turned again to Annie. "You haven't heard from Sergeant Strong today?"

Her sad eyes looked into Brandy's. "He'll call if they find..." she paused, choking on the words—"anything at all." Then, as if to hide tears, she turned, reached into a basket on the chickee platform, and handed Brandy her cell phone. "Thanks. I did use it."

"You're welcome," Brandy said. "I'm sorry I can't leave it with you, but the Sheriff's Office might call."

A sudden scowl darkened Fishhawk's square face. "I wish you'd tell the big detective to back off," he said, his lips scarcely moving. "The law's scaring away the witch who has her. If the deputies left us alone, I could get Daria back. I don't need their help."

Annie's eyes filled again. With trembling fingers, she pushed lank, black hair from her forehead. "I think we need the law's help," she said softly.

Grif eased closer. Brandy thought he meant to lay a sympathetic hand on Fishhawk's arm, but he seemed to think better of it and put his hand in his pocket. "She's all right somewhere," he said, "or they'd have found her.

Sorry, pal, but I need to pull you away, too, at least for now. You've got that burial in Tampa. I can't keep holding those bones. I'll be in trouble with the state and the Graves and Repatriation Act. You know that better than anyone."

The muscles in Fishhawk's face tensed. "I'm ready. I'm driving the pickup back tomorrow. We'll do the ceremony the next day, Sunday morning. I'm going to wait here through tonight. I need to clean up."

Clean up the area, Brandy wondered, or search for something besides Daria when Annie wasn't around?

"We'll meet at the Seminole Cultural Center. I'll call and tell them to prepare," Fishhawk was saying, his voice flat. "The cemetery's only a few miles from there." Something strange played across his features, dragged down his lips, gleamed in his black eyes, maybe anger. From a scrub oak beside the creek Brandy heard the shrill cry of a heron. Above the jagged cedars and palms an osprey sailed on the hunt. The male of the pair Brandy had watched had proved a better guardian of his young than Fishhawk. She wondered if he had used the medicine bag, and if Fishhawk would bring it to the ceremony. One thing she knew; she would never be told what role it played when the bones were finally buried.

"No problem," Grif said. "This afternoon I'm going to Gainesville. I've got to drop off the pottery the anthropology division wants to see. The registrar's arranged for it to be fumigated today." He looked down toward the creek. Brandy knew they must leave if he had to keep an afternoon appointment. It would take an hour and a half to drive to Gainesville. Grif turned to Fishhawk, his voice now insistent. "Tomorrow I'll bring the skeleton to Tampa in the van, maybe late afternoon. It's stowed in an airtight container. Nobody will see it, let alone touch it, until you do your thing the next morning. You can bury it in the same plastic container, as is, if you like. Before the ceremony, I'll help."

Brandy knew the ritual would be private. Whites could not be witnesses. Fishhawk's dark eyes swept over them both. "I'm coming back here," he said, his voice tight, "just as soon as I've done my part."

Brandy felt daring. "And what happens to the witch on the island?" she asked.

The Seminole spun around and looked at her for the first time with such malevolence that he startled her. What had she done to them except befriend Annie?

But he answered her question. "Oh, the witch is here," he said. "Has been here. But I don't think it will stay. I think its job is done."

The remark did not reveal much about his conception of the witch. Alma May was planning to sell her house; surely Melba would leave, too. Tugboat wouldn't stay on the island, and neither would Fishhawk himself, or anyone else. Everyone's job was done, but Daria was still lost.

In spite of Fishhawk's obvious bitterness, Brandy plunged on. "What about the ghosts—Hart's, the dead settlers'?"

For a moment the hardness went out of Fishhawk's eyes. He glanced toward the north end of the island. "I don't know. If they were Indian, the right ceremonies would help their ghosts go west. About whites, I don't know."

"But Mr. Hart, doesn't he have to be avenged?"

Fishhawk turned his gaze to the coarse wire grass at his feet and did not answer. For a moment Brandy had a mental image of plump, gullible Timothy Hart's ghost hovering like mist around the house and cistern, still seeking his treasure.

"Look," Grif said. "Maybe I could help out by taking Annie and her stuff back to town with us."

Fishhawk raised his head and faced the wind that blew clouds from the Gulf. "No," he said. "I took my eyes off my baby on this island. I'm not taking them off my wife."

As Brandy and Grif started back down the path, Brandy saw Fishhawk reach for Annie's hand. Several times Brandy looked back. Fishhawk stood staring after them until the two Indians disappeared from her view behind the shadowy cedars.

In silence Grif and Brandy pushed off and careened down the creek between high grasses until the pontoon boat reached the intersection with the canal and the Homosassa River. Beside the shoreline the Flint house rose against the bleak sky as quiet and still as it had the morning Brandy found Hart's body. She had thought Alma May would never give refuge to

Tugboat, but she was sure she had spotted him there earlier. Perhaps the two women had picked him up when they went out that morning. He might have leverage over them. He could tell the law about their own pottery theft.

Brandy glanced up at a heavy, gray sky. A sharp scent of rain hung again in the air. As the deputy near the cistern tipped his cap, she shouted "Stay dry!" She knew he wouldn't say whether the technician found useful tracks or prints. Maybe she could wheedle the facts from Sergeant Strong, if he ever called.

She settled herself on the rear bench, her back to the wind, and watched a long line of boaters stream past from the Gulf, trying to outrun the weather. Grif's own boat rocketed forward, gaining what distance he could before they reached the manatee "go slow" signs. With Tugboat on the loose again, Brandy felt anxious. She had expected the Sheriff's Office to hold him. Yet she knew Strong had only her word that he had threatened her life. What if he left no sign at the shack? She could only hope the Sheriff's Office could charge him with smuggling or vandalism or theft at the mound. At any rate, something had changed Melba since the Sheriff's Office decided to pick up her husband.

Time to throw in the towel and flee to the safety of her Gainesville apartment. She would probably never know who killed Timothy Hart, or what happened to his precious artifact.

Grif grinned back at her from the helm. "You want lunch?"

This time she shook her head. "Got to pack. Also need to ask a neighbor to take care of Carole's cat. I'll try to reach her tonight to tell her I'm leaving, and I'll leave a note." Brandy also wanted time alone, time to think, to try to make sense of the murder and the kidnapping. "Drop me at the marina. I need to drive Carole's car back."

In a few minutes Grif angled in next to the pier and reached with his boat hook to catch a post. "I'll bring Meg with me," Brandy said, rising. "She travels well."

"No problem. My stuff will be stowed in the back of the van. There's room for your pooch in the mid section." He checked his watch. "It's one o'clock. Be back for you in about an hour."

Brandy clambered out on the dock, dragging her crutches, then leaned on them and looked directly at Grif. "Remember, no misunderstandings. This is strictly a ride home."

Still grinning, he held up his right hand. "Scout's honor."

Brandy fought to keep down the discomfort she now felt from being alone with him.

For a moment she balanced with her crutches on the narrow pier while Grif backed into the canal to turn around. The wind slapped waves against his boat. Charcoal clouds rolled across the sky. "See you then, and thanks," she said, and made her way slowly toward Carole's car, glad she had the key in her bag.

As the first drops of rain began to fall, she pulled into her carport. In the yard she unfastened Meg's lead, banged through the screen door, and let Meg onto the porch. Made it in time, she thought, as rain began to pound the road before the canal and boat slips. She stumped into the kitchen. No message light. She dialed the Sheriff's Office in Inverness and asked for Detective Strong. He was out, a secretary said. He would call.

"Tell him to make it in the next half hour," Brandy said, disappointed.

Next she dialed the marina where her pontoon boat was held. Her pontoon was there, awaiting the detectives. In the bedroom she whipped back her pillow and snapped open the lid of the first aid kit. The pouch still lay in its moist bed. In the bathroom she poured a thin trickle of water on the deerskin, thrust the slick plastic box into a zippered bag from the kitchen, and laid it at the bottom of her suitcase. On top of it she piled nightgown, underwear, two pairs of shorts, and jeans. She stuffed her few soiled clothes into an empty garbage bag. After performing the cat chores, Brandy called the neighbor to ask if she'd mind the regal Persian and rinsed the breakfast dishes. She was grateful she had done a more thorough cleaning job before she'd been trapped in the cistern. Peanut butter and bread, a few raw carrots, and left-over iced tea would suffice for a meager lunch.

Stuffing her cell in a pants pocket, she leaned the crutches against the cabinet and shuffled back to the porch table with her meal on a tray. Meg raised her buff-colored nose from her paws and her tail thumped the floor. "Leaving soon," Brandy said. "And this time you go, too."

She tore a sheet of paper from her notebook and dashed off a long message to Carole. She'd keep the house key, give an extra one to the neighbor, and mail hers to Carole after her friend returned home.

Then she picked up her notebook from the porch table where she'd left it. Before thrusting it into the large canvas bag, she leafed through the last entries, then sat back, frowning. She'd been eager for some time to mull over her notes. Now she realized she hadn't thought with sufficient care about all the details. She turned back to the beginning. She might have enough facts about Hart and the artifact at least to pose a few questions. For one thing, what about Melba?

Brandy had been thinking of her almost as an appendage of Alma May, but Melba was smarter. She was a successful business woman, perfectly capable of acting independently. She'd been around Timothy Hart, even if her husband hadn't. And Brandy had seen her sneak something into Alma May's house through the back kitchen door. Melba knew about the journal, and she could climb down a rope as well as anyone. She might even be partnered with Tugboat in more ways than marriage. As for Hart's murderer, Brandy couldn't see how Tugboat could've pulled off the poisoning. He seemed more like a later opportunist.

For several minutes she read through the pages while the rain drummed on the aluminum roof. Brandy had almost despaired of Strong's call when the phone rang. She picked it up and listened with relief to his firm voice. "Sorry, little lady. Got your message, but I've been busy with a case in Inverness. Your experience at the cistern ought to finally teach you a lesson."

Brandy sat forward, her mouth tense. "What about Tugboat Grapple?"

Strong paused. "The news for you isn't too good. The detective who questioned him says he denies everything. The crab fisherman and his son can't verify your story. They didn't see him or the rifle. The narcotics guys couldn't find a trace of cocaine in the cabin. He had plenty of time to get rid of whatever you saw. All we got is maybe stolen pots. Not much to go on."

Her hands tightened on the phone. "And in the meantime, what happens to Tugboat?"

"His wife and Mrs. Flint came to the station in Homosassa Springs and his wife posted bail. The corporal says she looked scared to death, but she sprang him. Go figure."

"I think she's so frightened of him—or someone—she's almost sick. Any fingerprints or footprints that might help?"

"Too early to know. Anyway, I'm not sharing that information yet with the press."

Brandy almost signed off before she remembered why she had called the detective in the first place. "Sergeant, wait. I found an artifact in the cistern, not the valuable one Hart expected to find, but the tobacco or shot pouch the journal says it was stored in. It's rare itself. According to what I've read, no deerskin ones are left. I want to hand it over for your investigation. I think it proves there was an artifact in the cistern, one that's much more priceless."

Strong's voice rose again. "Who knows you have the pouch?"

"I haven't told anyone, but my husband might have. He doesn't know much about the case. He wasn't interested."

"Smart man. Probably didn't want you involved. Remember the cabin on the mound and the cistern trap? I've got some words for you to think about. You never listen, but I'm going to tell you all the same." He paused. He's recalling a quotation, Brandy thought, rubbing Meg behind the ear. He could always think of one that fit.

"This advice comes from the Psalms. Pay attention. 'I waited patiently for the Lord, and he inclined unto me, and heard my cry. He brought me up also out of a horrible pit, out of the miry clay, and set my feet upon a rock, and established my goings.'" Strong stopped for emphasis. He had managed to come up with a reference to her rescue from the cistern. "My own advice to you, Miss O'Bannon, is to take the Bible's. You're safe now. Keep your feet on that rock. Don't be going anywhere. Not even out of your house, and be sure the neighbors are there."

"Then you'll approve of my plans," she said. "I'm going home to Gainesville this afternoon. Getting out of Homosassa altogether. Tomorrow I'm driving to Tampa."

Strong's tone elevated. "Where your husband is?"

"Yes. John doesn't know I'm coming yet. I'll call him tonight." She dropped her voice. "Grif Hackett's driving me to Gainesville because I don't have my car. I can pick it up there, and then go on the next day to Tampa. Hackett's taking the Safety Harbor girl's bones to the Tampa reservation." She tapped her notebook. "Fishhawk and his wife will meet him at the Seminole Cultural Center. We'll all be there tomorrow, Saturday, and the service for the Safety Harbor child will be Sunday morning."

Brandy held the phone between her ear and her shoulder and lifted the notebook into the canvas bag. "I'm leaving here in a few minutes. Can you come to Gainesville today to get the pouch? I've got more to tell you." Brandy imagined his dark face, his big hand passing over his forehead, thinking. "And do you have any news about the search for Daria?"

"That's what we're working on. Be easier for me to come to Tampa tomorrow."

"Make it late afternoon," she said. "You can always reach me on my cell. I'll have the pouch. Come to the Seminole Cultural Center on Orient Road, just off Hillsborough Avenue." She gazed out into the glistening rain and visualized the gathering, some of the figures still in shadow. "But finding Daria's certainly your most important job."

The detective's voice sounded weary. "I've learned from sad experience that you probably won't take my advice."

When Brandy put down the phone, she sat waiting for Grif, still clinging to the canvas bag with her notebook. She'd been tearing from one place to another without enough reflection. When she was alone at her own apartment, she'd finish studying her notes. Several facts nagged at her, but she did not like where they seemed to lead. One thing she did know—she would be at the Seminole Cultural Center tomorrow. There she'd be safe, surrounded by people, and there she expected to find answers—as well as her biggest feature story yet.

CHAPTER 16

▼

As soon as Brandy spotted Grif's van turning in at the area entrance, she hobbled into the bedroom for her suitcase, pulled on her rain coat, and fastened her note on the refrigerator with a magnet. After locking the front door, she sank down on a chair by the porch door. Outside, rain still pounded the street and splashed in the canal. When Grif pulled into the carport, Brandy limped to the van door, dragging her suitcase behind her. He leapt out and helped hoist Meg and the pad for her bed onto the middle bench of the van. After giving the retriever a reassuring pat, Brandy climbed gingerly into the passenger seat. Although she could now walk without crutches, Grif spotted them on the porch and swung them into the van with her suitcase.

"Got everything?" he asked. She nodded, thinking more about his box with the Safety Harbor child's bones than about her suitcase. She'd spotted the box in the rear, resting on a coil of rope beside hand spades, small picks, and screens. The bones were secure in their plastic container, but in spite of the skeleton's age, the thought of its being in the van made her uneasy.

"The weather's going to slow us down," Grif said as he drove between the entrance pillars. She heard a car start up behind them and turned to peer out the back window. Through a curtain of blowing rain, she could make out the hood and bloated wheels of an over-sized pick-up similar to

Tugboat Grapple's. You're being paranoid, she told herself. It probably belongs to someone in the park.

The research center on the University of Florida campus was about seventy miles northeast of Homosassa, her own apartment three miles south of the university. Although the roads were good, they were only two lanes most of the way. Brandy felt frustrated. It would take more time than usual. She had a fierce desire to get this drive over with, to be back in her own apartment. When they reached U.S. 19, Grif drove north through the traffic of Crystal River, then past wide pastures rimmed with pine trees, and up the overpass above the Florida By-Pass Canal.

The truck still followed. Brandy tensed when Grif veered northeast onto an isolated road where slash pines rose on each side like sentinels. Only a few cars plowed on here through rain that still slashed down in torrents. Brandy listened again for the pick-up. When she heard a roar, she swiveled around, and looked out the back window. The pick-up bucked along a few yards behind them, its windshield wipers a blur of motion. She could see a large, shadowy figure behind the wheel, impossible to identify. Hackett gripped the steering wheel and frowned into the downpour.

"Do you know a truck's been behind us since we left Homosassa?" she asked.

He grunted. "Scoped it out way back," he said. The muscles in his cheek hardened as the dim bulk of the truck rumbled closer. "Can't believe that meat head wants to pass in this rain."

He sped up and the van and pick-up surged into a national forest where the pines stood in rows, veiled by rain, tall and straight, as far as Brandy could see. After Grif passed an empty logging trailer, abandoned on the road's wide shoulder, he pulled closer to the right. The pick-up honked, and nosed in behind them, its chassis high above the van, then began to swing out, its huge front tires almost even with their rear.

"Dumb ass!" Grif hissed between his teeth. "He's trying to force me off the road." He gunned the engine and shot ahead, opening a wide gap between van and truck.

Brandy's fingers clenched over the strap to her canvas bag. Tugboat, it's got to be Tugboat. He probably thought she had something that belonged on the Flint property. And she did, though not what he suspected. Hackett himself seemed agitated, his hands tight around the wheel, his lips compressed.

Through the wet gloom a light flashed from a dirt side road, flared across the highway, and caught the road in a cold glare. An enormous logging truck ground to a stop at the intersection, the formidable figure of a logger at the wheel. He gave a blast on his horn, waved Grif past, and swerved in behind the van.

Hackett settled back, his nervousness subsiding, and watched the logging truck bob along behind him, the pick-up awash in its ponderous wake. "Hope the logger's going to Williston," he said. "We'll stop there for coffee. There'll be more traffic from now on."

Brandy gave him a wan smile. "It'll be nice to have people around. You think that was Tugboat?"

"Yeah. He's got his knickers in a knot. I guess he thinks you have something on him. Or thinks we're stealing something he had the right to steal."

Brandy still felt tense. "You sure wouldn't want him pawing through your collection."

"No," he said. He gave her a sharp glance, but she understood the need to protect the bones and the valuable pots in his care.

Tugboat, Melba, Alma May—the whole lot of them could be after her. They knew she'd been in the cistern. Melba was smart enough to have a translation of the Seminole phrase by now. She knew about the hole filled with water and could tell her husband. Any of them might think Brandy had escaped with more than the pouch. Grif glanced periodically in his rear view mirror.

Still pelted by rain, they rolled past cattle sheltered under giant oaks, and parked beside a fast food service window on the outskirts of town. As Grif ordered coffees, Brandy watched the pick-up halt at a nearby truck stop, too far away for her to recognize the hazy figure inside. She wondered if a man who loved his dog would carry out an act of violence, even if he threatened one. She and Tugboat felt a similar emotion for their pets.

He was adept at frightening victims, but the possibility nagged her that he was mostly bluff. He'd backed down before Grif easily enough.

Grif reached through the window for the plastic cups, set one in a holder on the dash and handed her the other. "I've got to take the pots first thing to Ag and Engineering for fumigation. I cleaned them the best I could in the field lab, but we don't take chances on contaminating the collection." As he turned the key and stepped on the gas, Brandy saw the pick-up inch forward. Grif swore under his breath.

But within thirty minutes, insulated by traffic, they had shed their escort. Brandy relaxed her grip on her bag as Grif rounded a curve into the University of Florida campus and parked a few blocks farther down the street in front of a one-story yellow stucco building. He reached for a rain slicker on the seat behind him, pulled it on, and hurried around to open the back hatch. Soon he was rushing for the front door, carrying a stack of plastic containers.

Brandy had not spotted the pick-up since they turned off the expressway into Gainesville. Even in this weather students holding umbrellas or raincoats over their heads ran in and out of the parking garage and dorms. She was far from alone. If Tugboat did re-appear and wanted revenge because Brandy had turned him in, he wouldn't try anything here. She still feared what might've happened on the lonely road to Williston.

It was no secret now that she'd been down in the cistern. Although she removed only the valuable tobacco pouch, anyone who knew about the journal might think she had stolen the main treasure—unless one or all of them had already found it themselves. If Tugboat's income from drug running had made him independent of Melba, his wife might've lost what control she had over him. Brandy didn't like to think what might happen after Grif left her at her apartment. After all, her address was in the phone book.

"The indigenous Indian and Seminole material isn't on exhibit yet," Grif said a few minutes later, as he crawled back into his seat. "But the registrar for the anthropology division needs to log in this Safety Harbor stuff." He pulled into a space behind a red brick building labeled Dickinson Hall. "My office and work area is in here," he added. "You might as well see it. I need to check my mail. Your dog okay for a little while?"

Brandy leaned back and fondled Meg's ears. "Fortunately, it isn't hot today. Meg's a saint. Didn't I say you wouldn't know she was in the car?" To Meg she whispered, "Won't be long, girl," and settled her raincoat hood over her hair. After Grif locked the van with its precious cargo secure in the rear, she followed him down a flight of steps to a lower level, then along a narrow hall, hung with photographs of recent digs. Today Grif had dressed professionally in tailored blazer and silk tie. A handsome man, but one with costly tastes. No wonder he was restless in this job.

He waved to a lanky employee coming out of a storage area. "We missed you and your flakey grad student Bibi this week, old buddy," the man said. "She still helping at the Citrus County mound?"

Brandy remembered how the smitten girl had been far more interested in the professor than in the work.

Grif shrugged. "Not really. She's with whooping cranes now. It's hard to keep students interested in archaeology once they've been in the field. They run into the snakes and spiders. Sometimes poison ivy. That stuff cures them. Bibi Brier's a good example." Brandy marveled that Grif did not seem to understand how Bibi felt about him. Brandy had not bothered to tell him how much trouble his grad student had caused her with John. Grif himself treated Bibi with such disdain that Brandy did not want to embarrass him.

As the other man passed, Grif explained to Brandy, "the collections manager," and flung open his office door.

It was larger than Brandy had expected, crammed with overflowing bookcases, papier maché animals, fiber baskets, two paper-littered desks, and a computer. Beside the door stood a low coffee table, flanked by two upholstered chairs, and cluttered with sports car and gourmet cooking magazines, none of which interested her. While he accessed his e-mail and rifled through a basket of mail, she sank into a chair and admired the color photographs of Mayan and Peruvian ruins on one wall, and the relics on a nearby shelf. One squat terra cotta figure, about two feet tall, with bald skull, bulging eyes and lips, extended hands, and claw-like feet enthralled her. It stared back with timeless menace from black, protruding pupils. Grif followed her gaze.

"Funerary incense burner from Vera Cruz, Mexico. A copy, of course. The god of death, Miclantecuhtli."

"He looks the part," she said, both repulsed and fascinated "I suppose the original is valuable."

"Priceless."

In spite of their safe arrival, Grif seemed more strained than he had en route. Now, as he stuffed his mail into a briefcase, he gave a relieved smile. "Everything's okay here," he said. "Thought I might be hung out to dry. Some of the staff said I should use grad students to work the mound, or hire a private firm. But they're not always careful. Imagine if Bibi had that assignment! I'd rather do the work myself. But I do need to take care of some correspondence tonight and make some calls."

Brandy sighed. She'd love to ask for a tour of the hall, see into the areas marked "Ethnographic Storage," "Ceramic Specialist," and "Exhibit Coordinator," or view the curators' work areas where, through an open door, she glimpsed long tables with metal trays and small cardboard boxes, but there wasn't time.

"You going to take me to my apartment?" she asked. "It's only a few miles from here."

"Sure thing."

Carrying his briefcase, Grif ushered her out the door, up the flight of steps to ground level, and into a chill drizzle. It wasn't until they were backing out of the parking lot that Brandy spotted the monster pick-up again, waiting outside the brick building where campus police issued parking permits. Her heart dropped. Grif saw the truck about the same time. With sinking heart, she watched the pick-up wheel around and follow them off campus.

They finally lost sight of it in the early evening.traffic. By the time they pulled up to her apartment building, a two-story stucco with a ragged lawn and an overgrown ligustrum hedge, only a few people hurried along the sidewalk.

He leaped out of the van and opened the passenger door. "Let me take your suitcase," he said. "You're still a little gimpy."

She slung her canvas bag over her arm, thought of the Seminole tobacco pouch, nestled in its wet plastic box, and grabbed for the case. "Don't bother. I can manage fine." He frowned "It's okay," she added quickly. "I'm on the first floor. I'll leave the crutches in the van. You can return them to the motel next time you're in Homosassa. I'll be fine." No one else would touch that case, not while it held the pouch. He wouldn't want her to carry the plastic container with its bones, either. To each his own relics. Her ordeal was almost over. She just had to make it through tonight.

While Grif stood bare-headed in the rain, still scowling, she bit her lip and walked as straight as she could up the walkway, obedient Meg behind her, and turned at the foyer door to wave. He was still watching.

After unlocking and re-locking the door to her rear apartment, she plunked the suitcase on the small table in the dining alcove, unsnapped the first aid kit, and checked the pouch. Not disintegrating yet, thank goodness. She'd read enough Seminole history and studied enough photographs of tobacco and shot pouches to know this one was unique. Beaded ones were on display or stored in several museums, but none made of deerskin. She reminded herself that it was a treasure in itself. She'd be glad to hand it over to Detective Strong.

Ironically, it probably did belong to Alma May. After a hundred and fifty years, anything on her property belonged to her. Hart had not cinched the deal to buy her house and land. Alma May might eventually get the pouch back, and the Sheriff's Office might recover the more valuable artifact for her, too. At least Tugboat wouldn't profit, even if Melba did. But Fishhawk was a fly in the ointment. He would never believe that a treasure stolen from the Seminoles could belong to anyone else.

Brandy looked around her. As usual she'd left in a hurry, and she'd never mastered the knack of a place for everything and everything in its place. Obviously, John had not been back to the apartment. He would never litter the sideboard with papers, toss a jacket over the arm of a chair, leave a book open and face down on an end table, or stack dishes carelessly on the kitchen counter. She reached into the cupboard and dipped three cups of dry, unappetizing pellets from a container into Meg's bowl, then wandered into the bedroom at the rear of the apartment and surveyed the unmade bed.

Tidy John. He was now in his efficiency bachelor apartment in Tampa, as neat as the uncluttered desk in his office. She shook her head sadly. He might not want to come back here.

Outside the rain had at last slackened, but the view was growing darker. She hated to go outside. She'd be more vulnerable, but she'd better take Meg for a quick walk now. From the bedroom window the woods were shrouded in heavy mist. The sidewalk under the window had become a pale strip, lit only by a distant street lamp. She had liked their apartment because it backed up to a heavily forested park. Tonight untrimmed nature did not seem desirable. She searched until she found an umbrella in a kitchen corner, picked up her key and Meg's leash, and made her slow way out to the front sidewalk. Grif's van was gone.

At the corner a woman was stepping down from a bus and several children ran toward another apartment building. Lights and the sound of music came from a corner drugstore and a café. She gravitated toward it, giving Meg the choice of a public stretch of grass, and waited for her in the path of light shining from the small restaurant. She could see people inside, a few eating at tables in the rear. One man sat alone, gnawing on a large hamburger, his face turned away from the window—a tall, broad-backed man.

Brandy yanked the leash, startling Meg, and began her jerky way back to her building. Had she been spotted? It didn't matter, she reminded herself. Her address was not only in the phone book, but her apartment number was on the mailbox in the foyer. The outsized pick-up hunched in a side street, like a predator-in-waiting. She had not anticipated this situation when she made her plans. Although Tugboat had certainly trailed her, following wasn't illegal. Her own actions were the ones that were illegal. Because of Brandy, law enforcement officials now suspected him of cocaine trafficking. Tugboat would need to find another place for his stash and probably reorganize his operation. He had a reason to be angry, certainly, but she couldn't connect him to the death of Timothy Hart.

Hackett had reminded her that she also might run into Alma May and Melba tomorrow. They had become familiar with the Seminole Cultural Center by driving to the casino next door.

Back in her apartment Brandy limped again to the bedroom window, while Meg, sensing her uneasiness, paced along behind her. The ligustrum hedge had grown tall enough to hide the glass, would conceal anyone climbing in. With nervous fingers, she tested the Miami window. It had never locked properly and still didn't, one more defect the landlord had not yet corrected. Favoring her sore ankle, she made her way back into the living room and looked out into the dusk. For a moment she stood silent, heart racing, then gave a decisive nod, hobbled to the kitchen phone, checked the flip-top directory on the counter, and dialed. The woman who rented the apartment above hers could be flaky, but she was generous to a fault.

"Lily Anne? Brandy here." She kept her voice steady. "Gotta favor to ask."

Lily Anne's voice was low, drawn out, and friendly. "Whatever you say, sugar."

"Look," Brandy said. "John's still in Tampa. I think a man may be following me. I don't want to sleep in my apartment tonight. I'll leave town again tomorrow, early. Could I crash on your couch tonight?"

"Sure thing, sugar. But shouldn't you call the cops?"

Brandy swallowed. The set-up was too complicated to explain to Lily Anne. "Not yet."

"Well, okay. I'm going out soon myself." Lily Anne giggled softly. "Meeting a hot date. I may be out kinda late. Real late, know what I mean?" She paused. "Truth is, I may not get in 'til morning."

Brandy smiled to herself. "Look, I'll come up right away," she said. "You know, I'll have to bring Meg."

"No problem."

Brandy was already mentally ticking off what she had to take with her. "I'll be gone in the morning," she said. "I'll leave your key under that half-dead Shiffelera in the building foyer. I'll slip it under the first brick."

"Sure thing, sugar. No problem." Thank goodness, Brandy thought, for the Lily Anne's in the world.

In the bedroom Brandy searched a drawer for clean pajamas and gathered up a sweater, slacks, and a shirt for tomorrow. Then she took down a gray pant suit and a fresh white blouse from her closet and hung it in a garment bag, stuffed underwear and hose in the bottom, and pitched a pair of dress shoes into a plastic bag. She might be allowed to watch the Seminole funeral service from a distance. In any case, she wanted to appear respectful of the re-burial Sunday. Then she stuffed a can of vegetable beef soup, a pack of sandwich crackers, and a withered apple from the hydrator into a plastic bag and shouldered her canvas bag with the notebook. At the last minute she remembered to root around in a kitchen junk drawer, pull out a tattered Florida map, and thrust it into her bag as well. Then she picked up her suitcase, her confidence renewed. She had no intention of being a target again for anyone.

Loaded down and with Meg on a leash, Brandy climbed up one step at a time to Lily Anne's apartment, where she gave her slim neighbor a hug, admired her new silky black pants, her low-cut black cashmere sweater, and her bouffant hair. After Lily Anne had patted Meg's head and pointed out a pink quilt on the couch, Brandy waved her out the door. Then she dropped her canvas bag on the floor, sagged down on the soft cushions and elevated her leg. She'd better stay off her ankle for a while, or the swelling would never go down.

On the coffee table were the current issues of *Cosmopolitan* and *Working Woman*. Brandy flipped through them for a moment before realizing neither was of interest. It didn't matter because she wanted to re-read the detailed notes she'd made in Homosassa. After she'd plugged in her charger and cell, she struggled up again. She limped into the tiny kitchen, heated, and ate her meager supper at the counter. Then she poured herself a small glass of Lily Anne's cream sherry and used the kitchen phone to call the newsroom and explain that, while she was still on vacation, she was following up the Timothy Hart story.

Next she summoned her courage, drew a deep breath, and rang John's Tampa apartment. He should be home by now. She had to talk to him. Again her luck held.

"So you're actually driving to Tampa?" he asked, an edge to his voice.

"I'm meeting Sergeant Strong there tomorrow afternoon. The Safety Harbor child's bones are to be re-buried in Tampa the next day."

She tried to picture him. He would be rubbing his forehead, probably, like he did when he was perplexed or upset. "I didn't suppose you were coming to see me. Your archaeologist friend will be here, too, I imagine." He bore down sarcastically on the word "friend."

Brandy swallowed her rising indignation. "I'll be at your apartment tomorrow night. I want to explain everything to you clearly in person, especially who the trouble-maker is who called you about me. Will you be home?"

He bit off each word. "You bet I will." Brandy hoped he would understand that, Bibi Brier to the contrary, she was not having an affair.

After replacing the phone in its cradle, she rinsed the dishes and stacked them in the dishwasher before shuffling back into the living room, setting the wine on an end table, and settling herself on the couch. She remembered the state map and pulled it from her bag. Everyone would expect her to take Interstate 75 straight into Tampa, and exit where it passed near the Seminole Cultural Center. But another route suggested itself. It would take longer, but that was okay. Route 441 out of Gainesville connected to Route 301, once the major highway to Tampa. Route 301 passed even closer to the Center, but no one would select it as the best road to take today. She would use another precaution. No one would expect her to leave at dawn to make a two and a half hour trip.

At last she set her wrist watch alarm for 5:00 A.M. and picked up the glass. Time for the notebook. Had she missed anything? For several minutes she read, frowning, flipping back and forth between the pages. When she closed the book, she stared out at the darkened street, her fingers still gripping the cover. Brandy hoped she was wrong, but she had been overlooking important points. She felt like a cartoon character with a light bulb suddenly blazing above her head. She did not feel safer because of what she had read, but surprised. Her options were few.

Brandy began to relax as the last drops of the smooth, sweet sherry slid down her throat. She snapped off the lamp on the end table, and curled up under the quilt. Meg stretched out on the floor beside her, coppery head and pale muzzle resting on her paws. As Brandy closed her eyes, she knew Detective Strong, as usual, would not approve of her actions. Neither would John. Maybe if the Sergeant read Lieutenant Henry Hart's journal again, he would recall that the Seminole warrior had placed the artifact in a tobacco pouch before hiding it in a hole of water. That fact would show that the treasure Timothy Hart expected to find had actually been in the cistern and had been stolen. She would lend the detective her notebook. He should make the same deductions she did about the theft and murder. First, she would call and leave him a tip.

But the most priceless missing treasure of the tribe was not an artifact, but a vivacious, black-eyed little girl, worth more than all the relics in all the world's museums. Again Brandy felt the weight of sadness. She could not be as hopeful about finding Daria.

She dropped off to sleep, still thinking of Annie and her grief. About 1:00 A.M. she awoke to a tiny, repetitious sound, Meg's nails clicking on the hardwood floors. The retriever had prowled through the apartment and stationed herself at the back bedroom window. Deep in her throat, she was growling. Brandy slipped off the couch, crept into the bedroom, keeping in the shadows, and peered out into the blackness of a moonless night. She could neither see nor hear anything. At last she trudged back into the living room, Meg trailing after her. Brandy crawled again onto the couch and dozed fitfully until 4:45 A.M. If her conclusions last night were correct, she and Strong would discover the truth tomorrow.

CHAPTER 17

▼

When the alarm woke Brandy, she heard Meg whimper beside the couch and fumbled to turn off the ring. "Hurt your ears, girl? Want to go out-side?" Meg leaped up and danced in place. The joys of dog ownership. Brandy slipped on her scuffs, stepped into Lily Anne's bedroom to pull a terry cloth robe from the closet, and stuffed her apartment key into a pocket. Then she started downstairs with Meg on her leash. The night's rest had reduced the swelling in her ankle and she could walk with more comfort. Cautiously, she opened the rear door into the dark.

She could see no one. If Meg had heard someone downstairs in the night, that person was now gone. The rain had stopped, replaced by a chill wind. Only a faint light glowed in the east. She should be away by dawn. She peered around the corner of the building. The pick-up truck no longer lurked in the side street. While Meg sniffed an inviting patch of grass, Brandy checked out her own Toyota coupe in the parking lot, glad no one involved in the Hart case could identify it. She would be hard to spot and follow.

But as soon as she opened the door to her own apartment, a knot settled in her stomach. Every room had been ransacked—kitchen drawers pulled out, sofa cushions upended, bookcases emptied. Meg stiffened and stalked into the living room, ears lifted. In a daze Brandy marched on into the bedroom. More rummaging had gone on here. Bedclothes were strewn about, dresser drawers opened and the contents spilled, the dressing table moved, even the mattress pushed askew. Brandy sank down on the bed, shaking. The back window had been forced.

What if she had stayed in her apartment? To steady her hands, she gripped the sheets and tried to think rationally. As far as she could tell, nothing was missing. The television, VCR, and radios had not been touched. Brandy had nothing of value except the tobacco pouch, safely upstairs. Clearly, someone believed she had something worth much more. For a moment she thought of calling the Gainesville police immediately. But that would delay her. She had to get away. She would feel safer among people. She needed to be in Tampa, and this afternoon she'd be with Strong.

Brandy dragged from the bedroom closet a small, worn suitcase. She'd leave it in her car as a decoy. Into it she tossed cleaning rags from the utility room and empty aluminum cans from the trash. If someone wanted to steal from her, they'd probably go for the suitcase, hear the rattle, and think they had a box with an artifact. Then tugging on the leash, she stopped Meg from snuffling around the sill and the clothes on the floor, and pulled her toward the bedroom door. Even if Meg recognized the intruder by smell, she couldn't signal that identity to Brandy. She and Meg mustn't disturb anything else. The police might investigate a break-in later, but not this morning. In her kitchen she tossed two daily servings of Meg's dry food into a plastic container, looked around—still with disbelief—and closed and locked her apartment door.

Back upstairs, her mouth still felt dry and her chest tight. She pulled on blue slacks and a white shirt, wrapping a blue scarf at the neckline, and placed the first aid kit with the Seminole pouch under her notebook at the bottom of her canvas bag. She wanted to be ready to hand it to Strong. After she slung a sweater over her arm, she lifted the hanging bag with the gray suit and blouse out of the closet and picked up her dress shoes.

She didn't expect to be alone except on the trip down, and then she'd be on a well-traveled highway. The canvas bag with the pouch wouldn't leave her sight.

No time for breakfast now. She's stop a few miles south, a short distance from the Interstate, in the tiny town of Micanopy. She'd have to kill time. She saw no point in arriving at the Seminole Cultural Center before mid-afternoon when, as she'd told Strong, many involved in the Hart case would gather for tomorrow morning's ceremony. Grif would meet her there, as well as Strong. Tugboat, Melba, and Alma May had probably heard they were going to Tampa and might follow.

The night before Brandy had puzzled over her notes and carefully examined what she'd been told, what she'd seen, even what she had foolishly said herself. Then she had concentrated on all the facts as she relaxed into sleep. In the morning she had reached a conclusion. If her theory proved correct, the monster would be unmasked in Tampa.

Before she left Gainesville, Brandy put in a call to Detective Strong. He wouldn't be in his office at five-thirty in the morning, but someone would take calls for the Sheriff's Office. First she explained to the responding officer that someone had searched her apartment and gave her address. The officer was more surprised by the rest of her message. She gave him a brief summary of the facts she had recorded and made sure the officer wrote down the entire message

"Better have Sergeant Strong ask the Hillsborough County Sheriff's Office to stand by in Tampa," she added. A shiver raced through her. "He may need them. He may wind this whole case up today or tomorrow." Her main suggestion, though, she added in a one word tip, one she hoped might lead the detective to Daria.

By 6:00 A.M. Brandy had loaded her clothing for the trip and settled Meg in the back seat. A half an hour later she drove south down the oak-lined main street of Micanopy, one of Florida's oldest little towns, now a haven of antique and book stores. Her pulse slowed. No one here had ever heard of Timothy Hart. A few clouds shifted in the dim sky, and when she stopped and opened the car door, she drew in the sweet scent of early morning.

Fortunately, one restaurant was already open, catering to early Gainesville commuters or possibly to turkey hunters. She parked where she could watch Meg, tethered to a tree by the window, and between forkfuls of scrambled eggs and sausage, thought about the Seminole chief Micanopy, the town's namesake. Maybe the Indian who had been captured by Lieutenant Henry Hart had served under that chief. The community lay in the same general area as Homosassa, but inland. Back in the car, Brandy patted the box that contained the pouch. One of Micanopy's warriors could've carried it before he killed Alma May Flint's family, before he hid the artifact. Whoever that Indian was, he caused the murder of Timothy Hart more than a century and a half later.

Brandy meandered down the highway, grateful to feel more relaxed than she had in a week. There wasn't much traffic, but she kept the speedometer at fifty. She didn't plan to arrive early...After checking her map, she detoured west to small Dade Battlefield Historic State Park, where she studied the battlefield markers and toured the Visitor Center. Here she learned that a Seminole ambush of 107 soldiers in December of 1835 by Micanopy and his warriors left only three of the soldiers alive, and that event exploded into the Second Seminole War. Brandy was wryly amused that an engagement won by Indians became a "massacre," while another won by the army became a "battle." But the history of the war clarified why the hatred grew so intense among the army, settlers, and besieged Seminoles.

Brandy drove on at a leisurely pace and halted for a late lunch in Dade City, named for the major who had fought and lost to Micanopy's Seminoles. All during the trip she watched her rear view mirror. No out-sized pick-up loomed into view.

When Brandy swung onto Tampa's Orient Road, she checked her watch again. Still only 2:00 P.M. She and Strong had agreed on late afternoon. To kill more time she turned into the only fast food restaurant near the Seminole Reservation, planning to pick up a Tampa newspaper and buy a cup of coffee. As soon as she stepped into the cool interior, she spotted a familiar couple, a short, wiry woman with a pinched face and, seated across the table, a hat rack of a woman in a trim business suit. Melba spoke earnestly, punctuating each remark by brandishing her fork. "We get enough money, I'll be able to leave that awful man for good," she was saying.

Alma May saw Brandy and motioned to Melba to be quiet. "Looks like you got here ahead of that fellow works with bones," she said. "Haven't seen him go by yet. Figure you two got pretty thick back in Homosassa."

Brandy was startled, but not altogether surprised to see them near the Casino. She'd heard Tugboat claim they often came here. She saw no reason to be evasive. "I've come to cover the interment of the mound builder child. It'll be tomorrow morning," she explained. "Also, to visit my husband, who's working in Tampa."

Melba, as always, was more tactful than her friend. "I've got business appointments later this afternoon in Tampa," she said. "But we came early for a little bingo." Thankfully, the meeting was not developing into a confrontation, at least not until Alma May added her final touch. "I reckon them Indians will be here, too. Remember, my house and property is still mine. I never sold it to no one. Won't be a court in the land will hold any different."

Brandy wondered if they were staying at the nearby Seminole hotel. She nodded pleasantly, bought her coffee and newspaper, and carried them out to the car. When she turned into the Seminole Cultural Center grounds a few minutes later, she noted that the parking lot for the casino was packed and nearby a long line of cars waited before a tobacco shop for tax-free cigarettes. Ironic that the whole complex, including a large hotel and restaurant, was here as a happenstance of history.

During the Second Seminole War Tampa's Fort Brooke had provided protection for the settlements on Florida's west coast. In 1979, when a parking garage was built on the site, contractors found 150 Seminole skeletons in the old cemetery. To help the Seminoles properly inter these dead locally, the tribe was awarded a reservation of thirty-eight acres. The Indians built a museum around a memorial to their Fort Brooke dead, then crowded in the gift shop and a profitable bingo palace. Very shrewd.

Brandy was surprised that the tribe had allotted only a half dozen parking spaces in front of the large, tin-roofed gift shop and museum next to the casino. When she pulled in, she didn't see Strong's car or Grif's van, but felt a wave of relief that she also didn't see Tugboat's pick-up. She had completed the first phase of her plan successfully. Apparently, she had given Tugboat the slip. She wondered if Grif had. She also wondered exactly when Strong would arrive. He'd suggested late afternoon. She checked her watch—2:30 P.M. It would be foolish to wait out here for the detective. In spite of her efforts, she had arrived early.

Brandy laid her locked suitcase with its phony contents on the back seat, partly covered by an old jacket, as if she had tried to conceal it. She knew she might invite a broken window, but the risk seemed to be the cost of trapping her burglar, if not a killer. She sat for a moment, wishing she knew how to reach Annie, but she'd never asked for the Seminole couple's Tampa address or phone number. Anyway, Annie might not want to be bothered. She would have many supportive friends here. Brandy reached back and petted her patient golden retriever. Perhaps she could beg Meg's way in and ask to fill her water bowl. She could always count on Meg to behave.

At the entrance two totem poles with carvings of Seminoles in turbans and leggings towered by the door, along with a larger-than-life statue of a warrior sculpted from wood. The three stood beside soft drink dispensers. The large American flag decorating the window was embossed with a Seminole on horseback. Two cultures side by side, but separate. With Meg's shortened leash gripped in one hand and carrying the water bowl in the other, Brandy opened the gift shop door and stepped into a large room with a concrete floor. Long tables cluttered with Indian beads and jewelry filled the interior space, displaying palmetto fiber dolls, bright, multi-colored skirts and children's clothing, and racks of Seminole postcards. The walls were hung with large oil portraits. One she recognized as Fishhawk, resplendent in Medicine Man regalia, belted scarlet tunic and oval, scarlet hat decorated with a feather. She remembered how he had tried to cleanse Tiger Tail Island of its witch, how he had apparently failed.

The only other person in the room, a dark-skinned middle-aged woman with a long black braid down her back, stood at a counter near the door to the outside exhibit. Brandy had again expected more visitors. She approached the clerk.

"I'm Brandy O'Bannon, a newspaper reporter. I'm meeting Fish-hawk—Mr. Franklin Pine—here," she began.

The woman looked at her gravely with black, expressive eyes. Like Fish-hawk, she gave nothing away, "I've been expecting you," she said. "The reservation police were contacted by the Sheriff's Office. I'm told a detective from Citrus County is meeting you here as well."

"I'm working on a story about Fishhawk Pine and his wife," Brandy said. "And trying to help them."

The clerk glanced down at Meg and frowned. "Mrs. Pine called, too. She said to let you look at everything here. They'll see you tomorrow morning."

"I don't have a place to leave my dog." Brandy followed the clerk's gaze. "I'd like to get her some water in the rest room. She's well-behaved. May she stay?" The woman pursed her lips and looked again at the retriever. Brandy didn't wait for her answer. She hurried with Meg into the women's room, emerged with the water, and set it down for Meg.

"While I'm waiting," she said, "I'd like to pay the entrance fee and see the exhibits, especially the museum." It would have an attendant, and surely more customers. She glanced down meaningfully at Meg, who wagged her fluffy tail, rumbled a low, friendly greeting, and gazed up with what seemed like hopeful eyes.

"I don't know," the woman said. "Not supposed to. We've got animals here."

"I'll keep my dog on a tight leash. She won't bother any of them, honestly. Otherwise, I can't go in myself."

The woman frowned. "The docent needs to leave early today. If no one else is here, he'll lock up early."

Brandy took her answer as a "yes." She pulled her billfold from her bag, paid the $5.00 entrance fee, and added an extra two dollars for her pet. "I won't be long," she said. Silently, the cashier rang up the sale and unfastened a chain across the doorway.

As soon as Brandy stepped on the wooden walkway that bridged a narrow stream, several large white geese cackled loudly and strutted about, flapping their wings. Meg cringed and took refuge behind Brandy. "They're watchdogs like you, silly," she said and yanked the retriever on past. "They won't hurt you, but they do make a racket."

Before them rose a thatched presentation area and stage, attended only by a few wandering roosters and hens. Meg lunged at a Road Island Red and sent it squawking, but Brandy tugged her back onto the path and coiled the leash even more snugly around her wrist. To the right lay a small, fenced lagoon, where a number of medium-sized alligators lounged on an island, and beyond them, she saw a cage of snakes, mainly rattlers and fat water moccasins. Several almost dry, stale-smelling streams laced the grounds, spanned by little bridges. This was not Disney World—no manicured hedges or velvet lawns here. Mostly the grass was weedy, the banana plants, and ferns rank, the water covered with greenish scum, all intended, she supposed, to remain in its natural state.

Brandy paused under an oak, fringed with Spanish moss, then walked on past a stand of cabbage palms, motionless and untrimmed under the partly cloudy sky. No one else appeared in the area. To her left, beyond the open air auditorium, lay the ceremonial grounds, its many chickees vacant, and before her an overturned, thirty foot cypress canoe ringed by broad, green elephant ears and still under construction. She glanced around in vain for Fishhawk. One of his jobs was to demonstrate canoe making. But all was silent. Across a stream stood the octagonal museum, the burial place for the Indian bones from Fort Brooke.

She hurried over another bridge and inside the museum, relieved to find an elderly white man in attendance. He explained that the building was divided into eight areas like spokes of a wheel, representing the eight contemporary Seminole clans. One was designated Fishhawk's, the Panther Clan, the clan that included the tribe's medicine men, named for an animal that was fierce, secretive, and stealthy. The image fit. Brandy wondered if he came here often, if he contributed items from his own family for the exhibits.

In the center of the room the memorial itself dominated the scene. A copper-colored Seminole man's head rose from the gnarled roots of a cypress tree, a turban tied over shoulder-length hair, his expression unyielding. The Indians who remained at the end of the war retreated to the Everglades and never surrendered. But the warrior who had killed the Flints, who hoped to retrieve the artifact for his own medicine man, had been deported to Oklahoma. None ever came back. Brandy stared at the platform on which the memorial rested. Beneath it, cypress planks reached out in a circle. Under these lay the 150 burials. She had a sudden idea, although she would have to ask permission.

In Fishhawk's clan enclave hung colorful shoulder shawls, patchwork skirts, elaborate turbans, cloth tobacco or shot pouches studded with beads, but none of deerskin. The one she found must be unique, although a glass case held a deerskin medicine bundle tied with fiber. Brandy recognized turtle shell rattles used at the Green Corn Dance, a sifting basket, and a sofki ladle, like those she had seen at Fishhawk's camp. Beside an enormous drum with a head of animal hide stood a portrait of the ferocious warrior Osceola, driving a knife into a broken treaty. She didn't doubt that Fishhawk could be as determined. His camp had been authentic. He would fight to preserve this heritage.

Brandy turned to the docent, standing patiently by the door. "Does Franklin Pine, the medicine man Fishhawk, come in here often? Has he donated material?"

The man removed his glasses, rubbed them with a white handkerchief, and looked at the Panther Clan wing. "Sometimes. He gave us some things that belonged to his grandfather, as I recall. I'm sure he'd like to give more, but there's a big push to collect exhibits for the newer, bigger Ah-tah-thi-ki Museum off Alligator Alley. I expect he'd give whatever else of interest he has to it." Brandy nodded. Including a valuable treasure carried by a Seminole fighter during the Second Seminole War.

She stood silent, her gaze drawn once more to the Seminole carving in the building's center. This is where the Safety Harbor child's bones should await burial tomorrow morning, not in the rear of a van, in a hotel room, or under the counter of a commercial gift shop. These were probably her distant relatives, and they presented a fitting, Native American memorial.

The docent eyed Brandy and Meg, smiled, and rattled his keys. He had already kept the museum open past the time he had intended to leave. Time to go. And time to find Strong, Grif Hackett, and the Safety Harbor remains. Brandy thanked the docent and rushed along the path that circled back to the gift shop. She passed a sleeping black bear in a chain link cage, a restless panther in a large enclosure with two chain link sections, and in a second lagoon, an alligator so colossal that she had to stop in awe. According to the sign on the fence, the reptile stretched almost fifteen feet. Old Joe. He sprawled on a small island, his immense, jagged jaws open to the fading sunlight. But on she hurried. She must not forget why she was here, not forget her plan.

Brandy burst into the gift shop, Meg in tow, in time to see Grif standing at the counter, introducing himself to the cashier. "I have Indian bone relics to deliver to Fishhawk for proper burial," he said. Brandy remembered Fishhawk had called the Center.

Brandy signaled to him, then stopped at a distance from the clerk beside a tall, $60 Seminole doll. "Were you followed this time?" she asked when he joined her.

"I didn't see Grapple, if that's what you mean." Although Grif shrugged, he seemed on edge. The custody of the bones seemed finally to affect him, too.

Brandy moved closer. "Tugboat may come and cause trouble. I saw him near my apartment early last night. Later, while I was away, my apartment was ransacked. He'll know where we are. People in Homosassa talk. Did you leave the Safety Harbor bone relics in your van?"

He glanced toward the door. "The van's locked and the box is covered. I can take it to my room for the night."

"Why not bring it in here? You owe it to Fishhawk to keep it safe. I don't think Tugboat or Alma May would hesitate to break into your car or the hotel room. He was probably the one who got into my apartment last night. They're expecting someone to smuggle something out of Homosassa."

Grif frowned and drummed his fingers on the counter. "I've got to reach Fishhawk, and I've got to go out to eat. Guess I could leave it locked in here. There's an office behind the cashier." He nodded at a closed door a few feet from the clerk, then strode toward the parking lot. When he returned, he carried the container wrapped in a black, plastic bag, not a very dignified casket.

"Fishhawk and I have to make arrangements," he said to the clerk. "I'm checking into the tribe's motel next door."

"The bones will be safer locked here," Brandy said.

Grif gave her a sharp glance. "No one touches it," he said. "I promised Fishhawk. Not until time for the burial. I'll get it to him then. The tribe has its own casket."

Brandy glanced back at the cashier and realized she was staring at them, that she must have overheard. The clerk gave a nervous shake of her head, a startled look in her dark eyes. Grif hesitated, still unsure, walked to the outside door, peered out, then seemed to make a reluctant decision and walked with the box toward the counter. Brandy heard liquid slosh inside and realized Grif preserved the bones as she did the pouch, by keeping them wet. When she toured the Indian mound, he had explained that the skeletal remains had endured because of moisture in the high water table.

He held the box close to his chest and stepped up to the cashier. The woman took a step back. She was an educated Seminole living in the white man's world, but the cultures collided about bodies and bones. They still held an aura of danger and possible death. "I want to lock them securely in the office here," he said. "I have reason to think someone might disturb them at the hotel." He looked at Brandy. "Miss O'Bannon here's with me. Her newspaper story that will give publicity to the Indian Village, museum, and gift shop. We're meeting Fishhawk here in the morning." Brandy nodded.

The clerk bit her lip. These two had come in, acting as if they owned the shop, and now they wanted to store bones within a few feet of her. It wasn't quite time for closing at 5:00 P.M. But Brandy and Grif had evoked the names of Fishhawk and Annie Pine, powerful forces at the Center. And she had to consider the requests of the Seminole police and the Sheriff's Office, who were cooperating with these two. The woman frowned, her eyes on the box, her fingers twisting a scarf on the counter. Then she rose from her chair before the cash register, turned slowly and unlocked the office door. Grif darted in, and Brandy watched him slip the box far back under the desk. "Be sure to lock the door right away," he said. "I'll be at the hotel until I can give it to Fishhawk in the morning." He touched Brandy's arm. "You want to go with me?"

Brandy shook her head. "I'm committed to going into town tonight."

The woman continued standing, troubled, while Grif walked back outside and disappeared. Brandy edged closer and spoke softly. "I bet you'd like to have those bones moved completely out of the gift shop area. I understand. It's your tradition to avoid any part of a body or a skeleton. Until time for the ceremony, we could store them in the museum beside the memorial. They'd be near the other Indians' burial place. The museum's always securely locked. I'd take them there for you."

A look of relief washed over the woman's face. "I'm sure Dr. Hackett would agree they'd be safer there," Brandy added. "He just didn't think of it. All I need is the key to unlock the museum building. I'd be careful to lock it again. I could give it to Fishhawk first thing in the morning,"

Brandy waited while the woman hesitated. No one else had appeared in the shop. Finally she lifted a great ring of keys from a pocket in her patchwork skirt. "Be sure it goes to Mr. Pine," she murmured. "Don't wait until tomorrow. He usually checks the animals later. If I'm gone, give it to him before you leave."

Brandy dropped the key ring into the canvas bag looped by its straps over her arm. The clerk gestured toward a phone on the counter. "I almost forgot. I took a message for a you about half an hour ago." Alarmed, Brandy halted on her way toward the office. "A Sergeant Strong. Said he'd been delayed."

Brandy's pulse quickened. Today's first stroke of bad luck. "The best laid plans o' mice and men…" she began, but the clerk had already opened the office door and was unhooking the chain across the doorway to the outside exhibit. "Better hurry," she said.

Brandy smiled reassuringly. "You go on home. No one else is here. I'll take care of everything." As she reached under the desk and carefully picked up the box, she saw the hands of a wall clock pointed to 4:50 P.M. She heard the clerk open the door to the parking area and quickly close it behind her, glad to escape before the Tupperware box was carried through the room again. The woman would be relieved when the bones and Brandy were gone in the morning.

Brandy had not expected to be alone, but her task would take only a few minutes.

CHAPTER 18

▼

With Meg trotting on a leash behind her, Brandy clutched the box to her breast and marched through the door into the exhibit area. She didn't think of the black wrapped Tupperware container as potentially deadly, as the clerk did, but it made her uneasy. When the long-dead child's bones were properly buried among her Seminoles relatives, however distant, Brandy would be relieved. Now she felt a shiver of anxiety. The docent would be gone, and the clerk had left early. Brandy had not factored those departures into her plan. Until Strong arrived, she was alone.

Again the guardian geese erupted, cackling and flapping. She pushed her way past them, holding Meg's leash wrapped around her wrist, and started down the path toward the museum. All she needed to do was unlock the door, deposit the box beside the memorial, and scamper back to the gift shop to wait for Strong. Carefully, Brandy detached the key marked *Museum* from the others on the heavy ring and held it tightly as she passed the first alligator lagoon and crossed to the building itself.

She had managed to unlock the door and push it open when the geese again began their clamor. Brandy had read that Seminoles, hidden in the brush, learned they were being followed from the sudden flight of water birds. The geese could be sending her the same message. Thrusting the key ring back into her bag, she spun around and looked behind her. Beside the outdoor auditorium, a familiar massive figure loomed up on the walkway, moving fast. In a sudden panic, she shoved the box inside the entrance under a table, tossed the museum key after it, and slammed the door. It would lock automatically. She hoped the surrounding water would keep the precious little bones from shattering. Brandy wanted no one to desecrate the memory of that child any further. Then she wheeled around, intent on snaking past the lagoon and into the gift shop. Maybe Tugboat was looking for someone else. He might think Fishhawk or Grif had Hart's artifacts.

As if in slow motion she saw the *Grapple Guides* tee shirt, the tangled black beard, the mass of blue tattoos on arms like oak branches, the small eyes in the fleshy face. He spotted her at once and was striding toward her. Brandy had almost forgotten the fishing guide's brute force. She stiffened, for the moment paralyzed, reeling between a frantic urge to escape and the hopeless task of reasoning with Tugboat Grapple. Grif had gone to find Fishhawk, no one else was on the premises. The Casino patrons couldn't help her. Above the clatter and blare of the games, no one would hear her cries. At the back of the exhibit area she glimpsed a wide, wooden gate, probably to allow trucks access, but it was closed. She had never heard a sound from that direction.

Even as Brandy turned and bolted toward the gift shop, she heard Tugboat's heavy boots behind her. He grabbed her from the rear, his thick fingers sinking into her shoulders. Meg yelped and shrunk down on her haunches. He ripped the canvas bag from her arm. While she struggled to free herself, he shook it upside down, then dropped it. Keys for her car and the animal cages rattled onto the pavement. As he bent to fumble among keys and lipstick, compact, pens, note pad, pocket calendar, and address book, his grip loosened. Brandy quickly stooped and clutched the empty bag, felt the first aid kit caught in a deep side pocket, and sidled toward the bridge. But Tugboat was quick for his size. Reaching up, he wrenched her arms behind her.

"What do you want with me?" Brandy screamed. She still held the valuable tobacco pouch. Even Indian bones brought a price on the macabre scavengers' market. But he must think she had something more.

"Damned little thief!" he hissed. "Been stealing from ole' Alma May, have you? You and your damn boyfriend!" Somewhere in the back of

Brandy's mind she wondered if the two women were here, too, trolling for blood.

"I found your damned suitcase! Think I wouldn't get it open? Think ole' Tugboat's a damn idiot?" The decoy. It hadn't fooled Tugboat long.

Brandy's breath came in ragged gasps. Meg cringed and backed away as far as the taut leash would allow and bared her teeth. A good tracker, not an attacker. Tugboat drew back a heavy cowboy boot and kicked the retriever in the ribs. The dog yelped again and struggled frantically, but Tugboat had pinned Brandy's arms. She gritted her teeth. "Let the dog go! You've got a dog yourself! Don't hurt mine!"

He grinned, unmoved, his whiskey breath again on her cheek. She was pressed against his sweat-stained tee shirt. "Let's see what else you got, you little bitch." Still holding her with vise-like fingers, he snatched the canvas bag again. This time the first aid box dropped to the walkway. "Reckon I need to check that out." He grinned and thrust it into a sagging jacket pocket. "I just bet you got something else hid, something you wouldn't be carrying around in no bag." Again he stooped, swept up the ring of zoo keys.

"Now what to do with you? Maybe find a place to lock you up a spell. A place you can't dig out of this time. Might help you remember where that other thing is." His gaze shifted from her to the building and then the cages.

Brandy registered every detail around her. She was aware of the black bear, hunched asleep in the corner of his pen, of the panther slinking from a smaller cage into a larger, saw it stop to stare at her, saw it stretch its sleek head forward and gnaw the tufts of grass between the chain link fence, saw its long pointed teeth, saw the ripple of its muscles under the tawny skin. She was conscious of the late afternoon chill, of gathering clouds, and wondered if Grif had seen Tugboat's pick-up in the parking lot before he locked the box in the office—and yet all the time she focused on the wracking pain in her arms and the hovering strength of Tugboat.

"I don't have anything else!" Her heart hammered in her chest.

Tugboat squeezed the cage keys in one fat fist. When she swiveled under his hand, pain shot through her shoulder. His eyes turned toward the panther cage. "Reckon that ole' cat wouldn't let you claw your way outta his cage. He'd do the clawing hisself." Again he grinned at his own wit. He shook the key ring, focused on finding the right one. They were numbered, a corresponding number on each cage. When he pulled her forward, she tried to brace herself and lean backward. Her effort amused him. He laughed, jerked her arms together, shoved her to her knees, then dragged her forward. From his second guffaw, she knew he had found the right one. Suddenly the panther held the menace of a tiger. It leapt onto a high perch, baffled by the noise of the scuffle and the clank of the keys. Behind Brandy, Meg had struggled to her feet. When she began to bark, the great cat snarled.

Like a faint sound in a distant world, Brandy heard the geese again. She hoped that Tugboat didn't understand what their cackling meant. She could not turn to look. He had managed to hold her arms and insert the key in the padlock. His words came through gritted teeth. "Reckon a close look at this ole' cat will help your memory."

Above the racket of the geese, footsteps drummed over the wooden bridge, running. "Let her go!"

Brandy recognized the voice. Grif bounded down the path, his face twisted in rage. "I thought I saw your truck! I knew you were here." Effortlessly, he closed the gap between them. His voice dropped to a murderous calm. "The Seminoles have a police force, even here."

Startled, Tugboat relaxed his grip. Brandy sagged forward. Grif was in Tugboat's face now, his tone flat and harsh. "The police are on their way, and they're armed. You'd better get out of here fast."

Tugboat dropped the keys, grunted, and released Brandy's arm. Before she could stop herself, Brandy cried out. She didn't want to lose the tobacco pouch. "He's stealing! Check his coat pocket!" Not a smart thing to say, she quickly realized. She wanted to save the tobacco pouch for Detective Strong. Now, as Tugboat turned away, Grif grabbed the back of his jacket and yanked it off. The fishing guide paused. "I was just scaring her!" he panted. A look of panic flashed across his heavy face. He whirled and sprinted toward the door, his boots pounding over the bridge. The back door banged open and slammed shut.

Brandy stood shaken and breathing hard. She had not expected the battle with Tugboat, but she was even less prepared for Grif's reaction now. He stepped closer, his fury undiminished. He spat out the words "The office inside is open! The clerk's gone. Where's the box of bones? What else have you got?"

This scene was not in her plan. She rubbed her chafed wrists, stalling, and bent to pat Meg, who still trembled at her feet. When she hesitated, he picked up the keys, then took a firm hold on her arm, his fingers biting into her flesh. A chill ran through her. She'd just been through this. She remembered how he had frog-marched Tugboat out of a restaurant.

"You've got something that belongs to me!" His words fell like stones. "Where is it?" She had seen Grif angry before. Not this angry. Why did everyone think she had stolen a treasure? Was it because she had been in the well?

She squirmed in his grasp. "All I've got is in that first aid kit. Take a look. It may be valuable, but it should go to the Sheriff's Office. It may be evidence. You said the Seminole police were coming."

"Don't be stupid. That was to fool Tugboat."

He let go of her arm long enough to open the small metal box, look inside. She made her eyes wide, innocent. Maybe she could reason with him. This was an educated man. "There's a murder investigation, remember? Look, Grif. After all that's happened, let Jeremiah Strong handle everything from now on. He'll be here soon. He'll find whatever is missing. The box is safe. Let's just go back into the shop and wait."

In Homosassa, even at the Gainesville museum, Hackett had been smooth, assured, seductive. Now his electric blue eyes grew icy. She had felt certain they could. He thrust his face forward. "Think you can fool me like that big dumb ass? I'm not giving anything to the Sheriff's Office." Again he gripped her arm. "You're going to tell me where it is. You've been a spy for the Sheriff's Office all along. You couldn't just go along with me, have a little fun. You had to go on your own search."

What did he mean? Brandy was too frightened to think.

His voice sank. "Tell me where you've stashed it, and tell me now."

Brandy managed to squeak, "Or else?" Mistake. Bad mistake.

Grif glanced down at Meg. The golden retriever lifted her head, growled, and again bared her teeth.

"Or else you have a choice." He dragged Brandy to the rock wall, topped by a chain link fence that ringed Old Joe's pond and pressed her against the rough stone by the padlocked gate. Before she could stop him, he snapped the scarf from her neck and knotted her wrists together. When she let out a cry, he slipped off his belt, wrapped it around her head, forced it between her lips, buckled it to the metal gatepost, and drew it tight. She gagged, tasted the sweaty leather, felt her heart thump against her ribs. When he tore the leash from her arm, the sound from her throat was more moan than scream.

Before them on the lagoon's center island, the fifteen-foot alligator shifted his bulk. His narrow eyes flicked open. Another monster, Brandy thought numbly, on another island. Another Caliban. Grif rattled through the key ring, searching for matching numbers. Then he fitted a large key into the lock and twisted. The padlock sprang apart. In an instant Grif swept a rock up in one hand and pitched it hard over the fence. It thudded against the alligator's thick, scaly hide. Old Joe let out a hiss like a steam engine. His giant body slithered forward, splashed into the rank-smelling water. The long, gray-green head lifted among the pond scum, jaws gaping.

Meg hesitated, retreated a few paces, ears flattened, but was unwilling to abandon Brandy. Grif bent down and with both arms began to scoop up the trembling retriever. Meg yelped from the bruised ribs and lashed out with her legs. She snapped at his hand, struck flesh, drew blood, but Grif held on.

"Dinner time for Old Joe," he breathed. "One gulp and your dog's hamburger. Gators just love dogs." Brandy knew how alligators pulled prey under the water, rolled until they drowned them, then devoured them. They found dogs especially tasty. "Give it up," he said, "or your dog's dinner." A knot of horror rose in Brandy's throat. Frantic, she raised both wrists toward the belt and jerked her head up and down.

Grif's lips crooked upward. He dropped the retriever, who lay for a few seconds, the breath knocked out of her. After he forced the leather from

Brandy's teeth, she gasped, thinking wildly, he must mean the bone box. "In the museum!" While she tried not to vomit, he gave her an ugly smile and shoved the belt back across her mouth. Meg lunged at him as he turned toward the museum and caught his shirt in her teeth, but he kicked her away, grabbed her leash, and looped it over the metal post. It pulled hard against her neck. She whimpered while Grif dashed for the door, twisted the knob, held up the keys and flicked through them, trying one after another. Brandy strained against the leather band, but she made no sound. He would soon realize the key was gone, that she had somehow tricked him. He still could count on Old Joe.

In a few minutes Grif turned toward her, the muscles in his cheek twitching. "I can do without the belt," he said. "You and your mutt will stay right here, until I find someone who's got the right key. You're good at hiding things. Now it's the museum key. I'll tell them the kid's bones are in there. You'd better hope someone gives me another key."

Meg half hung from the post, twisting, her angry yelps muffled. She could choke, straining to break free. Already the sky was darkening and long shadows fell across the lagoon and the bridge. Strong would never know to look for her here. Tears blinded her. If she had stayed out of the Hart case, she would not be in such danger. Fishhawk would bury the Safety Harbor child's little bones, as planned; Meg would be safe; John would not be angry. Strong would discover who poisoned Hart without her help. She sniffled, then remembered: Daria would still be missing.

Grif still stood, making one last, futile try with the last key. Once he left to find the right one, how long would he be gone? What would he do to her when he returned and opened the museum? He spared her and Meg now, in case he needed her again. But after that?

Brandy's heightened senses registered a strange sound—a scratching. It came from the tall back gate, a noise like a door being dragged open over dirt. There must be a shed there for tools and animal rations. She was afraid to cry out. Meg was still in danger. She certainly was. She coughed as loudly as she could, shuffled her feet, and scraped them against the cement walk. Meg stopped battling the leash and growled.

Brandy strained to turn her head and caught a flicker of movement at the gate. It opened a crack. A figure slipped from the growing shadows. She heard a flurry of quiet footsteps, and a man darted forward. For a moment she recognized the set face, the graceful movements. Fishhawk. She had a glimpse of the fury in his eyes. His long arm flashed above the other man's head. A large wrench fell with a smashing blow, and Hackett crumpled on the walkway. Blood seeped through the tousled blond hair Brandy had once thought so attractive. The Seminole must have been watching. She slumped forward, lungs bursting, supported only by the belt.

Fishhawk lifted a whistle from his pocket and blew a shrill alarm. Then he moved toward Brandy, unfastened the belt, and released Meg. Brandy's legs buckled, and she held to the fence while Meg crouched, shaking and wheezing beside her. Brandy's voice came in tiny gusts. "Thank God you got here." She sat down heavily on the pavement.

But Fishhawk himself did not look pleased. Rescuing her did not seem to bring joy to anyone. "A Seminole police officer will be here in a minute," he said. He stared down at Hackett. His eyes showed the menace and contempt Brandy had seen earlier at his island camp. "Figured you two were in cahoots." He shook his head. "Maybe you were. Maybe this was a falling out of thieves." His words startled her. Tugboat had believed she was Grif's ally in some scheme, too.

"God, no!" Her voice quavered. "I only wanted to find the truth."

The Seminole gazed at her, pain now in his eyes. "Maybe you did. Maybe you found some of the truth. It hasn't helped anyone."

Head down, Brandy crawled to the spot where Grif had dropped the first aid kit with its Seminole tobacco pouch, lifted it in gentle hands, and sat on the walkway cradling it in her lap, while Meg crept to her side. When Hackett groaned and moved an arm, the retriever growled, and Brandy pushed herself farther from him. She didn't yet trust her legs to stand.

She scarcely noticed the thick set police officer in black pants and light blue shirt who came running through the truck entrance. He spoke in low tones to Fishhawk, then knelt beside the archaeologist and felt his pulse.

"You really clobbered him, Pine," the officer said. "But looks like he'll live. Lucky for you." Dimly Brandy heard an ambulance siren on the street outside.

"He had the woman tied up. He was trying to get into the museum."

The officer turned and stared at her. "You all right, Miss?"

Brandy forced an answer. "I'm not really hurt. Shaken, maybe." After an accident she'd often read that someone was "badly shaken." From the ache in her quivering muscles, she knew exactly what the phrase meant now. As medics trotted through the gift shop door, the officer directed them to Hackett. Brandy set down the kit. With both hands, she grasped the rough wall beside the alligator pit, then clung to the chain link fence, and pulled herself to her feet. The medics hoisted a litter that held a limp Grif Hackett.

Fishhawk waited, unmoving, where he had stood since he struck the blow. As the medics were leaving, he stepped over to the sleeping bear's cage, flipped open a small door at the bottom, slid out the water dish, and refilled it from a nearby spigot, his movements mechanical. Numbly, Brandy remembered that the clerk had said Fkshhawk would check the animals after she left. That was why he had come. He repeated the service for the panther, now aroused and pacing back and forth between its two enclosures, ears flattened. The beasts that she had feared might be her death had saved her. Fishhawk ignored Old Joe, whose long, furrowed back gradually submerged, leaving only his eyes staring out from their scaly knots above the water.

Brandy turned from the giant alligator to Fishhawk. "The clerk inside said I could put the Safety Harbor relics in the museum until morning," she said. "Beside the memorial. It seemed more fitting. That way they won't be left in the gift shop. When I saw I was going to be attacked, I threw the key into the museum and locked the door."

Wordlessly Fishhawk reached down, picked up the key ring from the walkway where it had fallen and, after stuffing the scattered contents of her canvas bag back into it, handed the bag to her. Then he trudged silently back down the path, past the geese, and into the gift shop. While Meg trailed behind, dragging, her leash, Brandy retrieved the first aid kit and limped after him in the failing afternoon light. "I should tell you," she said, "that Detective Strong promised to meet me here soon."

Fishhawk gave an uninterested grunt, switched on the overhead light, and disappeared into the office, leaving the door open. Better take care of Meg before I collapse, Brandy thought. She picked up the retriever's dish, and shuffled out to the car to fill it with dry dog food. When she led the bruised retriever back inside, Fishhawk moved in behind her and locked the outside door. They walked into the gift shop, past Fishhawk's resplendent portrait, and into the barren little office, where she found herself a bench.

Fishhawk himself sagged into a chair behind a wooden desk under a window, his bronzed face like a house with closed shutters. If he had any further concern about her, those vacant eyes did not show it. Clearly, not a time to talk. She set Meg's supper on the floor beside a straight chair and took a seat. After her dinner, the retriever flopped on the floor beside Brandy, pale gold muzzle on her front paws, exhausted. It seemed like a full day since Brandy first strolled into the Cultural Center. It had only been four hours.

In silence they waited for the detective. Strong hadn't disappointed her yet. He said he would be here. She frowned. If he had been on time, her plan would have worked. She wouldn't have been attacked, twice. The child might not still be in danger. They might even have the treasure. In the bleak setting of the small office, facing a stoic, unbending Fishhawk, Brandy felt crushed. She had not meant the day to unfold in the way it had. If the Sergeant arrived now, he might be too late. She slumped on the bench, head down, hands hanging between her knees. Occasionally she bent to rumple one of Meg's ears.

The attacks at the Center showed that she was either a suspect or a danger to both Tugboat and Hackett. Melba and Alma May might lurk in the background, ready to pounce or already conducting some related, clandestine business. But nothing yet proved who had the treasure, who killed Timothy Hart, or—most important—what had happened to the little Seminole girl.

Fishhawk stirred and dropped his head in his hands. He muttered more to himself than to Brandy, "I've lost any hope of finding Daria now."

CHAPTER 19

▼

After what seemed like hours, but according to her watch was only forty minutes, Brandy heard a car pull to a stop in a gift shop parking space. When headlights flashed in the window and shut off, Fishhawk stiffened, waiting. The front door rattled and then opened. Someone had a key. Brandy's heart lifted. Could be Sergeant Strong. The reservation police officer would surely give him one. Voices echoed through the large room, a man's and woman's, followed by footsteps. Fishhawk rose, still tense. Brandy hovered close behind him.

Next came the most welcome sound that Brandy had ever heard—a child's piping treble. Fishhawk leaped toward the door, eyes suddenly bright and alive. An excited little voice called, "Go, go!" Small feet pattered over the gift shop floor.

Brandy recognized Annie's almost hysterical laugh. Fishhawk lunged through the office door, Brandy close behind. Past the long counters Daria toddled, coming toward her father. Annie hurried after her. The little girl's usually neat hair was uncombed, her shirt untucked, her overalls smudged with dirt. Chubby arms reached out. "Da, Da!" While Fishhawk swept the little girl up in his arms, Brandy ran to Annie with tears in her eyes and hugged her.

"She's safe!" Annie cried. "Thank God. Only a little dirty. We didn't take time to clean her up." She smiled and brushed her glistening eyes with a tissue.

"It's what I prayed for," Brandy said, and watched Fishhawk's little family scramble into the office, laughing and talking at once. When Daria began to tug on the retriever's fluffy tail, Brandy called Meg to come outside the room, then knelt in the doorway and held out her arms. The little girl sidled toward her, gave her a searching look with those dark, long-lashed eyes, then wheeled and trotted back to her mother. Brandy stood. For a moment she longed to feel Daria's warm breath on her own face again, as she had on the island trail, but Daria's mother and daddy were who mattered now. This was a family affair. She shouldn't intrude.

"Don't go home just yet, please, Mr. Pine," Brandy called. "The Sergeant may want to see you."

Fishhawk stood up beside the desk. "Tell him I've got to go back to the island tomorrow and close up the chickee. I hauled our provisions to Tampa today."

Brandy turned away and finally noticed the tall figure standing quietly beside a display of palmetto dolls and patchwork skirts.

The detective bestowed on Brandy one of his rare grins. "Chassahowitzka," he said. Brandy nodded. She had called the Sheriff's Office before she drove out of Gainesville, and the detailed message she left for Strong had surprised the deputy. "Chassahowitzka" was the final, one-word tip. "I owe you for the head's up," Strong added. "Baby was in a beat-up trailer, way out in the National Wildlife Refuge. Protection for the whooping cranes kept us from making a thorough search earlier."

"I began to suspect that's where she'd be. Who was with her?"

"That's the bad part. No one. Whoever took her had gone. We found car tracks, remnants of food for someone besides the little girl. Poor little thing was drugged. We're so late because we had to take her straight to Seven Rivers Hospital for a check-up. The doctors got the stuff out of her system. A tranquillizer. I don't know if the plan was ever to tell the parents where she was. Annie left a message for Fishhawk at their apartment."

Even in this joyous moment, Strong remembered his Bible. He had a clear vision of punishment for Daria's kidnapper. "It were better for him that a millstone were hanged about his neck, and he cast into the sea, than he should offend one of these little ones.'"

Brandy smiled, agreeing. "And where's Tugboat and the others?"

"Soon the fishing guide, his wife, and her friend Mrs. Flint will all be guests of the Sheriff's Office. Seems some very old Indian pots were stashed in Mrs. Grapple's trunk at the Casino, mixed in with a few spoons and pewter ware from the plantation site. The women are people of interest to the law. Deputies will soon have Grapple, and Hackett's still under guard at the hospital. All the vehicles will get a good going over."

"Good. I'll sleep easier tonight." Brandy felt sure the deputies would make a thorough search of the pots. She wondered if they would also check Fishhawk's utensils and provisions. The treasure was still missing. She fixed the detective with an anxious gaze. "You will stay until tomorrow morning, won't you? That's when the funeral service and burial take place."

Strong glanced through the open office door at the happy mother and child. "I'll be here overnight. The Seminole police officer said you tangled with Grapple and Hackett. I need to talk to both. Guess you didn't figure on being attacked. It's lucky you're still standing there." He looked toward Annie. "Also Mrs. Pine asked for my help in the morning, before the funeral ceremony. I need to substitute for Dr. Hackett."

The sergeant looked exhausted. His usual erect posture sagged, and his eyes were gray with fatigue. Brandy stared out into the brief Florida twilight, beyond the bridge and lagoon, in the direction of the museum.

"I see," she said. "In the morning someone needs to collect the box of bones and transport it. I imagine the Seminoles had rather not handle it, at least until the burial. You have suitable authority." She lowered her voice, almost to a whisper. "I hope you'll get some rest tonight. If we're lucky, everything may fall in place tomorrow. We may finally see the 'thing of darkness,' the thing that frightened the Seminole warrior over a hundred years ago, the thing that caused Daria's ordeal and Hart's death."

*   *   *   *

About 7:00 P.M. that evening Brandy pulled into the driveway of a Victorian house with a second floor turret and a wrap-around porch. The fragrance of confederate jasmine hung in the air. John had chosen to rent a small apartment in this old restored home. No sterile honeycomb of an apartment complex for him, but this white, three-story frame house on the fringe of a historic neighborhood.

She felt wound tight, her heart like a fist. A few minutes ago John had sounded non-committal when she called him on her cell, but he had said, "Come on. I've got a pot of vegetable soup on the stove." John was in his remote phase, still hurt and backing way from possible pain, but civil. He had not forgotten about Grif's motel room.

When Brandy told him briefly what had happened at the Cultural Center, his response was a muted, "Glad you weren't injured—this time."

Now she stood on the porch and rang the bell, a symptom of what had happened in their relationship. She had no key. Her task would not be easy, and she felt as wrung out as Sergeant Strong. John opened the door in jeans and tee shirt, bare-footed, then stepped back and brushed long fingers over his mustache. A nervous gesture. He, too, was like a coiled spring. In the living room Brandy recognized a few pieces of furniture they had bought or made together—a glass-fronted secretary with a display of unusual rocks, a well-worn leather couch, a book case of bricks and boards. From the CD player came the strains of a Bach fugue.

"The boyfriend turned out to be dangerous, so you came back," John said, turning down the music. His mouth took a wry twist and he held his back rigid. "Any port in a storm, I see."

From the tiny kitchen Brandy could smell a tempting aroma of simmering tomatoes, beef, potatoes, green beans, bouillon. Her recipe. She laid a hand on his arm and pulled him toward the old couch. "I'll eat later. First, I've got to make you understand." Haltingly, he allowed himself to be guided. She settled next to him, still holding his arm as if he might flee into the kitchen.

"At first, Grif Hackett was nothing to me but a man with an interesting job," she began, "one I wanted to learn about. Then he became one of the keys to a murder and a kidnapping. I had to know what he knew. It's true he tried to start something with me. I think he wanted to get my mind off the case and get me out of Homosassa. He had his own agenda."

John arched his eyebrows. "And the motel?"

"Pottery, truly. He lured me up there to show me the artifacts he culled from the mound. A field lab, he called his suite. The pots were astonishing. When he tried to hit on me, I left in a hurry. His grad student has a crush on him. She jumped to conclusions and called you." Brandy paused, trying to think how to begin. "It all started with the murder of a nice little guy. Then the baby was snatched." She dropped her voice, choked for a moment. "I'd become fond of her, and I was obsessed with finding her. I couldn't afford to make an enemy of anyone. Everything's in my notes."

For the first time he met her eyes. "I heard gossip."

"There's not much excitement in Homosassa. For entertainment they dream up rumors. They were based on a few dinners together in public restaurants, each trying to get information from the other, the pottery display, and a drive from Homosassa to Gainesville. There's no public transportation, and I had to pick up my car to come here. That's it. Besides," she added, "I really didn't like Grif Hackett. He was too cynical. He had no respect for marriage—and none at all for bones."

Again the raised brows.

"It didn't matter to me, or to the Seminoles, that the little girl's bones were four hundred years old. A millisecond in the history of human culture. They were still what remained of a child."

John clasped his hands between his knees, head down, then looked up at her. "You've worried me a lot, Bran, but I've never known you to lie."

Quickly she bent toward him, kissed his cheek. "I haven't, and I won't. We can work things out. We need each other's support." She admitted to herself that Hackett had briefly seemed attractive, but only because she felt John had rejected her. But Hackett focused solely on his own interests. He would certainly never be guilty of wanting a family. She had seen that from the beginning. John was unselfish, loyal, easily wounded, but a man she could always count on. Even when she had angered him, he came searching for her. He did not give up until he pulled her out of a premature tomb. He was the man she had loved and still did.

"I want to believe we both need each other," he said at last, quietly. "I've got problems in my job, too."

She kissed him again, this time on the lips. He held her for a moment against him—his first sign of real warmth since the Hart case began—then helped her to her feet beside him. "Let's have that bowl of soup with some French bread," he said. "You must be starved."

Brandy sat down at a round table next to the kitchen and turned to watch as he carried in steaming bowls and a basket of crusty bread and real butter. "Can you meet me in the morning about nine-thirty at the Seminole Cultural Center?" she asked. "I'll need to see Detective Strong at the Center first, even earlier." Brandy looked out into the dark street with its canopy of drooping live oaks and suddenly felt anxious. She drew in a quick breath. What if her theory was wrong? Other possibilities existed.

She turned back to John. "I want you to go with me to an unusual funeral service at ten. The Seminole couple will allow us in the cemetery, but at a distance. It's only because I helped find Daria. We can watch the little Safety Harbor girl finally be laid to rest."

Brandy saw the hint of a smile. "You take me to such interesting places."

He carried the dishes into the kitchen, then held out both hands to her. "I don't have any fascinating pieces of pottery, but I'd like to show you my bedroom." In spite of her weariness, Brandy felt a familiar surge of warm anticipation. Taking his hands, she pulled him against her and kissed him again, deeply.

Much later, they stretched out on the bed together. A breeze from the bay blew across them through an open window, carrying the scent of jasmine. Brandy turned to John and curled her arm around his bare chest. "When I was scrambling through the underbrush, before I fell into the cistern, I looked up and saw resurrection fern. Our marriage is like that plant. Sometimes it seems withered, but that's an illusion. It will spring back, greener than ever."

John's brown eyes grew suddenly solemn. "We haven't yet solved the biggest problem between us."

She tapped one finger against his lips. "Tomorrow, when I'm not so tired. We do have something else to talk about.

*   *   *   *

The next morning dawned clear and unusually crisp for a Florida spring. Brandy dressed with care in the gray suit she had brought from Gainesville. She took the Interstate before rush hour, and drove into the Seminole Cultural Center. Once inside, she frowned in disappointment. The detective was not in the gift shop. The clerk greeted Brandy with scant enthusiasm. She would surely be glad to see the lot of them gone. Brandy stepped to the counter. "The Sergeant must be delayed," she said. "We'll need to get into the museum before it opens. I left the original key with the box of skeletal remains in the museum. I was alone, and there were prowlers around. I was afraid it would be stolen." She didn't dare ask for the back-up key herself.

She was morosely examining the cornhusk dolls when Fishhawk hurried in. Brandy could see Annie waiting in their truck with Daria. "The big detective's not here yet?" The medicine man glanced down at his shirt and jeans, then looked at Brandy. "You get the box, then. You won't mind handling it. I've got to change."

Brandy noticed the disapproving expression on the clerk's face. She had given the key to Brandy once and the result was disastrous. Brandy turned to Fishhawk. "Will you please open the museum and re-lock it first? I'll carry the box carefully to my car and wait with it there. Surely Sergeant Strong will be here soon."

Fishhawk nodded. The clerk's dark eyes were still guarded, but after a few seconds, she tossed a braid back over one shoulder, and reached into a pocket of her colorful skirt. "One of our policemen left this duplicate." She pointedly handed it to Fishhawk, while looking at Brandy. "Please re-lock the door, Mr. Pine, and bring it back to me."

Inside the exhibit area, the immense alligator lay in a languid torpor. The panther stretched out asleep on its shelf. At the museum, the medicine man unlocked the heavy door and swung it wide. Through the high windows the early sunlight cast a glow over the cypress head of the warrior. Brandy glanced around the circular room, conscious of the power of the giant drum and the magnetism of the Seminole portraits and clan displays. Silently, she knelt beside the Tupperware container, pulled the black plastic cover more tightly around it, and lifted up the box. It felt light for the burden of emotion it carried.

After taking it to her coupe, she placed it on the front seat and sat beside it. Half an hour later Fishhawk emerged from the doorway to speak to Annie. To officiate at the burial service, he wore the costume in the portrait: a scarlet tunic, a wide belt studded with silver discs, a round pill-box turban with a feather, and buckskin leggings.

A few minutes later Brandy spotted John's minivan turning into the street ahead. She checked her watch and noted with alarm that it was already 9:30 A.M. John pulled in beside her car, parked, and swung his long legs out of the driver's side. Always dependable. Brandy smiled fondly and gave him a discreet kiss. He will be where he says he will be, and when he says he will be there. But where was the detective? Her plan had been disrupted enough. All would be lost if Strong did not come. She needed the law beside her.

Fishhawk strolled over to them. "We'd better head out." To Brandy he said, "Looks like you have to be our helper here." He did not look pleased. "The cemetery schedules its burials, and we can't change the time."

She gave him a glum nod. "We'll come." To John she added, "If it's okay, I'd like to move the Tupperware container into your minivan. As a hearse, it looks better than my car." John raised his eyebrows, but he carried it around, lifted the hatch, re-covered the box in black, and stowed it as she asked.

He drove the few miles to the cemetery, following Fishhawk's truck and a few other cars bringing Seminoles, friends the medicine man had recruited as witnesses and mourners. They all parked beside a road bordering graves that dated back to the last century. The twisted limbs of live oaks, shrouded in Spanish moss, encircled the grounds, but there was no fence. Here the dead excluded no one.

Brandy felt drained. Her big moment was being denied. All her careful note taking, her study, her thoughtful deductions would come to zero without the protection and authority of Sergeant Strong. She glanced around and saw no Seminole officer on the scene. This was her last chance, and she didn't dare act alone.

CHAPTER 20

▼

Brandy heard the detective's Ford before she saw it. He came careening through the gates, plowed to a stop in front of their minivan, and bounded out of his car and up to their driver's window in almost one motion. "Sorry!" he panted. "I was called to Tampa International Airport. An emergency." He looked past John at Brandy. "You'll be interested in the outcome." The detective wore his uniform today, a tacit signal to the Seminoles that he was acting in his capacity as law enforcement officer.

Brandy took a hasty look at Fishhawk in his truck. He seemed to be waiting with a cemetery official for something. She knew he would be eager to finish the ordeal.

"Hurry," Brandy said. "We've got one more job to do before you hand over the Indian girl's skeleton."

Strong looked puzzled, but Brandy was already out of her seat and hurrying to the back of the minivan. She pulled up the hatchback. "You've got to open the container, Sergeant," she said. "I think you'll find more than bones."

For once he did not stop to question her. "You better know what you're talking about, young lady," he said. "It's against the law to tamper with Indian bones."

But he stepped to his own car and reached for his detective's kit. Brandy nodded. She knew it would hold a camera and the implements he might need. "The box is the perfect hiding place," she said. "By law no one can disturb it. I think you will find what Timothy Hart searched for and what he died for." She held her breath while Strong removed his penknife from a pocket and forced the lid. The musty smell of stale water and old fabric lifted into the air. Through a film of moisture, at first Brandy saw only the slender, broken femurs, a fragile clavicle, tiny teeth, the scrap of matting.

"You needn't remove the skeleton parts," she added. "Fishhawk will know if they need to come out of the Tupperware box." She prayed her hunch would be right. Among the bones they both could see the edge of a plastic bag.

Strong lifted a small camera from the kit and snapped a photograph. Then he pulled on a pair of thin gloves, lifted the plastic bag out of the water and unwound a layer of bubble wrap. His eyes widened in surprise. Then with great care he spread out on the minivan carpet Hart's treasure—a long necklace of twelve large, grinning golden skulls, all strung together on two lengthy strands of turquoise beads. Their round turquoise eyes radiated malignancy; their fleshless lips stretched in the cruel parody of a grin.

Again the camera flashed. From his kit, the detective lifted a little cardboard box. Skulls, Brandy thought. The thing of darkness was a universal symbol of death, skeletal heads that Indians would avoid at all costs, but made of the gold that white men craved. No wonder the nineteenth century warrior had found them horrifying, had said the necklace should go to a medicine man. No wonder he wanted to keep it from his enemies and use its power against them. It would certainly terrify anyone who believed skeletons brought pain and death, yet it was an object of enormous value to collectors. The necklace would be much older than the150 years it waited discovery in Homosassa, and the workmanship was exquisite.

Brandy slipped around to John's window. "Come back here," she whispered. "This is your chance to see Timothy Hart's treasure."

Strong spoke slowly. "Dr. Hackett was the only one who had charge of the bones or the box." He arranged the golden necklace in the smaller box, scrawled a label on the lid, and stowed it in his trunk with the kit. "Then he must be the murderer."

"He checks out, motive and opportunity," Brandy said. "Hackett was desperate to leave his dull job in Florida and take part in the exciting Mayan digs. With what this artifact would bring, he could afford to. And he liked expensive things."

The final Seminole mourner had pulled into the cemetery. From his truck Fishhawk called to the Sergeant, "Glad you got here!" He walked a few paces toward them. "Bring the box and follow me." While Strong slid the lid firmly back onto the Tupperware container, Brandy and John stepped to one side and stood watching. She knew they had been asked to come no nearer to the service.

From the distance of a small knoll, sheltered from the morning sun by over hanging branches, they watched Strong make a dignified transfer of the covered box of bones to Fishhawk. A few women in long skirts and capes, banded in blue, yellow, white and red, gathered around the small plot, along with men in colorful matching jackets.

Fishhawk raised what appeared to be a gourd above the grave. Brandy could make out the child-size, oblong casket resting on the grass, could see the welcoming portal in the ground, but she could not understand the solemn, muffled chant—too far away, too Indian. Brandy wondered if Fishhawk would use his medicine bundle. She knew she would never know.

She edged closer, touching John's shoulder. "Grif Hackett himself helped me understand how the treasure got into the Safety Harbor mound. He told me that in the sixteenth century Indians dived on Spanish shipwrecks along the Gulf coast. They murdered the survivors and then salvaged the treasure the Spaniards had stolen from Mexico and South America. For a few years, the Spaniards didn't melt down gold artifacts."

A slight wind carried faint sounds of the ritual toward them. Still watching the figures across the graveyard, John asked, "And the artifact—the necklace? Where did it come from?"

"From what I've read about Mexican treasures, it's probably Mixtec from the state of Oaxaca. They're famous for gold and silver work. I remember a similar skull necklace in the Pre-Columbian exhibit at Dumbarton Oaks in D.C. The Seminole warrior must've found this one near the old Safety Harbor village when he was digging for clams."

Brandy entwined her fingers with John's. "I doubt Hackett originally meant to kill Hart. He thought he'd make off with the necklace and Hart would never know. But Fishhawk could read the journal, too, in spite of what he said. He staked out the cistern. He must've seen Hackett find the necklace and told Hart. Then the poor guy was a danger to Hackett.

"After I got involved, Hackett considered me a spy, or else another person after the artifact. He became really anxious when I looked into the box of bones in his motel room. He must've thought I saw the plastic bag hidden in the burial bundle, so I needed to be silenced. Ironically, I never saw it." She smiled with sudden satisfaction. "Strong thinks they can match the rope I saw in Hackett's van with the cut-off rope on the hickory tree at the cistern.

"I finally began to realize the murderer had to be Hackett. Tugboat had no way to persuade Hart to eat pokeweed, but Hart trusted Hackett. Poisoning wasn't a method Tugboat would choose, anyway."

The ceremony before them was winding down. Brandy thought she saw the casket lowered. Behind them a car pulled up beside the cemetery gates.

"Then there was the cistern trap," she added. "Tugboat had no way of knowing I'd search that end of the island, or when. But I told Hackett myself the night after Daria disappeared."

John tilted his head and looked down at her. "What about the two women, the home owner and her Realtor friend?"

"If Alma May or Melba had found the necklace—or even knew where to look—they wouldn't still be digging holes in the area. I'm sure Tugboat pried the story out of Melba, but he hadn't a clue where to look. He figured someone had found the treasure, and he was after whoever had it. In the meantime, he threatened Melba, probably Alma May, too, if they told the Sheriff about his pot hunting and drug running. Of course, they got involved with the pot selling, too. I once thought they might be holding Daria, but Strong said the sound I heard in a room there was just what Alma May claimed it was—a sick cat.

"Both Strong and I suspected Fishhawk for a time because he didn't want deputies searching for Daria. We know now he was afraid of what

Hackett would do to her. He believed I was in on the theft and the kidnapping because I was Hackett's friend."

John tugged at his tie. He'd come dressed for a formal occasion that he could scarcely see, and the sun was growing hotter. Brandy patted his arm.

"Actually, Hackett's girl friend was his grad student. This morning Strong told me she was caught at the airport trying to leave the country. She'd held poor little Daria in the wildlife preserve. At the hospital, deputies found two one-way tickets to Mexico on Hackett. Now Bibi Brier's singing like a bird."

"And what happens to the necklace?"

"It belongs to Alma May. She'll sell it for thousands to a Mexican collector, like Hackett planned to. It'll go back where it belongs. As for Melba, Tugboat's in the tank to stay for a while. It gives her a chance to sell out in Homosassa and move back to New Jersey, sadder but wiser, I'd say."

"And the Seminole tobacco pouch you were so concerned about?"

"I gave it to Sergeant Strong. He thinks he can persuade Alma to sell it through a middle-man to the Ah-Tah-Thi-Ki museum off Alligator Alley. It really belongs in a Seminole collection. Fishhawk will like that."

They heard the scramble of small feet and turned to see a flash of red and blue. Annie and Daria had come in the car they'd just heard arrive. The little girl scampered to Brandy, her wide, fluted collar fluttering above a skirt ringed with red and white bands, each brightened by a lightning motif. She raised her hands to be picked up. Brandy smiled, encircled the squirming body in her arms and laid her head against Daria's cheek.

"That something else we need to talk about," she said to John. "I've been thinking." She looked into the child's dark eyes, at the round, laughing face.

"I'd like to spend more time in Tampa, as long as you're here. I might even look for a job on one of the Tampa Bay papers. I might try my luck at freelancing. I want to write that article about Tiger Tail Island. Maybe more about the Seminoles. I think I could find markets."

"Wait for Mother!" Annie called, rushing up in another skirt of brilliant horizontal stripes. She swept Daria into her own arms and peered toward the figures at the far side of the cemetery. "Didn't want little miss here to interrupt the ceremony."

In front of their minivan, Sergeant Strong was striding toward his car. He waved briskly. "Got to get back to Citrus County." He paused a moment. "You worry me to death, O'Bannon, but I got to admit, you get a few good ideas." He gave a vigorous nod to his head. "There is nothing covered that shall not be revealed; neither hid, that shall not be known." Brandy agreed that the Biblical quotation was relevant to their morning's discovery. Smiling, she waved back as he climbed into the driver's seat.

Fishhawk had finished and was hurrying with the others toward the road that wound between gravesites. He had released the Safety Harbor child's spirit to go west. Brandy wondered if Fishhawk's chants and medicine bundle had been able to send those other spirits west, the slaughtered settlers on Tiger Tail Island, Timothy Hart himself.

"Some day I'd like to go back to the island," she said, "and see if I get the same awful feeling there."

John raised his eyebrows. "Of course, you won't. You won't expect to. Those presences you feel are in your mind, Bran. They're not external." When she looked stricken, he pressed her hand. "It's not a bad thing, you know, to be aware of the suffering of others."

Brandy knew she couldn't explain a sensation that she couldn't prove. She brushed back her damp, coppery hair, glanced at mother and child as they rushed to greet Fishhawk, and spoke softly. "I wanted to tell you, you were right about a family now."

John's arm crept around her waist and tightened.

She thought of all that had happened since she first saw Timothy Hart at the Tiki Bar. Especially, she remembered Hackett, crumpled on the Cultural Center walkway. The monster on Tiger Tail Island had been conquered, and the sorcerer had laid aside his staff and book. "The Hart murder case is over," she said. "I guess our revels now are ended."

"Not if what you say is true." With both hands, John tilted her face up to his. "I'd say our revels have just begun."

Reference books, in alphabetical order by author, used as sources

Carter, W. Horace, *The Nature Coast Tales and Truths*, Tabor, N. C.: Atlantic Publishing Co., 1993; *Nature's Masterpiece at Homosassa. Tabor, N.C.:* Atlantic Publishing Co.,1981.

Downs, Dorothy, *Art of the Florida Seminole and Miccosukee Indians.* Gainesville, FL et al: University of Florida Press, 1995.

Hall, Francis Wyly, *Be Careful in Florida: Know These Poisonous Snakes, Insects, Plants.* St. Petersburg. FL: Great Outdoors Publishing Co.,1980.

Jumper, Betty Mae, *Legends of the Seminole.* Sarasota, FL : Pineapple Press, Inc., 1994.

Mahon, John K. *History of the Second Seminole War 1835-1842.* Gainesville, FL et al: University Press of Florida, 1985.

Milanich, Jerald T., *Archaeology of Pre-Columbian Florida.* Gainesville, FL et al: University Press of Florida, 1994; *Florida's Indians and the Invasion from Europe.* Gainesville, FL et al: University Press of Florida, 1995; *Florida's Indians from Ancient Times to the Present.* Gainesville, Fl et al: University Press of Florida, 1998.

Perry, I. Mac, *Indian Mounds You Can Visit, 165 Aboriginal Sites on Florida's West Coast.* St. Petersburg, FL: Great Outdoors Publishing Co., 1993.

Seminole Tribune, 1994–1999. 6300 Stirling Road, Hollywood, FL 33024

Singer, Steven D., *Shipwrecks of Florida: A Comprehensive Listing*. Sarasota, FL: Pineapple Press Inc. 1998.

Snow, Alice Micco and Susan Enns Stans, *Healing Plants, Medicine of the Florida Seminole Indians*. Gainesville, FL et al: University Press of Florida, 2001.

Weisman, Brent Richards, *Like Beads on a String: A Culture History of the Seminole Indians in North Peninsular Florida*. Tuscaloosa and London: University of Alabama Press, 1989; *Unconquered People; Florida's Seminole and Miccosukee Indians*. Tuscaloosa and London: University Press of Florida, 1999.

Wickman, Patricia Riles, *Osceola's Legacy*. Tuscaloosa and London: University of Alabama Press 1994; *The Tree That Bends: Discourse, Power, and the Survival of the Maskoki People*. Tuscaloosa and London: University of Alabama Press, 1999.

0-595-34466-6

Printed in the United States
203047BV00011B/12/A